Bob, Son of Battle

:VANT'S

Bob, Son of Battle

The Last Gray Dog of Kenmuir

A NEW VERSION BY

Lydia Davis

Illustrated by Marguerite Kirmse

THE NEW YORK REVIEW CHILDREN'S COLLECTION

NEW YORK

THIS IS A NEW YORK REVIEW BOOK
PUBLISHED BY THE NEW YORK REVIEW OF BOOKS
435 Hudson Street, New York, NY 10014
www.nyrb.com

Library of Congress Cataloging-in-Publication Data
Davis, Lydia, 1947–
 Bob, Son of Battle: The Last Gray Dog of Kenmuir / by Alfred Ollivant ; a
new version by Lydia Davis.
     pages cm. — (New York Review children's collection)
 Summary: On the border of Scotland and England beginning in the early
1880s, two sheep farmers and their sheepdogs engage in a years-long battle to
prove their superiority in handling sheep—a battle which must end in death.
 ISBN 978-1-59017-729-7 (hardback)
[1. Farm life—Great Britain—Fiction. 2. Sheep dogs—Fiction. 3. Dogs—Fic-
tion. 4. Great Britain—History—Victoria, 1837–1901—Fiction.] I. Ollivant,
Alfred, 1874–1927. Bob, son of Battle. II. Title. III. Title: Bob, son of Battle.
 PZ7.D29478Alf 2014
 [Fic]—dc23
                              2013050865

Cover design by Louise Fili Ltd.
Cover illustration by Lauren Nassef

ISBN 978-1-59017-729-7
Available as an electronic book; ISBN 978-1-59017-746-4

Printed in the United States of America on acid-free paper.
10 9 8 7 6 5 4 3 2 1

Contents

PART ONE

The Coming of the Tailless Tyke

CHAPTER I

The Gray Dog

THE SUN stared boldly down on a gray farmhouse lying long and low in the shadow of the sharp summit of Muir Pike; it shone on the ruins of a fortified tower and a rampart, left from the time of the Scottish raids; on rows of white-washed outbuildings; on a crowd of dark-thatched haystacks.

In the yard where the stacks were kept, behind the long row of stables, two men were covering them with thatch to protect them from rain. One lay sprawled over the top of a haystack, the other stood perched on a ladder down below.

The man on the ladder, small, old, and with a clever nut-brown face, was Tammas Thornton, who had worked for the Moores of Kenmuir for more than half a century. The other, on top of the stack, seemed wrapped in his own unhappy thoughts. This was Sammel Todd, a sturdy Dalesman, with huge hands and hairy arms; around his face an odd-looking halo of stiff, red hair; and on his face, a sad look.

"Ay, the Gray Dogs, bless them!" the old man was saying. "You can't beat 'em. I've known 'em sixty years now, and never knew a bad one yet. Not that I'm saying, mind you, that any of them is the equal of Rex, son of Rally. Ah, he was a one, was Rex! We never won the Cup again after his day."

"Nor ever shall again, you may count on that," said the other gloomily.

Tammas clucked his tongue irritably.

"Come, come, Sammel Todd!" he cried. "You're never happy unless you're making yourself miserable. I've never seen such a chap. Never win again? Why, our young Bob will be a fine example, I tell you, and I should know. Not that he'll be anything like as great as Rex, son of Rally, mind you! I remember how—"

The big man interrupted him hastily.

"I've heard it before, Tammas, I really have," he said.

Tammas paused and looked up angrily.

"You've heard it before, have you, Sammel Todd?" he asked sharply. "And what have you heard before?"

"Your stories, old lad—your stories about Rex, son of Rally."

"Which of 'em?"

"All of 'em, Tammas, all of 'em—many a time. I'm quite sick of 'em, Tammas, I really am," he pleaded.

The old man gasped. He brought down his mallet with a vicious smack.

"I'll never tell you a tale again, Sammel Todd, not if you was to go down on your bended knee for it. Nay; it's no use talking. Never again, says I."

"I never asked you," declared honest Sammel.

"And it wouldn't have been any use if you had," said the other viciously. "I'll never tell you a tale again if I was to live to be a hundred."

"You'll not live to be a hundred, Tammas Thornton—nowhere near it," said Sammel brutally.

"I'll live as long as some, I guarantee you," the old man

replied with spirit. "I'll live to see the Cup back at Kenmuir, as I've said before."

"If you do," the other declared, "Sammel Todd never spoke a true word. Nay, nay, lad; you're old, you're wobbly, your time's nearly run out or I'm quite mistaken."

"For mercy's sake, hold your tongue, Sammel Todd! It's clack-clack all day—" The old man broke off suddenly, and bent over his work with suspicious energy. "Get back to your work, lad," he whispered. "Here's Master and our Bob."

As he spoke, a tall man with a strong, thin, serious, weather-beaten face and the blue-gray eyes of the hill country came striding into the yard, his lower legs wrapped in leather. And trotting quietly at his heels, with the gravest, saddest eyes you ever saw, was a sheepdog puppy.

The puppy was a rare dark gray, his long coat splashed here and there with lighter touches, like a stormy sea under the moonlight. On his chest was a patch of the purest white, and the top of his head was sprinkled with white, as though with a shower of snow. Perfectly solid, utterly limber, and supremely graceful with his smooth motions, every inch the gentleman; you could not help but stare at him—Owd Bob of Kenmuir.

At the foot of the ladder the two stopped. And the young dog, placing his forepaws on a lower rung, looked up, slowly waving his silvery brush of a tail.

"A proper Gray Dog!" murmured Tammas, gazing down into the dark face beneath him. "Small, yet big; light-footed when he's moving behind his sheep, yet not too light. With a coat rough on top to keep out the Daleland weather, soft as sealskin beneath. And with them sorrowful eyes that you never see except on a good one. He almost reminds me of Rex, son of Rally."

"Oh, dear! Oh, dear!" groaned Sammel. But the old man did not hear him.

"Did Henry Farewether tell you what he did this morning, Master?" he asked, speaking to the man at the foot of the ladder.

"Nay," said the other, his stern eyes lighting up.

"Why, it was this way, it seems," Tammas continued. "The young bull gets loose somehow and marches out into the yard, overturns the milk pail, and pokes the old pigs in the ribs. And as he stands looking about him, thinking what he'll be up to next, our Bob sees him. 'And what are you doin' here, Mr. Bull?' he seems to say, cocking his ears and trotting up gaily. With that, Mr. Bull swells up fit to burst himself, lashes his tail, waggles his head, and gets ready to charge. But Bob leaps out of the way, quick as lightning yet cool as butter, and when he's done with his fooling drives him back again."

"Who saw all this?" Sammel broke in, as though he didn't quite believe it.

"Henry Farewether from up in the loft. So there, Fat-head!" Tammas replied, and went on with his tale. "So they continues; bull charging and Bob driving him back over and over, hopping in and out again, quiet as a cucumber, but determined. At last Mr. Bull sees it's no good that way, so he turns around, rears up, and tries to jump the wall. No use. Our young dog jumps in at 'im and nips 'im by the tail. With that, our bull tumbles down in a hurry, turns with a kind of a groan, and marches back into the stall, Bob after him. And then, dang me!"—the old man beat the ladder as he offered this last tidbit—"if he doesn't sit himself down in the doorway like a sentry guard till Henry Farewether come up. How's that for a little tyke not yet one year old?"

Even Sammel Todd was moved by the tale.

"Well done, our Bob!" he cried.

"Good lad!" said the Master, laying a hand on the dark head at this knee.

"You may well say that," cried Tammas with delight. "A

proper Gray Dog, I tell you. As clever as any person, and as gentle as the spring sunshine. Ah, you can't beat 'em, the Gray Dogs of Kenmuir!"

The patter of cheerful feet rang out on the bridge below, a simple one made of thick boards that lay across a little stream. Tammas glanced around.

"Here's David," he said. "He's late this morning."

A fair-haired boy came hurrying up the slope, his face glowing from his effort. Immediately, the young dog dashed off to meet him with a fiery speed nothing like his earlier sober behavior. The two raced back together into the yard.

"Poor lad!" said Sammel gloomily, gazing at the boy.

"Poor heart!" muttered Tammas, while the Master's face softened. Yet there seemed to be little to pity in this jolly, rollicking boy with his tousled fair hair and fresh, rosy face.

"Good morning, Mister Moore! Morning, Tammas! Morning, Sammel!" he panted as he passed; and he ran on through the hay-carpeted yard, around the corner of the stable, and into the house.

The kitchen was a long room with a floor of red tiles and windows covered in patterns of crisscrossing ironwork. In it, a woman in a white apron with a delicate face was bustling about her morning work. A strong little bare-legged boy was holding tight to her skirts; while at the oak table in the center of the room, a girl with brown eyes and straggling hair sat in front of a bowl of bread and milk.

"So you've come at last, David!" the woman cried, as the boy entered; and, bending, greeted him with a tender, motherly kiss, which he returned as warmly. "I really thought you'd forgot us this morning. Now you sit down beside our Maggie." And soon he was bending over his own bowl of bread and milk.

The two children munched away in silence, while the little

bare-legged boy watched them carefully. At last, bothered by his long staring, David turned on him.

"Well, little Andrew," he said, speaking in the fatherly way which one small boy likes to use towards another. "Well, my little lad, aren't you coming along just fine." He leaned back in his chair, the better to study the smaller boy. But Andrew, who was slow to speak, like all the Moores, did not react, but went on quietly sucking his chubby thumb and watching the older boy as though he did not quite trust him.

David did not like the look on the boy's face, and half rose to his feet.

"You change that expression, Andrew Moore," he cried threateningly, "or I'll change it for you."

Maggie, however, stopped him just in time.

"Did your father beat you last night?" she asked in a low voice; and there was a shade of worry in the soft brown eyes.

"Nay," the boy answered; "he was going to, but he never did. Drunk," he added in explanation.

"What was he going to beat you for, David?" asked Mrs. Moore.

"What for? Why, for the fun of it—to see me wiggle and squirm," the boy answered, and laughed bitterly.

"You shouldn't speak that way about your dad, David," the woman scolded, though not very severely, as it was not in her nature to be severe.

"Dad! A fine dad he is! I'd dad him if I had the chance," the boy muttered under his breath. Then, to change the conversation:

"We should be starting, Maggie," he said, and, going to the door, "Bob!" he called, "Owd Bob, lad! Are you coming with us?"

The gray dog came springing up like an antelope, and the three started off for school together.

Mrs. Moore stood in the doorway, holding Andrew by the hand, and watched them as they went away.

"They make a pretty pair, Master, surely," she said softly to her husband, who came up to her just then.

"Ay, he'll be a fine lad if his father will let him," the tall man answered.

"It's a shame Mr. McAdam does not give him a better life," the woman went on, troubled at the unfairness of it. She laid a hand on her husband's arm, and looked up at him persuasively.

"Couldn't you say something to him, Master, don't you think? Maybe he'd listen to you," she asked. For Mrs. Moore thought that there could not be anyone who would not be glad to listen to whatever James Moore, Master of Kenmuir, might say. "He's not a bad man at heart, I do believe," she went on. "He was never like this before his dear wife died. Oh, he was so fond of her."

Her husband shook his head.

"Nay, mother," he said. "It would only make things worse for the lad. McAdam listens to no one, and certainly not me." And indeed he was right; for McAdam, who lived not far away, across the stream on a farm called the Grange, made no secret of how much he disliked his neighbor, the honest, plain-speaking Mr. Moore.

◆ ◆ ◆

Our Bob, in the meantime, had gone with the children as far as the woods at the edge of the lane that leads to the village. Now he crept quietly back to the yard, and settled down behind the water barrel.

We do not need to know just how he played and how he laughed; how he teased old Whitecap, the gray goose, till the bird nearly died of helpless surprise; how he made the brown bull-calf run, and roused the bitter fury of a fat sow, the mother of many piglets.

At last, in the midst of his merry mischief, a stern voice stopped him.

"Bob, lad, I see that it's time we started your own schooling."

And so the serious business of life began, for that dog whom the simple farming people of the Daleland still love to talk about—Bob, son of Battle, the last of the Gray Dogs of Kenmuir.

CHAPTER 2

A Son of Hagar

THE COUNTRYSIDE around the village of Wastrel-dale is a lonely one.

The minister, Parson Leggy Hornbut, will tell you that his church is the smallest, and his parish the biggest, north of the Derwent River, and that his parish has more square miles in it than it has people. It includes moors and ravines, swift streams and lakes; with a little village standing far away in one spot and a sheep-farm alone up on a hilltop in another. It is a countryside in which sheep are the most important thing; and every other Dalesman works at sheep-herding, a job as old as Abel in the Bible. And what the men here talk about is sheep, and again sheep—wethers and gimmers and tup-hoggs and ewe tegs in wool, and other things that are only strange words to you and me; and always they talk about the good deeds and the wrong-doings, the intelligence and the stupidity, of their helpers, the sheepdogs.

Of all the Daleland, the country from the Black Water to Grammoch Pike is the wildest. Above the tiny, stone-built village of Wastrel-dale, the Muir Pike lifts its massive head. To the west, the desolate Mere Marches—which give their name to the great estate of the Sylvester family—stretch away in mile upon mile of sheep-filled, wind-swept moorland. On the far side of the Marches is that twin valley where the gentle stream called the Silver Lea flows. And it is there, in the fenced plots of grassy land behind the inn called the Dalesman's Daughter, that, in the late summer months, the famous sheep-dog Trials of the North are held. It is there that the battle for the Dale Cup, the world-renowned Shepherds' Trophy, is fought.

Past the little inn, the main road leads into the central market-town of the area—Grammoch-town. At the bottom of the fenced enclosures, in back of the inn, winds the stream called the Silver Lea. Just there, a wooden plank-bridge crosses the water, and, beyond, the Murk Muir Pass crawls up the steep side of the bare rock face known as the Scaur and on to the Mere Marches.

At the head of the Pass, before it opens out into those lonely sheep-walks which divide the two valleys, is that hollow place, shuddering with dark possibilities, that is rightly called the Devil's Bowl. In its center, the Lone Tarn, a pool of water that suggests strange and fanciful ideas, lifts its motionless face to the sky. It was beside that black, frozen water, across whose cold surface a storm was swirling in ghostly white shapes, that, many, many years ago (not in this century), old Andrew Moore came upon the mother of the Gray Dogs of Kenmuir.

In the North, everyone who has heard of the Muir Pike—and who has not?—has heard of the Gray Dogs of Kenmuir; everyone who has heard of the Shepherds' Trophy—and who has not?—knows how famous the Gray Dogs are. In that country of good dogs and jealous masters, the highest place has long been held unchallenged. Whatever line may claim to come after them, the Gray Dogs are always at the very front. And there is a saying in the land: "Faithful as the Moores and their dogs."

◆ ◆ ◆

On the top cupboard to the right of the fireplace in the kitchen of Kenmuir lies the family Bible. At the back of it you will find a loose sheet of paper—the pedigree of the Gray Dogs; at the beginning, pasted on the inside, another sheet of paper, almost the same, long since yellowed with age—the family record of the Moores of Kenmuir.

If you run your eye down the loose page, once, twice, and a third time, your attention will be caught by a small red cross beneath a name, and under the cross the one word: "Cup." Lastly, opposite the name of Rex, son of Rally, are two of those proud, meaningful marks. The "cup" is the famous Dale Cup—the Champion Challenge Dale Cup, open to everyone in the world. If Rex had won it just one more time, the Shepherds' Trophy, which many men have spent their whole lives trying to win, and failed to win, would have come to rest forever in the little gray house below the Pike.

It was not to be, however. Comparing the two sheets of paper, you will read beneath the dog's name a date and a sad handwritten note; and on the other page, in the handwriting of Andrew Moore's son when he was still a boy, the name of Andrew Moore and beneath it the same date and the same note.

On that day, young James Moore, though he was only a boy, became the master of Kenmuir.

Past Grip and Rex and Rally, and a hundred others, at the

foot of the page, you will come to that last name—Bob, son
of Battle.

❖ ❖ ❖

From the very beginning, the young dog took to his work in
a way that amazed even James Moore. For a while he watched
his mother, Meg, doing her job, and that seemed to be all he
needed to master the most important moves in handling
sheep.

Rarely had such fiery spirit been seen on the slopes of Muir
Pike; and with it the young dog combined an unusual steadiness, an admirable patience, so that he did indeed deserve the
name by which they liked to call him—"Old" Bob, or "Owd"
Bob, as they said it. He worked silently, and with determination; and even in those days, he had that famous trick of per-
suading the sheep to do as he wished—he seemed to be as
clever as any person, as Tammas had said, and at the same
time as gentle as the spring sunshine.

Parson Leggy, who was believed to be the best judge of a
sheep or a sheepdog between the River Tyne, to the south,
and the River Tweed, to the north, summed him up with the
one word "Genius." And James Moore himself, a cautious
man, was more than pleased.

In the village, the Dalesmen, who took a personal pride in
the Gray Dogs of Kenmuir, began nodding wisely when "our"
Bob was mentioned. Jim Mason, the postman, who was
trusted by the villagers as completely as Parson Leggy was
trusted by the wealthy landowners, declared that he had
never seen such a charming and excellent young pup.

That winter it became quite the usual thing, when they had
gathered at night around the fire, in the tavern called the Syl-

vester Arms, with Tammas in the center, old Jonas Maddow on his right, Rob Saunderson of the Holt farm on his left, and the others surrounding them, for someone to begin with:

"Well, and what about our Bob, Mr. Thornton?"

To which Tammas would always reply:

"Oh, you ask Sammel there. He'll tell you better than I"— and would then immediately plunge into a story himself.

And the way in which, as the story went on, Tupper of Swinsthwaite winked at Ned Hoppin of Fellsgarth, and Long Kirby, the blacksmith, poked Jem Burton, the tavern-keeper, in the ribs, and Sexton Ross said, "My word, lad!" said more than enough about what they felt.

There was only one man who never joined in the chorus of admiration. Sitting always alone in the background, little McAdam would listen with a smile of disbelief on his sickly, yellowish face.

"Oh, of course! The dog's full of the devil! He's by no means as clever as all that!" he would keep exclaiming, as Tammas told his story.

❖ ❖ ❖

In the Daleland you rarely see a stranger's face. Wandering through the wild country surrounding the twin valleys at the time of this story, you might have met Parson Leggy, walking briskly along with a couple of troublesome terriers at his heels, and by his side young Cyril Gilbraith, whom he was teaching both to tie flies on a hook, for fishing trout, and to fear God; or you might have met Jim Mason, whose job was postman, but whose favorite hobby was to hunt small animals, even on private land, an honest man and a sportsman by nature, hurrying along with the mailbags on his shoulder, a rabbit in his pocket, and his faithful dog Betsy a yard behind him. Besides these, you might have come upon a quiet shepherd and a wise-faced dog; or Squire Sylvester, the large landowner in the region, making his rounds upon a sturdy cob horse; or, if you were lucky, his wife, sweet Lady Eleanour, on some errand to lend a helping hand to one of the Sylvesters' many tenants.

It was while the Squire's lady was driving through the village on a visit* to Tammas's drooling grandson—shortly after young Billy Thornton was born—that little McAdam, standing in the door of the Sylvester Arms, with a twig in his mouth and a nasty smile fading from his lips, made the remark that was never forgotten:

"Sall!" he exclaimed, in his Scots dialect, speaking in a low, serious voice; "'tis a muckle wumman." (Which meant: "Damn! What a fine woman!")

"What? What are ye saying, man?" cried old Jonas, startled out of his usual indifference.

McAdam turned sharply on the old man.

"I said the woman is wearing a fine hat!" he snapped.

Although he had tried to deny it, the comment is still remembered now—a compliment born of honest admiration. Doubtless the Recording Angel did not overlook it. That one statement about the gentle lady of the manor is the only personal remark little McAdam was ever known to make that was not hurtful and unkind. And that is why it will always be remembered.

---

*It was this visit that was described in the Grammoch-town *Argus* (a local radical newspaper) under the headline "Alleged Wholesale Corruption by Tory Agents." Which was why, on the following market day, the reporter Herbert Trotter, a former gentleman and Secretary of the Dale Trials, who had written the article, found himself thrown in the public horse-trough.

The little Scotsman with the mean smile had lived at the Grange for many years; yet he had never grown used to the land of the English. With his shrunken little body and weak legs, surrounded by the sturdy, straight-limbed sons of the hill-country, he looked like some brown, wrinkled leaf holding its place in a galaxy of green. And just as he was different from them in his body, he was also different in his nature.

He did not understand them, and he did not try to. The North-country character was a mystery he could not solve, even after ten years of studying them. "They doubt one half of what you say, and they let you see that they doubt it; the other half they don't believe, and they tell you so," he once said. And that explained his attitude toward them, and, in response, their attitude toward him.

He was entirely alone; he was an outcast like the son of Hagar in the Bible, who was sent out into the wilderness, and he mocked those around him. His sharp, ill-natured tongue was rarely quiet, and always bitter. There was hardly a man in the land, from Langholm Hollow to the cross in the center of the Grammoch-town marketplace, who had not at one time or another been stung by it and put up with it in silence—for these men of the moors and lakes are slow to speak—and was nursing his anger until he had a chance for revenge, a chance which always comes sooner or later. And there was a round of clapping at the Sylvester Arms when, one of the few times McAdam was not in the room, Tammas neatly described the little man in that historic phrase of his: "When he's drunk, he's violent, and when he ain't, he's vicious." Even the world-weary heart of Tammas Thornton was pleased by the applause.

Yet it was not until his wife died that the little man showed his ill nature so freely. Now that her firm and gentle hand was no longer there to guide him, his ill nature burst into new life.

And because he was alone in the world with David as his only company, all the poison of his vicious personality was constantly turned against the boy. It was as though he believed that his fair-haired son had caused his everlasting sorrow. This was all the stranger because poor Flora McAdam had treasured the boy, during her lifetime, as though he were her very own heart. And the lad was growing up to be the very opposite of his father. Big and strong, with never an ache or an ailment in the whole of his sturdy young body; his face direct and open; while even his speech was slow and he trilled his *r*'s like any native Dale boy. And all of this, along with the fact that the lad was clearly more an Englishman than a Scot— yes, and was glad of it—irritated the little man, who was loyal to his native Scotland above all, so much so that he itched to fight in its defense. And then, on top of all this, David was amazingly, boldly rude to him, which would have roused the anger of even a better man than Adam McAdam.

When his wife died, kind Elizabeth Moore had come to see him more than once, offering to help the lonely little man by doing those things in the house that his wife used to do. On the last of these visits, after she had crossed the Stony Bottom, which marks the boundary between the two farms, and made her way with some effort up the hill to the Grange, she had met McAdam in the door.

"You must let me tidy up your things a bit for you, mister," she had said shyly; for she was afraid of the little man.

"Thank ye, Mrs. Moore," he had answered with the sour smile the Dalesmen knew so well, "but ye must think I'm a woeful cripple." And there he had stood, grinning scornfully and placing his small body in the very center of the doorway.

Mrs. Moore had turned and gone back down the hill, puzzled and hurt at the way he had greeted her offer of help; and her husband, who was all too proud, had told her she must not make the offer again. Still, her motherly heart went out in great tenderness for the little orphan David. She knew how unhappy his life was, how his father disliked him, and what would come of that.

And so it became the usual thing for the boy to stop in at Kenmuir every morning and trot off to the village school with Maggie Moore. And soon he came to look upon Kenmuir as his true home, and James and Elizabeth Moore as his real parents. His greatest happiness was to be away from the Grange. And the ferret-eyed little man there noticed this, was bitterly angry at it, and showed his ill humor.

He felt that James Moore was taking away his own command of his son, and this was the main reason for his bad feeling toward Mr. Moore. He was thinking of the Master of Kenmuir when he remarked, one day, at the Arms: "I myself always prefer the good man who does not go to church, to the bad man who does. But then, as ye say, Mr. Burton, I'm a bit strange."

The little man's treatment of David, which was made out to be even worse than it really was by the villagers because they were so eager to believe the worst, at last became such a scandal to the Dale that Parson Leggy decided to speak to him about it.

Now McAdam was the person whom the minister liked least in the world. The bluff old parson, with his brusque manner and big heart, wanted nothing to do with the man, who never went to church, was always drinking liquor, and never spoke good of his neighbors. Yet he began the conversation fully determined not to allow himself to express any feelings that were not worthy of him; rather, he would appeal to the little man's better nature.

The conversation had not been going on for more than two minutes, however, before he knew that, although he had meant to be calm and convincing, he was quickly becoming excited and insulting.

"You, Mr. Hornbut," the little man was saying, "with James Moore to help you, may look after the lad's soul—I'll take care of his body."

The parson's thick gray eyebrows lowered threateningly over his eyes.

"You should be ashamed of yourself talking like that. Which d'you think is more important, soul or body? Shouldn't you, his father, be the very first to care for the boy's soul? If not, who should? Answer me, sir."

The little man stood smirking and sucking the twig that was always there in his mouth, entirely unmoved by the other man's agitation.

"Ye're right, Mr. Hornbut, as ye always are. But my argument is this: that I get at his soul best through his little carcass."

The honest parson brought down his stick with an angry thud.

"McAdam, you're a brute—a brute!" he shouted. At which outburst the little man had a fit of silent laughter.

"A fond dad first, a brute afterward, perhaps—he, he! Ah, Mr. Hornbut! Ye amuse me greatly, ye do indeed—" he said, and he added a line from his favorite, the Scottish poet Robert Burns—"'my loved, my honored, much-respected friend.'"

"If you paid as much attention to your boy's welfare as you do to the bad poetry of that immoral farmer—"

An angry gleam shot into the other's eyes.

"Do ye know what blasphemy is, Mr. Hornbut?" he asked, thrusting himself forward a step.

For the first time in the argument, the parson thought he was about to score a point, and so he was calm.

"I should. I think I have an example of a blasphemous man in front of me now. And do you know what impertinence is?"

"I should. I think I have—I would say it's what gentlemen often display if their mothers did not whip them when they were lads."

For a moment the parson looked as if he were about to grab his opponent and shake him.

"McAdam," he roared, "I won't stand here putting up with your insolent remarks!"

The little man turned, hurried indoors, and came running back with a chair.

"Allow me!" he said smoothly, holding it in front of him like a hair-cutter for a customer.

The parson turned and walked away. At the gap in the hedge he paused.

"I'll say only one thing more," he called slowly. "When your wife, whom I think we all loved, lay dying in that room above you, she said to you in my presence—"

It was McAdam's turn to be angry. He took a step forward with burning face.

"Once and for all, Mr. Hornbut," he cried passionately, "understand that I'll not have you and the likes of you lay your tongues on my wife's memory whenever it suits ye. You can say what ye like about me—lies, sneers, insults—and I'll say nothing. I don't ask ye to respect me; I think ye might at least respect her, poor lass. She never harmed ye. If you cannot let her remain in peace where she lies down yonder"—he waved in the direction of the churchyard—"ye'll not be welcome on my land. Though she is dead, she's mine."

Standing in front of his house, with flushed face and big eyes, the little man looked almost noble in his indignation. And the parson, striding away down the hill, was uneasily aware that he had not won this battle.

CHAPTER 3

Red Wull

THE WINTER came and went; the season in which the lambs were born was past, and spring was already shyly kissing the land. And now that the hardest work of the year was done, and her master was well started on the new season, McAdam's old collie, Cuttie Sark, lay down one evening and passed quietly away.

The little black-and-tan lady, Parson Leggy used to say, had been the only thing on earth that McAdam cared for. Certainly the two had been wonderfully devoted to each other; and now, on many a market day, the Dalesmen missed the shrill, chuckling cry which told them the pair were approaching: "Well done, Cuttie Sark!"

The little man missed her sorely, and, as was his habit, he took out his misery on David and the Dalesmen. In return, Tammas, who was skilled at inventing insults that had a good ring to them, called him, behind his back, "A venomous, virulent viper!" (a highly poisonous snake)—and the men clinked their pewter mugs in approval.

A shepherd without his dog is like a ship without a rudder

to steer it by, and McAdam felt his loss in a practical way as well as in his heart. This was especially so on a day when he had to take a batch of older ewes over to richer pasture in Grammoch-town. To help him, Jem Burton had loaned him the use of his small-waisted, small-hearted greyhound, Monkey. But before they came to the top of Braithwaite Brow, which leads from the village onto the "marches," or border country, McAdam was standing in the path with a rock in his hand, a smile on his face, and the gentlest flattery in his voice as he coaxed the dog to come to him. Master Monkey knew too much to do that. However, after he had been frolicking a while longer in the middle of the flock, a large rock, better aimed than those before it, struck him on his hip and sent him back to the Sylvester Arms with a sore tail and a subdued heart.

In the end, McAdam would never have made his way over the sheep-filled marches alone with his ewes if it had not been for old Saunderson and Shep, who happened to overtake him on the path and helped him.

It was in a very angry mood that he walked into the Dalesman's Daughter in Silverdale on his way home.

The only occupants of the taproom, as he entered, were Teddy Bolstock, the innkeeper; Jim Mason, with the faithful Betsy beneath his chair and the mailbags flung into the corner; and a long-limbed fellow, a stranger, who had the look of a drover, that is, one of those hardy and solitary men whose profession it is to drive animals to market over long, lonely distances.

"And he comes up to Mr. Moore," Teddy was saying, "and he says, 'I'll give ye twelve pound for that gray dog of yours.' 'Ah,' says Moore, 'you may give me twelve hundred and yet you'll not get my Bob.'—Eh, Jim?"

"He did indeed," agreed Jim. "'Twelve hundred,' says he."

"James Moore and his dog again!" snapped McAdam. "There's others in the world besides them two."

"Ay, but none like them," said loyal Jim.

"No, thanks be to God. If there were, there'd be no room for Adam McAdam in this 'melancholy vale'"—echoing his favorite poet again.

There was silence for a moment, and then—:

"You're wanting a dog, ain't you, Mr. McAdam?" Jim asked.

The little man jumped around quickly.

"What!" he cried, pretending eagerness and scanning the yellow mongrel beneath the chair. "Betsy for sale! Goodness! Where's my check-book?" In response to which Jim, a man easily insulted, slumped in his chair.

McAdam took off his dripping coat and crossed the room to hang it on the back of a chair. The stranger watched the scrawny, shirt-clad figure with shifty eyes; then he buried his face in his mug.

McAdam reached out a hand for the chair; and as he did so, a bomb in yellow leapt out from beneath it, and, growling horribly, attacked his ankles.

"Curse ye!" cried McAdam, starting back. "Ye devil, let me alone!" Then, turning fiercely on the drover, "Yours, mister?" he asked. The man nodded. "Then call him off, can't ye? Damn ye!" At which Teddy Bolstock went away, snickering; and Jim Mason slung the mailbags onto his shoulder and plunged out into the rain, the faithful Betsy following unwillingly.

The cause of the disturbance, having beaten off the attacking force, had withdrawn again beneath its chair. McAdam stooped down, still cursing, his wet coat on his arm, and saw a tiny yellow puppy, crouching defiantly in the dark, and glaring out with fiery light-colored eyes. Seeing that it was noticed, it bared its little teeth, raised its little hackles, and growled a hideous threat.

A sense of humor is a quality that comes to the rescue for many a person, and it was McAdam's one good quality. The little man saw how laughable it was that such a small particle of life should be so fierce in defying him. Delighted at such a display of evil in such a young creature, he began to chuckle.

"Ye little devil!" he laughed. "He! he! ye little devil!" and snapped his fingers in vain, trying to coax the puppy to come to him.

But it growled, and glared more terribly.

"Stop it, ye little snake, or I'll flatten you!" cried the big drover, and shuffled his feet threateningly. Whereat the puppy, gurgling like hot water in a kettle, darted forward as though to rid the world of these two bad men at one blow.

McAdam laughed again, and slapped his leg.

"Keep a civil tongue in your head and keep your distance," says he, "or I'll have to force you to. Though he's only as big as a man's thumb, a dog's a dog for all that—he! he! the little devil." And he began snapping his fingers again.

"Are you maybe wanting a dog?" asked the stranger. "Your friend said so."

"My friend lied; it's his way," McAdam answered.

"I'm willing to part with him," the other went on.

The little man yawned. "Well, I'll take him to oblige ye," he said indifferently.

The drover rose to his feet.

"I'd be giving him to you, plain giving him to you, you know! But I'll do it!"—he smacked his great fist into his hollow palm. "You may have the dog for a pound—I'll only ask you for a pound," and he walked away to the window.

McAdam drew back, the better to scan this man who seemed to be doing him a favor; his lower jaw dropped, and he eyed the stranger with a comical air, as though he hardly believed him.

"A pound, man! A pound—for that noble dog!" he pointed a crooked forefinger at the little creature, whose scowling mask peered from beneath the chair. "Man, I couldn't do it. No, no; my conscience wouldn't permit me. It would be plain robbing you. Ah, you Englishmen!" He spoke half to himself, and sadly, as if he was sorry about the unhappy accident of his being born Scottish; "It's your grand, open-hearted generosity that seizes a poor Scotsman by the throat. A pound! and for that!" He wagged his head mournfully, tipping it sideways the better to study the little creature.

"Take him or leave him," ordered the stranger crossly, still gazing out of the window.

"With your permission I'll leave him," McAdam answered quietly.

"I'm short of cash," the big man went on, "or I wouldn't part with him. If I could afford to wait, there's many who'd be glad to give me ten pounds for one of that breed—" He broke off quickly and then went on "—for a dog like that."

"And yet ye offer him to me for a pound! Generous of you, indeed!"

Still, the little man had noticed the other man's slip and hasty correction. Again he approached the puppy, dangling his coat before him to protect his ankles; and again the little wild beast sprang out, seized the coat in its small jaws, and wrestled with it savagely.

McAdam stooped quickly and picked up his tiny attacker; and the puppy, suspended by its neck, gurgled and slobbered; then, wriggling desperately around, closed its teeth on its enemy's shirt. At which McAdam shook it gently and laughed. Then he started examining it.

It seemed to be about six weeks old; had a tan coat, fiery eyes, a square head with small, clipped ears, and an immense jaw for its size; the whole promised great strength, though not great beauty. And adding to this impression was the fact that its tail had been cut nearly off. For the miserable stump, still raw, looked like little more than a red button sticking to the puppy's backside.

McAdam examined every part of the pup with careful attention; he left nothing out, from the square muzzle to the pill-like stub of a tail. And every now and then he cast a quick glance at the man by the window, who was watching this examination a little uneasily.

"Ye've cut his tail short," McAdam said at last, swinging around toward the drover.

"Ay; makes their backs strong," the big man answered, looking away.

McAdam's chin went up in the air; his mouth opened a little and his eyelids closed a little as he gazed at the man who had offered this information.

"Oh, ay," he said.

"Give him back to me," ordered the drover grimly. He took the puppy and set it on the floor; upon which it immediately returned to its earlier safe position under the chair. "You're no buyer; I knew that all along by that face of yours," he said in insulting tones.

"Ye bought him yourself, no doubt?" McAdam asked, carelessly.

"Of course; if you say so."

"Or perhaps you bred him?"

"Maybe I did."

"You're not from around here?"

"I'm not?"

A smile of real pleasure came over McAdam's face. He laid his hand on the other man's arm.

"Man," he said gently, "ye remind me of home." Then, almost in the same breath: "Ye said ye found him?"

It was the stranger's turn to laugh.

"Ha, ha! You tickle me, little man. Found him? No; I was given him by a friend. But there's nothing wrong with his breeding, you may believe me."

The large fellow walked over to the chair under which the puppy lay. It leapt out like a lion, and fastened its teeth on his huge boot.

"Unusual breeding, he has, look! Uncommon spirit! My word, he's a big-hearted one! Look at his back; look at his jaws; see how plucky he is!" He shook his booted foot fiercely, tossing his leg to and fro like a tree in the wind. But the little creature, who was first flung up toward the ceiling, then dashed to the ground, held on stubbornly, till its small jaw was bloody and its muzzle wrinkled with the effort.

"Ay, ay, that's enough," McAdam said, irritably, in order to stop him.

The drover stopped.

"Now, I'll make you a last offer." He thrust his head down to the level of the smaller man, thrusting out his neck. "And you know, this is handing him to you. You won't be buying him—don't fool yourself. You may have him for fifteen shillings. Why do this, you ask? Why, cause I think you'll be kind to him." The puppy meanwhile was retreating to its chair, leaving a spotted trail of red along the floor.

"Ay, ye wouldn't be happy unless you thought he'd have a comfortable home, kind man that you are?" McAdam answered, looking at the dark trail on the floor. Then he put on his coat.

"No, no, he's not for me. Well, I won't keep you. Goodnight to you, mister!" and he headed towards the door.

"He'll be a great worker," called the drover after him.

"Ay; great work he'll do among the sheep, with such a jaw and such a temper. Well, I must be going. Goodnight to you."

"You'll never have another chance like it."

"Nor never wish to. No, no; he'll never make a sheepdog." And the little man turned up the collar of his coat.

"Won't he, now?" cried the other scornfully. "There never yet was one of that line—" He stopped abruptly.

The little man spun around.

"Yes?" he said, as innocent as a child. "What's that you were saying?"

The other man turned to the window and watched the rain falling steadily.

"You'll miss the rain if you don't go," he said cleverly.

"Ay, we could use a bit of damp. And he'll never make a sheepdog." He shoved his cap down on his head. "Well, goodnight to ye!" and he stepped out into the rain.

◆ ◆ ◆

It was long after dark before the two men finally came to an agreement.

Little Red Wull, as he was called, became the property of Adam McAdam in exchange for the following: ninepence in cash—three copper pennies and a suspicious-looking six-pence; a lump of chewing tobacco of doubtful quality, in a well-worn pouch; and an old watch.

"I might as well be clean giving him to you," said the stranger bitterly, at the end of the deal.

"It's more charity that's making me so generous to you," McAdam answered gently. "I wouldn't want to see you pinched for cash."

"Thank ye kindly," the big man replied rather sourly, and plunged out into the darkness and rain. Nor was that long-legged drover ever seen in the neighborhood again. And the puppy's history—whether the stranger had come by him honestly or not, whether he was, indeed, descended from the famous Red McCulloch* line, remained forever afterwards a mystery in the Daleland.

---

*You may recognize a Red McCulloch anywhere by the ring of white on his tail about two inches from the base of it.

CHAPTER 4

First Blood

AFTER that first meeting in the Dalesman's Daughter, Red Wull—for that was the name McAdam gave to him—calmly accepted his situation; realizing, perhaps, that this was his fate.

From then on, the sour little man and the vicious puppy seemed to grow together until they were one creature. They were never apart. Wherever McAdam was, there was sure to be his absurdly tiny companion, bristling defiance as he kept guard over his master.

The little man and his dog were inseparable. McAdam never left him behind, even at the Grange.

"I couldn't trust my Wullie at home alone with the dear lad," was the way he explained it. "I know I'd come back to find a little corpse on the floor, and David singing:

'My heart is sair, I daur na tell,
My heart is sair for somebody.'

(My heart is sore, I dare not tell,
My heart is sore for somebody.)

"Ay, and he'd be sore somewhere else, too, by the time I was done with him—he, he!"

The sneer at David's expense was as typical as it was unfair. For although the puppy and the boy were already sworn enemies, the lad would have scorned the idea of hurting so small a foe. And David told many a story at Kenmuir about Red Wull's viciousness, about the dog's hatred of him (David), and his loyalty to his master; how, whether he was burying his nose in the pig-bucket or chasing a fleeting rabbit, he would stop at once, if he heard his master call, and hurry up to him, panting; how he would hunt out the tom cat and drive him from the kitchen; and how he would climb onto David's bed and seized him murderously by the nose.

Lately, relations between McAdam and James Moore had been even tenser than usual. Though they were neighbors, they rarely spoke to each other; and it was for the first time in many a long day that, on an afternoon shortly after McAdam had acquired little Red Wull, he entered the yard of Kenmuir, for the purpose of jeering at the master for, in his opinion, trespassing through the Stony Bottom.

"With your permission, Mr. Moore," said the little man, "I'll whistle for my dog." And, turning, he whistled a shrill, peculiar note like the cry of the black-and-white moorland lapwing when startled from its nest.

Immediately there came scurrying desperately up, ears back, head down, tongue out, as if the world depended on his speed, a little tawny beetle of a thing, who placed his forepaws against his master's ankles and looked up into his face; then, catching sight of the strangers, hurriedly he took up his position between them and McAdam, assuming his natural pose of dreadful defiance. He made such a laughable spectacle, that tiny warlike creature, standing at bay with bristles up and teeth bared, that even James Moore smiled.

"My word! Have you brought his muzzle, man?" cried old Tammas, the humorist; and, turning, climbed hastily onto an upturned bucket that stood nearby. At this, the puppy, made all the more bold by his enemy's retreat, advanced savagely to the attack, buzzing around the slippery pail like a wasp on a windowpane, in a vain attempt to reach the old man.

Tammas stood on the top, pulling up his trousers and looking down at his attacker, the picture of deathly fear.

"Help! Oh, help!" he bawled. "Send for the soldiers! Fetch the police! For goodness sake, call him off, man!" Even Sammel Todd, watching the scene from the cart shed, was tickled and burst into a loud guffaw, heartily joined by two of the other farm workers, Henry and old Job. McAdam remarked: "You're more suited to the stage than a stable bucket, Mr. Thornton."

"How did you come by him?" asked Tammas, nodding at the puppy.

"Found him," the little man replied, sucking his twig. "Found him in my stocking on my birthday. A present from my little David for his old dad, I suspect."

"Well, that's a bit hard to believe," said Tammas, and was seized with a sudden attack of mysterious merriment. For, looking up as McAdam was speaking, he had caught a glimpse of a boy's blond head peering cautiously around the cow shed, and, behind him, the flutter of short petticoats. They disappeared as silently as they had come; and two small figures, just returned from school, glided away and took shelter in the friendly darkness of a coal-hole.

"Come away, Maggie, come away! It's the old one himself," whispered a disrespectful voice.

McAdam looked around suspiciously.

"What's that?" he asked sharply.

At the same moment, however, Mrs. Moore put he
out of the kitchen window.

"Come in, Mister McAdam, and have a bit of tea, she
called hospitably.

"Thank you kindly, Mrs. Moore, I will," he answered, po-
litely for him. And we must admit this one good thing about
Adam McAdam: that, although there was only one woman he
had ever been known to praise, there was also only one, in
the whole course of his life, against whom he had ever spoken
an evil word—and that was years later, when men said his
brain was weakened. He had insults and jeers for every man,
but a woman, good or bad, was sacred to him. For he had a
feeling of tenderness and reverence for women in general,
the sex to which his mother and his wife belonged, and if a
man has that feeling, we know he cannot be altogether bad.
As he turned to go into the house he looked back at Red Wull.

"Ay, we can leave him there," he said. "That is, if you're not
afraid, Mr. Thornton?"

◆ ◆ ◆

It is enough to say two things about what happened while the
men were inside. First, that Owd Bob was no bully. Second,
this: In the code of honor among sheepdogs, one word is
written in stark black letters; and opposite it is another word,
written large in the color of blood. The first word is "Sheep-
murder"; the second, "Death." Sheep-murder is the only
crime that must be punished with bloodshed; and to accuse a
dog of that crime is to offer the one unforgivable insult. Every
sheepdog knows it, and so does every shepherd.

That afternoon, while the men were still talking, the quiet
echoes of the farm rang with a furious animal cry, repeated

twice: "Shot for sheep-murder"—"Shot for sheep-murder";
followed by a hollow stillness.

◆ ◆ ◆

The two men finished their conversation. The business was
concluded peacefully, mainly because of the soothing influence of Mrs. Moore. Together, the three went out into the
yard; Mrs. Moore taking the opportunity to speak up shyly for
David.

"He's such a good little lad, I do think," she was saying.

"You should know, Mrs. Moore," the little man answered,
somewhat bitterly. "You see enough of him."

"You must be very proud of him, mister," the woman continued, paying no attention to the sneer. "He is growing into
such a fine lad."

McAdam shrugged his shoulders.

"I barely know the lad," he said. "I know him by sight, of
course, but barely to speak to. He's not often at home."

"And how proud his mother would be if she could see
him," the woman continued, well aware of his one tender
spot. "Oh, she was fond of him, she was."

An angry flush stole over the little man's face. He understood the implied rebuke very well; and it hurt him like a
knife.

"Yes, yes, Mrs. Moore," he began. Then, breaking off, and
looking about him—"Where's my Wullie?" he cried excit-
edly. "James Moore!" whipping around toward the Master,
"my Wullie's gone—gone, I say!"

Elizabeth Moore turned away indignantly.

"I do declare he takes more trouble over that little yellow
beast than ever he does over his own flesh and blood," she
muttered.

"Wullie, my little doggy! Wullie, where are ye? James Moore, he's gone—my Wullie's gone!" cried the little man, running around the yard, searching everywhere.

"He cannot have gone far," said the Master, reassuringly, looking about him.

"You can never tell," said Sammel, appearing on the scene, pig-bucket in hand. "I doubt you'll ever see your dog again, mister." He turned sorrowfully to McAdam.

That little man, all disheveled, and with the sweat standing out on his face, came hurrying from the cow shed and danced up to the Master.

"I've been robbed—robbed, I tell you!" he cried recklessly. "My little Wull's been stolen while I was at your house, James Moore!"

"You mustn't say that, my man. No robbing at Kenmuir," the Master answered sternly.

"Then where is he? It's for you to say."

"I've my own idea, I have," Sammel announced just then, holding the pig-bucket up in the air.

McAdam turned on him.

"What, man? What is it?"

"I doubt you'll ever see your dog again, mister," Sammel repeated, as if he were supplying the key to the mystery.

"Now, Sammel, if you know anything, tell it," ordered his master.

Sammel grunted sulkily.

"Where's our Bob, then?" he asked.

At that, McAdam turned on the Master.

"That's it, no doubt. It's your gray dog, James Moore, yer blasted dog. I might have known it"—and he let fly a volley of foul words.

"Swearing will not find him," said the Master coldly. "Now, Sammel."

The big man shifted his feet and looked mournfully at Mc-
Adam.

"It was, maybe, half an hour ago when I saw our Bob going
out of the yard with the little yellow tyke in his mouth. In a
minute I looked again—and there! the little yellow one was
gone, and our Bob was sitting and licking his chops. Gone
forever, I do suppose. Ah, you may well have a fit, Tammas
Thornton!" For the old man was rolling around the yard,
bent double with laughter.

McAdam turned on the Master, resigned and despairing.

"Man, Moore," he cried piteously, "it's your gray dog that
has murdered my little Wull! You heard it from your own
man."

"Nonsense," said the Master encouragingly. "It has only
wandered off somewhere."

Sammel tossed his head and snorted.

"Come, then, and I'll show you," he said, and led the way
out of the yard. And there below them on the slope that led
down to the stream, sitting like a judge at the court of law,
was our Bob.

Immediately, Sammel, who was usually as solemn as old
Ross, the church warden, burst into loud laughter. "Why is he
sitting so still, do you think? Ho, ho! See him licking his
chops—ha, ha!"—and he roared again, while in the distance
you could hear the chuckling of Henry and Our Job.

At the sight, McAdam burst into a storm of passionate cursing, and would have rushed at the dog if James Moore had not
held him back by force.

"Bob, lad," called the Master, "come here!"

But even as he spoke, the gray dog cocked his ears, listened
a moment, and then shot down the slope. At the same moment, Tammas called out: "There he is! There's the yellow

tyke over there, coming out of the drain! You see, Sammel!"
And there, indeed, on the slope below them, a little angry,
smutty-faced figure was crawling out of a rabbit-burrow.

"You murdering devil, how dare you touch my Wullie?"
yelled McAdam, and, breaking away, ran madly after him
down the hill; for the gray dog had picked up the puppy as
easily as a swallow snatches a bug in mid-air, and was racing
on, his captive in his mouth, toward the stream.

Behind them hurried James Moore and Sammel, wondering what the outcome of this comedy would be, and after
them toddled old Tammas, chuckling. Meanwhile, a little
cluster of heads had appeared above the wall of the yard: it
was Henry, Old Job, Maggie and David, and Violet Thornton,
the dairy-maid.

Straight onto the plank-bridge galloped Owd Bob. In the
middle he halted, leaned over, and dropped his prisoner, who
fell with a cool plop into the running water beneath.

In another moment, McAdam had reached the bank of the
stream. In he plunged, splashing and cursing, and seized the
struggling puppy; then waded back, the waters surging
around his waist, with Red Wull, limp as a wet rag, in his
hand. The little man's hair was dripping, for his cap was gone;
his clothes clung to him, revealing how miserably thin his
body was; and his eyes blazed like hot ashes in his wet face.

He sprang onto the bank, and, beside himself with passion, rushed at Owd Bob.

"Curse you for a—"

"Stand back, or you'll have him at your throat!" shouted
the Master, running hard toward him. "Stand back, I say, you
fool!" And, when the little man kept on charging forward, he
reached out his hand and hurled him back; at the same moment, bending, he buried the other hand deep in Owd Bob's

shaggy neck. It was only just in time; for if ever a pair of gray eyes gleamed with the fierce desire for a fight, the young dog's eyes were those gray eyes, as McAdam came toward him.

The little man staggered, tottered, and fell heavily. At the shock, the blood gushed from his nose, and, mixing with the water on his face, ran down in washy red streams, dripping off his chin; while Red Wull, who had been jerked from his grasp, was thrown far off, and lay motionless.

"Curse you!" McAdam screamed, his face dead white except for the red around his jaw. "Curse you for a cowardly Englishman!" and, struggling to his feet, he lunged toward the Master.

But Sammel put the great bulk of his body between the two.

"Easy, little man," he said calmly, gazing at the small fury before him with mournful interest. "Eh, you're a little spitfire, you are!"

James Moore stood breathing deeply, his hand still buried in Owd Bob's coat.

"If you had touched him," he explained, "I couldn't have stopped him. He'd have mauled you before I could have got him off you. They're hard to hold, the Gray Dogs, when they're roused."

"Ay, my word, they are!" agreed Tammas, speaking from his experience of sixty years. "Once they're on you, you cannot get them off."

The little man turned away.

"You're all against me," he said, and his voice shook. He was a pitiful figure, standing there with the water dripping off him. A red stream ran slowly from his chin; his head was bare, and his features were moving in agitation.

James Moore stood watching him with some pity and some contempt. Behind them was Tammas, enjoying the scene. Sammel gazed at them all with a serene melancholy.

McAdam turned away and bent over Red Wull, who still lay like a dead thing. As his master handled him, the button-like tail quivered feebly; he opened his eyes, looked about him, snarled faintly, and glared with devilish hatred at the gray dog and the group with him.

The little man picked him up, stroking him tenderly. Then he turned away and stepped onto the plank-bridge. Halfway across, he stopped. It rattled beneath him, for he was still trembling like a man in a violent fever.

"Man, Moore!" he called, trying to quiet the disturbance in his voice—"I would shoot that dog."

Once he was across the bridge, he turned again.

"Man, Moore!" he called and paused. "You won't forget this day." And with that, the blood flared up a dull crimson in his white face.

PART TWO
The Little Man

CHAPTER 5

A Man's Son

THE STORM had long threatened, and now that it had burst, McAdam gave free rein to his bitter hatred of James Moore.

The two often met. For the little man often returned home from the village along the path across Kenmuir. It was out of his way, but he preferred it, in order to annoy his enemy and keep an eye on his doings.

He haunted Kenmuir like its evil spirit. His sickly pale face was perpetually turning up at odd moments. When Kenmuir Queen, the prize short-horn heifer, gave birth to a calf unexpectedly and alone in the hollow by the lane, Tammas and the Master, summoned hurriedly by Owd Bob, came running up to find the little man leaning against the steps over the fence, shaking with silent laughter. On another day, poor old Staggy, still bold and adventurous though feeble-minded with age, took a fall while scrambling over the steep banks of the Stony Bottom. There he lay for hours, unnoticed and kicking, until, when he was nearly exhausted, James Moore and Owd Bob at last came upon him. But McAdam was there before them.

Standing on the far bank with Red Wull by his side, he called across the gully with a pretense of concern: "He's been like that since last night." Often James Moore, despite all his great strength of character, could barely control himself.

There were two attempts to patch up the feud. Jim Mason, who went about in the world trying to do good, tried in his shy way to set things right. But McAdam and his Red Wull between them soon shut him and Betsy up.

"You look after your letters and your telegrams, Mr. Poacher-Mailman. Ay, I saw them both: the one down by the Haughs, the other in the Bottom. And there's Wullie, the fanciful child, having a great game with Betsy." There, indeed, lay the faithful Betsy, on her back pleading for mercy, her paws up, her throat exposed, while Red Wull, now a very large puppy, stood over her, his habitually evil expression intensified into a fiendish grin, as, with wrinkled muzzle and savage wheeze, he waited for her to move so that he would have an excuse to pin her down: "Wullie, let the lady alone—you've had your dinner."

The minister, Parson Leggy, was the other who attempted to play the role of peace-maker; for he hated to see the two most important members of his tiny parish on bad terms with each other. First he addressed James Moore on the subject; but that man of few words cut him short with, "I have nothing against the little man," and would say no more. And, indeed, he had not been the one who started the quarrel.

As for the parson's conversation with McAdam, it is enough to say here that, in the end, the angry old minister would certainly have attacked his mocking opponent if Cyril Gilbraith had not held him back by force.

And after that, the feud was left to take its own course with no attempt to stop it.

David was now the only link between the two farms. Despite his father's angry commands, the boy clung to his close friendship with the Moores with a stubbornness that no amount of beating could conquer. Every minute of the day, when he was out of school, and on holidays and Sundays as well, he spent at Kenmuir. It was not until late at night that he would sneak back to his home, the Grange, and creep quietly up to his tiny bare room under the roof—not without his supper, indeed, since the motherly Mrs. Moore had taken care of that. And there he would lie awake and listen with fierce contempt as his father, hours later, staggered into the kitchen below, drunkenly singing a verse from a song by his favorite Robert Burns:

> We are na fou, we're nae that fou
> But just a drappie in our e'e;
> The cock may craw, the day may daw',
> And ay we'll taste the barley bree!

> (We're not so full—ay, not at all,
> We've just a sparkle in our eye;
> The day may dawn, the cock may crow,
> And still we'll taste the barley brew!")

And in the morning, the boy would slip quietly out of the house while his father was still asleep; only Red Wull would thrust out his savage head as the boy passed, and snarl hungrily.

In this way, father and son would sometimes go for weeks without seeing each other. And that was David's purpose—to avoid attention. It was only because he was clever at this game of keeping out of his father's way that he escaped being beaten.

The little man seemed to have no natural affection for his son. He lavished all the fondness in his small nature on the Tailless Tyke—as Red Wull was called by the Dalesmen. And he treated the dog with a careful tenderness that made David smile bitterly.

The little man and his dog were as alike morally as they were different physically. Each held a grudge against the world and was determined to pay it back. Each was like Ishmael, the son of Hagar, an outcast among his fellows.

You saw them this way, standing apart, like lepers, in the turmoil of life; and it was quite a revelation to come upon them by chance in some quiet spot at night, playing together, each wrapped up in the game, innocent, tender, forgetful of the hostile world.

The two were never separated except when McAdam came home by the path across Kenmuir. After that first misadventure he never allowed his friend to accompany him on the journey through the enemy's country; for he knew well that sheep dogs have long memories.

As far as the stile in the lane, then, that little set of steps that led up and over the fence, Red Wull would follow him. There he would stand, his great head poked through the rails, watching his master till he was out of sight; and then he would turn and trot, self-reliant and defiant, sturdy and surly, down the very center of the road through the village—no playing, no tempting away, and woe to man or dog who tried to stop him as he went! And on, past Mother Ross's shop, past the Sylvester Arms, to the right by Kirby's blacksmith shop, over the Wastrel by the Haughs, to wait for his master at the edge of the Stony Bottom.

The little man, when thus crossing Kenmuir, often met Owd Bob, who had the free run of the farm. On these occasions he passed discreetly by; for, though he was no cow-ard, it is a bad idea to attack a Gray Dog of Kenmuir single-handedly. As for the dog, he trotted soberly on his way, only a steely glint in the big gray eyes betraying his knowledge of the presence of his enemy. If ever, however, the little man, in his desire to spy over the bare land, wandered off the public path, a gray figure that seemed to spring out of the blue would come fiercely, silently racing down on him; and he would turn and run for his life, amid the uproarious jeers of any of the farmhands who had witnessed the encounter.

On these occasions, David was just as full of mockery as Tammas, at his father's expense.

"Good for you, little one!" he roared from behind a wall, on one occasion.

"Isn't he quick on his feet, now?" yelled Tammas, not to be outdone. "Look at him fly along—ho, ho!"

"See how his knees wobble!" said the undutiful son, de-lighted. "If I had knees like him, I'd wear petticoats." As he spoke, a swinging punch on his ear nearly knocked the young scamp down.

"D'you think God gave you a dad for you to jeer at? You ought to be ashamed of yourself. It'll serve you right if he does thrash you when you get home." And David, turning around, found James Moore close behind him, his heavy eye-brows lowering over his eyes.

Luckily, McAdam had not heard his son's voice among the others. But David was afraid that he had; for on the following morning, the little man said to him:

"David, you will come home immediately after school today."

"Will I?" said David rudely.

"You will."

"Why?"

"Because I tell you to, my lad"; and that was all the reason he would give. Had he told the simple fact that he wanted help in giving a dose of medicine to a ewe with a bad cough, things might have gone differently. As it was, David turned away defiantly down the hill.

The afternoon wore on. School time was long over; still there was no David.

The little man waited at the door of the Grange, fuming, hopping from one leg to the other, talking to Red Wull, who lay at his feet, his head on his paws, like a tiger waiting for his prey.

At last he could restrain himself no longer, and he set off running down the hill, his heart burning with indignation.

"Wait till we lay hands on you, my lad," he muttered as he ran. "We'll warm you, we'll teach you."

At the edge of the Stony Bottom he left Red Wull, as always. Crossing it himself, and rounding Langholm Hollow, he caught sight of James Moore, David, and Owd Bob walking away from him in the direction of Kenmuir. The gray dog and David were playing together, wrestling, racing, and rolling. The boy hadn't a thought for his father.

The little man ran up behind them, unseen and unheard, his feet softly pattering on the grass. His hand had fallen on David's shoulder before the boy guessed he was approaching.

"Did I tell you to come home after school, David?" he asked, concealing his anger beneath a suspiciously smooth and polite tone.

"Maybe. Did I say I would come?"

The rudeness of his tone and words both fanned his father's ill will into a blaze of anger. In a burst of passion he lunged forward at the boy with his stick. But as he hit him, a gray whirlwind struck him squarely on the chest, and he fell like a snapped stick and lay, half stunned, with a dark muzzle an inch from his throat.

"Get back, Bob!" shouted James Moore, hurrying up. "Get back, I tell you!" He bent over the figure lying flat on the ground, and propped him up anxiously. "Are you hurt, Mc-Adam? Eh, I am sorry. He thought you were going to strike the lad."

David had now run up, and he, too, bent over his father with a very scared face.

"Are you hurt, father?" he asked, his voice trembling.

The little man rose unsteadily to his feet and shook off the other two as they tried to hold him up. His face was twitching, and he stood, covered in dust, looking at his son.

"Perhaps you're content, now that you've seen your father's gray head bowed in the dust," he said.

"It was an accident," pleaded James Moore. "But I *am* sorry. He thought you were going to beat the lad."

"I was—and I will."

"If anyone is to be beaten, it should be my Bob here, though he only thought he was doing right. And you *were* off the path."

The little man looked at his enemy, a sneer on his face.

"You can't thrash him for doing what you tell him to do. You may set your dog on me, if you will, but don't beat him when he does what you ask!"

"I did not set him on you, as you know," the Master replied with some emotion.

McAdam shrugged his shoulders.

"I won't argue with you, James Moore," he said. "I'll leave you and what you call your conscience to settle that. My business is not with you.—David!" he said, turning to his son.

A stranger might well have been confused as to which man was the boy's father. For David stood now, holding the Master's arm; while a few paces above them was the little man, pale but determined, the expression on his face revealing his awareness of the strangeness of the situation.

"Will you come home with me and have it now, or stay here with him and wait till you get it?" he asked the boy.

"McAdam, I'd like you to—"

"None of that, James Moore.—David, what do you say?"

David looked up into his protector's face.

"You'd best go with your father, lad," said the Master at last, in a low voice. The boy hesitated, and clung tighter to the protective arm; then he walked slowly to his father.

A bitter smile spread over the little man's face as he noted this new test of the boy's obedience to the other man.

"To obey his friend, he denies himself the pleasure of disobeying his father," he muttered. "Noble!" Then he turned homeward, and the boy followed in his footsteps.

James Moore and the gray dog stood looking after them.

"I know you won't take out your anger against me on the boy's head, McAdam," he called, almost pleading.

"I'll do my duty quite fairly, thank you, James Moore," the little man cried back, never turning.

Father and son walked away, one behind the other, like a man and his dog, and not a word was said between them. Across the Stony Bottom, Red Wull, scowling with bared teeth at David, joined them. Together the three went up the hill to the Grange.

In the kitchen McAdam turned.

"Now, I'm going to give you the grandest thrashing you ever dreamed of. Take off your coat!"

The boy obeyed, and stood up in his thin shirt, his face as

white and still as a statue's. Red Wull seated himself on his haunches close by, his ears pricked, licking his lips, all attention.

The little man bent the long, supple stick of ash-wood back and forth in his hands and raised it. But the expression on the boy's face stopped his arm.

"Say you're sorry and I'll let you off easy."

"I won't."

"One more chance—your last! Say you're ashamed of yourself!"

"I'm not."

The little man brandished his cruel, white weapon, and Red Wull shifted a little to obtain a better view.

"Get on with it," ordered David angrily.

The little man raised the stick again and— threw it into the farthest corner of the room.

It fell with a rattle on the floor, and McAdam turned away.

"You're the most pitiful son a man ever had," he cried brokenly. "If a man's son doesn't stick by him, who will?—no one. You're undutiful, you're disrespectful, you're most everything you shouldn't be; there's only one thing I thought you were not—a coward. And as to that, you don't have enough spirit to say you're sorry, when God knows you might be. I can't thrash you today. But you won't go to school anymore. I send you there to learn. You won't learn—you've learned nothing except disobedience to me—you will stay at home and work."

His father's rare emotion, his broken voice and wretched expression, moved David as all the taunts and whiplashes had failed to do. His conscience pained him. For the first time in his life, it dimly dawned on him that perhaps his father, too, had reason to complain; that perhaps he was not a good son.

He half turned.

"Father—"

"Get out of my sight!" McAdam cried.

And the boy turned and went.

CHAPTER 6

A Licking or a Lie

FROM THEN on, David buckled down to his chores at home, and in one respect only, father and son resembled each other—they were both hard workers. A drunkard McAdam might be, but not a lazy man.

The boy worked at the Grange with tireless, resolute energy; yet he could never satisfy his father.

The little man would stand with a sneer on his face and his thin lips contemptuously curled, and mock the boy's brave labors.

"Isn't he a grand worker, Wullie? 'Tis a pleasure to watch him, his hands in his pockets, his eyes turned up toward the heavens!" he would say, as the boy snatched a hard-earned moment's rest. "You and I, Wullie, we'll break ourselves slaving for him while he looks on and laughs."

And so it went, the whole day through, week in, week out; till the boy was sick with weariness of it all.

In his darkest hours, David sometimes thought of running away. He was miserably alone in the cold heart of the world. The very fact that he was the son of his father isolated him in the Daleland. Quiet and reserved by nature, he did not have a single friend outside Kenmuir. And it was only the thought of his friends there that stopped him. He could not bring himself to leave them; they were all he had in the world.

So he worked on at the Grange, miserably, stubbornly, enduring his father's blows and taunts alike in burning silence. But every evening, when work was done, he walked away to his other home beyond the Stony Bottom. And on Sundays and holidays—for he took these days without asking, as his by rights—he would spend the whole day, from the time the cock crowed until the sun went down, at Kenmuir. In this one matter, the boy held firm. Nothing his father could say or do would break him of the habit. He endured everything with white-lipped, silent doggedness, and kept to his way.

Once he was past the Stony Bottom, he cast his troubles behind him with a courage that did him honor. Of all the people at Kenmuir, only two ever imagined the whole depth of his unhappiness, and this was not because of anything David said. James Moore suspected some part of it, because he knew more about McAdam than the others did. And Owd Bob knew it better than anyone. He could tell it from the touch of the boy's hand on his head; and the story was writ large on his face for a dog to read. And he would follow the boy about with a sympathy in his sad gray eyes that was greater than words.

David might well compare his gray friend at Kenmuir with that other one at the Grange.

The Tailless Tyke had now grown into an immense dog, with heavy muscles and huge bones. A great bull head; his lower jaw stuck out beyond the upper, square and long and terrible; his eyes were a vicious, gleaming yellow; his ears cropped; and his expression utterly savage. His coat was a tawny, lion-like yellow, short, rough, and dense; and his back, running up from shoulder to hips, ended abruptly in the knob-like tail. He looked like the devil in a dog's hell. And his reputation was as bad as his looks. He never attacked unless provoked; but he never ignored a challenge, and he was greedy for insults. Already he had nearly killed Rob Saunderson's collie, Shep; Jem Burton's dog, Monkey, ran headlong at the sound of his approach; and he had even fought one round with that fearful trio, the Vexer, Venus, and Van Tromp.

Nor, when it came to fighting, did he limit himself to his own kind. His huge strength and invincible courage made him a match for almost anything that moved. Long Kirby once threatened him with a broomstick; the blacksmith never did it again. While in the Border Ram, he attacked Big Bell, one of the guards of the Squire's forest, with such murderous fury that it took all the men in the room to pull him off.

More than once, he and Owd Bob had tried to wipe out memories of past encounters; and of all his fights, these were the only ones that Red Wull himself provoked. As yet, however, though they dashed in and out for a moment, looking for that deadly grip on the throat, the value of which they both knew so well, James Moore had always found the chance to intervene.

"That's right, hide him behind yer petticoats," sneered McAdam on one of these occasions.

"Hide? He won't be the one that I'll hide, I warn you, McAdam," the Master answered grimly, as he stood twirling his good oak stick between the would-be fighters. At which there was a loud laugh at the little man's expense.

It seemed there were to be other areas in which the two dogs were rivals, besides their memories. For in all of the Daleland, when it came to Red Wull's actual business, the handling of sheep, it was becoming clear that he would be second to none but the Gray Dog of Kenmuir. And McAdam was patient and painstaking in the training of his Wullie, so much so that David was astonished. It would have been touching, if it had not been so unnatural, considering his treatment of his own son, to watch the tender care with which the little man molded the dog beneath his hands. After a promising display from Red Wull, he would stand rubbing his palms together, as nearly content as he ever was.

"Well done, Wullie! Well done. Wait a little longer and we'll show 'em a thing or two, you and I, Wullie.

'The warld's wrack we share o't,
The warstle and the care o't.'

(The wreck of the world—we share in it,
The struggle and the care of it.)

"For it's you and I alone, lad." And the dog would trot up to him, place his great forepaws on his shoulders, and stand thus with his great head higher than his master's, his ears back, his stump of a tail vibrating.

You saw them at their best when they were thus together, each displaying his one soft side to the other.

From the very first, David and Red Wull were open enemies: under the circumstances, indeed, nothing else was possible. Sometimes the great dog would follow on the boy's heels with surly, greedy eyes, never leaving him from sunrise to sundown, until David could hardly stop himself from leaping at the dog.

So matters went on for a never-ending year. Then there came a climax.

One evening, on a day throughout which Red Wull had trailed behind him in this hungry way, David, his work finished, went to pick up his coat, which he had left nearby. On it was lying Red Wull.

"Get off my coat!" the boy ordered angrily, marching up. But the huge dog did not stir: he lifted his upper lip to show a fence of even white teeth, and seemed to sink even lower in the ground; his head on his paws, his eyes in his forehead.

"Come and take it!" he seemed to be saying.

Now, what David had endured that day, between master and dog, was almost more than he could bear.

"Oh you won't, won't you, you brute!" he shouted, and bending, snatched a corner of the coat and tried to jerk it away. At that, Red Wull rose shivering to his feet, and with a low gurgle sprang at the boy.

Quick as a flash, David dodged, bent, and picked up an ugly stake that lay at his feet. Spinning around, all in a moment, he swung the stake and struck the dog hard on the side of the head. Dazed from the blow, the big dog fell; then, recovering himself, with a terrible, deep roar he sprang again. At this point it would have gone badly for the boy, even though he was a well-grown, muscular young giant. For Red Wull was now in the first bloom of that great strength which afterwards was to earn him undying fame in the land.

As it happened, however, McAdam had been watching the scene from the kitchen. And now he came hurrying out of the house, shrieking commands and curses at the two fighters. As Red Wull sprang, the little man stepped between them, his head back and his eyes flashing. His small body received the full shock of the charge. He staggered, but recovered, and in a firm voice ordered the dog to heel.

Then he turned on David, seized the stake from his hand, and began furiously beating the boy.

"I'll teach ye to strike—a poor—dumb—harmless—crea-ture, ye—cruel—cruel—lad!" he cried. "How dare you strike —my—Wullie? your—father's—Wullie? Adam—McAdam's —Red Wull?" He was panting from his exertions, and his eyes were blazing. "I put up as best I can with all kinds of disrespect to myself; but when it comes to my poor Wullie, I cannot endure it. Have you no heart?" he asked, unconscious of the irony of the question.

"As much as some, I reckon," David muttered.

"Eh, what's that? What did you say?"

"You may thrash me till you're blind; and you say it's no more than your duty; but if anyone dares so much as to look at your Wullie, you're mad," the boy answered bitterly. And with that he turned away defiantly and openly in the direc-tion of Kenmuir.

McAdam took a step forward, and then stopped.

"I'll see ye again, my lad, this evening," he cried with cruel meaning.

"I doubt but you'll be too drunk to see anything at all—ex-cept, maybe, your bottle," the boy shouted back; and swag-gered down the hill.

◆ ◆ ◆

At Kenmuir that night, the particular, noticeable kindness of Elizabeth Moore was too much for the overstrung lad. Deeply affected by the contrast of her sweet motherliness, he burst into a storm of abuse against his father, his home, his life— everything.

"Don't, Davie. Don't, dearie!" cried Mrs. Moore, much dis-tressed. And taking him into her arms, she talked to the great, sobbing boy as though he were a child. At length he lifted his face and looked up; and, seeing the exhausted, pale face of his dear comforter, was struck with tender remorse that he had given way and pained her; she looked so frail and thin herself.

He mastered himself with an effort, and for the rest of the evening was his usual cheery self. He teased Maggie till she cried; he joked with stolid little Andrew; and bantered with Sammel Todd until the usually peaceful man threatened to bash his nose in.

Yet it was with a feeling of tightness in his throat that, later, he headed down the slope for home. James Moore and Parson Leggy went with him to the bridge over the Wastrel, and stood for a while watching as he disappeared into the summer night.

"He's a good lad," said the Master, half to himself.

"Yes," the parson answered. "I always thought there was good in the boy, if only his father would give him a chance. And look at the way Owd Bob there follows him. There's not another soul outside Kenmuir he would do that for."

"Yes, sir," said the Master. "Bob knows a man when he sees one."

"He does," agreed the other. "And by the way, James, they're saying in the village that you've decided not to run him for the Cup. Is that so?"

The Master nodded.

"It is, sir. They're all wild for me to do it, but I must oppose them. They say he's reached his prime—and so he has, in his body, but not in his brain. And a sheepdog, unlike other dogs, is not at his best till his brain is at its best—and that takes a while to develop, same as in a man, I reckon."

"Well, well," said the parson, trotting out a favorite phrase of his, "to wait is to win—to wait is to win."

❖ ❖ ❖

David slipped up into his room and into bed—unseen, he hoped. Alone in the darkness, he allowed himself the rare relief of tears; and at length fell asleep. He awoke to find his father standing at his bedside. The little man held a spindly homemade candle in his hand, and it lit his pale face in crude black and white. In the doorway, dimly outlined, was the large figure of Red Wull.

"Where have ye been all day?" the little man asked. Then, looking down at the white tear-stained face beneath him, he added hurriedly: "If ye choose to lie, I'll believe ye."

David was out of bed and standing up in his nightshirt. He looked at his father with contempt.

"I've been at Kenmuir. I won't lie for you or your sort," he said proudly.

The little man shrugged his shoulders.

"'Tell a lie and stick to it,' is my rule, and a good one, too, in honest England. I, for one, will not think any the worse of ye if your memory plays tricks on you."

"Do ye think I care at all what ye think of me?" the boy asked brutally. "No; there's enough liars in this family without me."

The candle trembled and was still again.

"A licking or a lie—take yer choice!"

The boy looked scornfully down on his father. Standing on his naked feet, he already towered half a head above the other and was twice the man.

"Do you think I'm afraid of a thrashing from you? Good gracious me!" he sneered. "Why, I'd just as soon let old Gramma Maddow beat me, for all I care."

A hint about his small size was sure to provoke the man's anger, like putting a lit match to gunpowder.

"Ye must be cold, standin' there like that. Run down and

fetch our little friend"—he meant a certain strap that hung in the kitchen. "I'll see if I can warm ye."

David turned and stumbled down the unlit, narrow stairs. The hard, cold boards struck like death against his naked feet. At his heels followed Red Wull, his hot breath fanning the boy's bare legs.

So into the kitchen and back up the stairs, and Red Wull always following.

"I won't despair, yet, of teaching ye the fifth commandment, to honor thy father, though I kill myself doing it!" cried the little man, seizing the strap from the boy's numb grasp.

◆ ◆ ◆

When it was over, McAdam turned away, breathless. At the threshold of the room he stopped and looked around, a dimly lit, devilish little figure, framed in the door; while from the blackness behind, Red Wull's eyes gleamed yellow.

Glancing back, the little man caught sight of such an expression on David's face that for once he was afraid. He banged the door and hobbled quickly down the stairs.

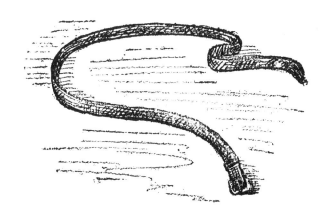

CHAPTER 7
The White Winter

McADAM, in his sober moments at least, never touched David again; instead, he devoted himself to the more agreeable exercise of lashing him with his tongue. And he was wise to restrain himself; for David, who was already nearly a head taller, and handsome and strong in proportion, could have, if he wished, taken his father in the hollow of his hand and crumpled him like a dry leaf. Moreover, with his tongue, at least, the little man enjoyed the noble pleasure of making the boy wince. And so the war was carried on just as spitefully.

Meanwhile, another summer was passing away, and every day brought fresh proofs of the superior prowess of Owd Bob. Tammas, whose supply of stories about Rex, son of Rally, had, after forty years of repetition, become a little dull even to the loyal ears of old Jonas, found no lack of new material now. In the local taverns, the Dalesman's Daughter in Silverdale and the Border Ram at Grammoch-town, a fresh tale was passed around each market day, week after week. Men told how the gray dog had outdone Gypsy Jack, such an expert "sheep-sneak"; how Owd Bob had slipped into the very center of Londesley's flock and separated out a shearling (a year-old sheep that has been sheared once) that belonged to Kenmuir; and a thousand stories of the same sort.

The Gray Dogs of Kenmuir have always been both heroes and favorites in the Daleland. And the Dalesmen now had absolute confidence in Owd Bob. Sometimes on market days he would perform some move that was impossible to explain, and a shepherd who had come into the area from somewhere else would ask: "What's that gray dog up to?" To which the nearest Dalesman would answer: "Well, I can't tell! But he knows what he's doing. It's Owd Bob of Kenmuir."

Whereupon the stranger would prick up his ears and watch with close attention.

"So that's Owd Bob of Kenmuir, is it?" he would say; for already the name was becoming known among the shepherds in the region. And never in such a case did the young dog fail to justify the faith of his supporters.

It therefore came as a keen disappointment to every Dalesman, from Herbert Trotter, Secretary of the Trials, to little Billy Thornton, when the Master stood firm in his decision not to enter the dog for the Cup in the approaching Dale Trials; and he stood firm even though the parson, the Squire, and Lady Eleanour herself tried to shake his resolve. Nearly fifty years had passed by now since Rex, son of Rally, had won back the Trophy for the land where it had first come into being; it was time, they thought, for a Daleland dog, a Gray Dog of Kenmuir—which was almost the same thing—to bring it home again. And Tammas, who had such a way with words, was only expressing the feelings of every Dalesman in the room when, one night at the Arms, he said, about Owd Bob, that "to have run was to have won." At which McAdam snickered audibly and winked at Red Wull. "To have run was to have one—a beating, I mean; to run next year will be to—"

"To win next year," Tammas interrupted stubbornly. "Unless"—with shivering sarcasm—"you and your Wullie are
thinking of winning."

The little man rose from his solitary seat at the back of the
room and came pattering across the floor.

"Wullie and I are thinking of it," he whispered loudly in
the old man's ear. "And one more thing. Take note of this, Mr.
Thornton: what Adam McAdam and his Red Wull think of
doing, they will do. Next year we will run, and next year—
we will win. Come, Wullie, we'll leave them to chew on
that"; and he marched out of the room amid the jeers of the
crowd of men. When quiet was restored, it was Jim Mason
who declared: "One thing is certain—win or not, they'll not
be far off."

◆ ◆ ◆

Meanwhile, the summer ended abruptly. Hard on the heels of
a sweltering autumn, the winter came down. That year, the
Daleland covered itself very early in its cloak of white. The
waters of the Silver Mere were soon veiled in ice; the course
of the Wastrel rolled sullenly down below Kenmuir, its pools
and quiet places tented with jagged sheets of ice; while the
towering Scaur and Muir Pike raised their white heads against
the frosty blue. It was the season still remembered in the
North as the White Winter—the worst, they say, since the
famous winter of 1808.

For days on end, the postman Jim Mason was stuck with
his bags of mail in the Dalesman's Daughter, and there was no
communication between the two valleys. On the Mere
Marches, the snow piled up deep, too deep to cross, in thick,
billowy drifts. In the Devil's Bowl, men said it lay twenty feet

deep or more. And sheep, looking for shelter in the ravines and protected spots, were buried and lost by the hundreds.

This is the time of year that tests the hearts of shepherds and sheepdogs, when the wind runs ice-cold across the empty stretches of white, and the low woods on the upland walks shiver black through a veil of snow, and sheep must be found and brought back into the safety of the fold, or they will be lost: it is a test of the mind as well as the heart, of a shepherd's resourcefulness as well as his resolve.

During that winter, more than one man, and many a dog, lost his life in the quiet performance of his duty, gliding to his death over the slippery snow-shelves, or buried beneath an avalanche of warm, suffocating white: "smoored," as they call it. Many a deed was done, many a death died, that was recorded only in the Book which contains the names of those—men or animals, souls or no souls—who Tried.

They found old Wrottesley, the Squire's head shepherd, lying one morning at the foot of Gill's Peak, like a statue in its white bed, the snow gently blowing about the dignified old face, calm and beautiful in death. And lying stretched out on his chest, with her master's hand, blue and stiff, still clasped around her neck, was his old dog Jess. She had huddled there, as a last hope, to keep her dear, dead master warm, her great heart broken, hoping where there was no hope.

That night she followed him to herd sheep in a better land. Death from exposure, said Dingley, the vet; but as little McAdam, his eyes dimmer than usual, declared in a husky voice, "We know better, Wullie."

Cyril Gilbraith, not usually a very emotional young man, told with a sob in his voice how, at the terrible Rowan Rock, Jim Mason the postman had stood helpless, silent, wide-eyed, as he watched Betsy—Betsy, his friend and partner of the last ten years—slip over the ice-cold surface, silently appealing to the hand that had never failed her before, sliding away to Eternity.

In the Daleland that winter, the endurance of many a shepherd and his dog was strained past the breaking point. From the frozen Black Water to the white-peaked Grammoch Pike, only two men, each with his shaggy helper always by his side, never admitted defeat; never turned back, never failed in anything they tried.

In the following spring, Mr. Tinkerton, the Squire's agent, declared that James Moore and Adam McAdam—or rather Owd Bob and Red Wull—had, between them, lost fewer sheep than any single farmer on the whole March Mere Estate—a proud record.

Many a tale was told that winter about those two. They could not be beaten, they were unlike any other; they were worthy rivals.

It was Owd Bob who, when he could not *drive* the herd of black-face sheep over the narrow Razorback which led to safety, persuaded them to *follow* him across that ten-inch-wide death-trail, one by one, like children behind their school-teacher. It was Red Wull who was seen coming down the steep Saddler's How, supporting that grand old gentleman, King o' the Dale, whose leg was broken.

It was the gray dog who found Cyril Gilbraith by the White Stones, with a cigarette and a sprained ankle, on the night the whole village was out with lanterns searching for the well-loved young rascal. It was the Tailless Tyke and his master who, one bitter evening, came upon little Mrs. Burton lying in a huddle beneath the meadow of Druid's Pillar, whitening quickly with the falling snow, her newest baby lying on her chest. It was little McAdam who took off his coat and wrapped the child in it; little McAdam who unwound his scarf, threw it like a sash across the dog's great chest, and tied the ends around the weary woman's waist. It was Red Wull who dragged her back to the Sylvester Arms and to life, straining like a giant through the snow, while his master staggered behind with the baby in his arms. When they reached the inn it was McAdam who, with a smile on his face, told the landlord what he thought of him for sending his wife across the Marches on such a day and on an errand for him. To which the honest Jem pleaded: "I had a cold."

For days at a time, David could not cross the Stony Bottom to Kenmuir. His forced imprisonment in the Grange resulted, however, in no more frequent quarrels than usual with his father. For McAdam and Red Wull were out at all hours, in all weathers, night and day, toiling at their work of salvation.

At last, one afternoon, David managed to cross the Bottom at a point where a fallen thorn-tree gave him a bridge over the soft snow. He stayed only a little while at Kenmuir, yet when he started for home it was snowing again.

By the time he had crossed the ice-draped bridge over the Wastrel, a blizzard was raging. The wind roared past him, striking him so hard he could barely stand; and the snow leaped at him so that he could not see. But he held on doggedly; slipping, sliding, tripping, down and up again, with one arm shielding his face. On, on, into the white darkness, blindly on, sobbing, stumbling, dazed.

At last, nearly dead, he reached the edge of the Stony Bottom. He looked up and he looked down, but nowhere in that blinding mist could he see the fallen thorn-tree. He took a step forward into the deep drift of wet white snow, and sank up to his thigh. He struggled feebly to free himself, and sank deeper. The snow twisted and coiled around him like a white flame, and he collapsed, softly crying, on that soft bed.

"I can't—I can't!" he moaned.

Little Mrs. Moore, her face whiter and more delicate than ever, stood at the window, looking out into the storm.

"I can't rest for thinking of the lad," she said. Then, turning, she saw her husband, his fur cap down over his ears, buttoning his heavy wool pilot-coat around his throat, while Owd Bob stood at his feet, waiting.

"You're not going out, James?" she asked, anxiously.

"Yes I am, lass," he answered; and she knew him too well to say more.

So the two, man and dog, went quietly out, either to save a life, or to lose their own, without counting the cost.

Down a wind-shattered slope—over a spar of ice—up an eternal hill—a forlorn hope.

In a whirlwind chaos of snow, the tempest storming at them, the white earth lashing them, they fought a good fight. In front, Owd Bob, the snow clogging his shaggy coat, his hair cutting like lashes of steel across his eyes, his head lowered as though he followed the finger of God; and close behind, James Moore, his back stiff and straight against the storm, firm and resolute still, yet swaying like a tree before the wind.

So they battled through to the edge of the Stony Bottom— only to arrive too late.

For, just as the Master, peering about him, had caught sight of a shapeless lump lying motionless in front, there loomed across the snow-choked gulf, through the white riot of the storm, a gigantic figure pushing his way steadily forward, his great head down to meet the hurricane. And close behind, battered and bruised, stiff and staggering, a little fearless figure holding stubbornly on, clutching with one hand at the gale; and a shrill voice, whirled away on the trumpet tones of the wind, crying:

"Now, Wullie, with me!

'Scots wha' hae wi' Wallace bled!
Scots wham Bruce has often led!
Welcome to—!'

(Scots who have with Wallace bled!
Scots whom Bruce has often led!
Welcome to—!)

"Here he is, Wullie!

'—or to victorie!'"

The brave little voice died away. The search was over; the lost sheep found. And the last James Moore saw of them was the same small, gallant form, half carrying, half dragging the rescued boy out of the Valley of the Shadow of Death and away.

David was none the worse for his adventure, for on reaching home McAdam produced a familiar bottle.

"Here's something to warm yer insides, and"—making a show of reaching for the strap on the wall—"here's something to do the same by your— But, Wullie, out again!"

And out they went—unreckoned heroes.

❖ ❖ ❖

It was only a week later, in the very heart of the bitter season, that there came a day when, from the gray dawn to the grayer evening, neither James Moore nor Owd Bob stirred out into the wintry white. And the Master's face was hard and motionless, as it always was in a time of trouble.

Outside, the wind screamed down the Dale, while the

snow fell without stopping, softly fingering the windows, blocking the doors, and piling deep against the walls. Inside the house, there was a strange quiet; no sound except for hushed voices, and upstairs the shuffling of muffled feet.

Downstairs, Owd Bob paced back and forth in the hall all day long, like a silent gray ghost.

Once, there came a low knocking at the door; and David, his face and hair and cap smothered in the whiteness that was everywhere in the air outside, came in with a whirling gust of cold snow. He patted Owd Bob and moved on tiptoe into the kitchen. Maggie came to him softly, her shoes in her hand, with a white, frightened face. The two whispered anxiously awhile like brother and sister, as they seemed to be; then the boy crept quietly away; only a little pool of water on the floor and wet, slippery footprints leading to the door gave evidence of the visitor.

Toward evening the wind died down, but the sad flakes still fell.

With the darkening of night Owd Bob retreated to the entryway and lay down on his blanket. The light from the lamp at the head of the stairs shone through the crack of the open door on his dark head and the eyes that never slept.

The hours passed, and the gray knight still kept watch. Alone in the darkness—alone, it almost seemed, in the house —he lay awake. His head rested motionless along his paws, but the steady gray eyes never flinched or drooped.

Time tramped on, on leaden foot, and still he waited; and the pain of hovering anxiety was stamped ever deeper in the gray eyes.

At last it grew past enduring; the hollow stillness of the house was too much for him. He arose, pushed open the door, and softly pattered across the hall.

At the foot of the stairs he halted, his forepaws on the first step, his grave face and pleading eyes uplifted, as though he were praying. The dim light fell on the raised head; and the white blaze on his chest shone out like the "snow on Zalmon," as it is sung in the Bible.

At last, with a sound like a sob, he stepped back from the stairs and stood listening, his tail drooping and head raised. Then he turned and began softly pacing up and down, like some velvet-footed sentinel at the gate of death.

Up and down, up and down, as softly as the falling snow, for a weary, weary while.

Again he stopped and stood, listening intently, at the foot of the stairs; and his gray coat quivered as though there were a draft.

Suddenly, the deathly stillness of the house was broken. Upstairs, feet were running hurriedly. There was a cry, and again silence.

A life was coming in; a life was going out.

The minutes passed; the hours passed; and, when the sunless dawn came, that life was gone.

And all through that night of age-long agony, the gray figure stood, still as a statue, at the foot of the stairs. At last, with the first chilly breath of the morning, a dry sob, quickly stifled, was heard, the sob of a strong man sorrowing for his wife of twenty years, and after it the tiny cry of a newborn child, wailing because its mother was not there. Only then, when these cries came down to his ears, did the Gray Watchman drop his head on his chest, and, with a little whimper, creep back to his blanket.

A little later the door above opened, and James Moore came down the stairs with a slow, heavy step. He looked taller and thinner than usual, but there was no sign of emotion on his face.

At the foot of the stairs Owd Bob stole out to meet him. He

came crouching up, head and tail down, in a way no man had ever seen before or ever saw again. At his master's feet, he stopped and whined pitifully.

Then, for one short moment, James Moore's whole face quivered.

"Well, lad," he said, quite softly, and his voice broke; "She's gone!"

That was all; for they were a pair who did not make a great display of their feelings.

Then they turned and went out together into the bleak morning.

CHAPTER 8

McAdam and His Coat

To DAVID McAdam, the loss of gentle Elizabeth Moore was as real a grief as to her children. Yet he bravely quieted his own aching heart and devoted himself to comforting the mourners at Kenmuir.

In the days following Mrs. Moore's death, the boy recklessly avoided his duties at the Grange. But little McAdam did not scold him. At times, indeed, he tried, without ever going out of his way, to be kind. David, however, was too deeply sunk in his great sorrow to notice the change.

The day of the funeral came. The earth was throwing off its chains of ice; and the Dale was lost in a melancholy mist.

In the afternoon, McAdam was standing at the window of the kitchen, studying the endless desolation of the scene, when the door of the house opened and shut noiselessly. Red Wull raised himself up to the windowsill and growled, and David hurried past the window heading for Kenmuir. Mc-Adam watched the passing figure indifferently; then with an angry curse sprang to the window.

"Bring me back that coat, ye thief!" he cried, tapping

75

fiercely on the windowpane. "Take it off at once, ye great fool, or I'll come and tear it off ye. Did ye see him, Wullie? The great idiot has my coat—my black coat, new last Michaelmas, and it raining enough to melt it."

He threw the window up with a bang and leaned out.

"Bring it back, I tell ye, ye undutiful lad, or I'll serve ye with a summons of the law. Though ye've no respect for me, you might have for my clothes. You're too big for yer own boots, let alone my coat. Did ye think I had it made for an elephant? It's bursting on you, I tell ye. Take it off! Fetch it here, or I'll send Wullie to bring it!"

David paid no attention except to begin running heavily down the hill. The coat was stretched in wrinkled agony across his back; his big, red wrists stuck out like shank-bones from the sleeves; and the little coattails flapped wearily in vain attempts to reach the wearer's legs.

McAdam, bubbling over with indignation, scrambled halfway through the open window. Then, tickled by the amazing impudence of the thing, he paused, smiled, dropped to the ground again, and watched the awkward retreating figure with chuckling amusement.

"Did ye ever see anything like it, Wullie?" he muttered. "My poor coat—poor little coatie! It makes me cry to see her in such pain. A man's coat, Wullie, is often remarkably small for his son's back; and David there is straining and stretching her near to breaking, for all the world as he does my patience. And what does he care about the one or the other?—not a jot."

As he stood watching the disappearing figure, there began the slow tolling of the funeral bell, once every minute, in the little Dale church. Now it sounded close by, now far away, now loud, now muffled, and its dull chant rang out through the mist like the slow-dropping tears of a mourning world.

McAdam listened, almost worshipfully, as the bell tolled

on, the only sound in the quiet Dale. Outside, a drizzling rain was falling; the snow dribbled down the hill in muddy trickles, and the trees and roofs and windows dripped.

And still the bell tolled on and on, calling up sad memories of an earlier time.

It was on just such another dreary day, in just such another December, and not so many years ago, that the light had gone out of his life forever.

The whole picture rose instantly to his eyes, as if it had been yesterday. That bell tolling on and on brought the scene surging back to him: the dismal day; the drizzle; the few mourners; little David dressed in black, his fair hair bright against his gloomy clothes, his face swollen with weeping; the Dale as quiet as though it were dead, except for the ringing of the bell; and his love had left him and gone to the happy land the hymn-books talk about.

Red Wull, who had been watching him uneasily, now came up and shoved his muzzle into his master's hand. The cold touch brought the little man back to earth. He shook himself, turned with a tired step away from the window, and went to the door of the house.

He stood there looking out; and all around him the drip, drip of the thaw went on and on. The wind died down, and again the funeral bell tolled out clear and steady, determined to remind him of what was and what had been.

With a choking gasp, the little man turned back into the house and ran up the stairs and into his room. He dropped on his knees beside the great chest in the corner and unlocked the bottom drawer, the key turning noisily in its socket.

In the drawer he searched with feverish fingers, and at last brought out a little paper packet tied up with a stained yellow ribbon. It was the ribbon she used to weave into her soft hair on Sundays.

Inside the packet was a cheap, heart-shaped frame, and in it a photograph.

Up there in his room, it was too dark to see. The little man ran down the stairs, Red Wull bumping against him as he went, and hurried to the window in the kitchen.

It was a sweet, laughing face that looked up at him from the frame, modest and yet playful, shy and yet impish—a face to gaze at and a face to love.

As he gazed, a wintry smile, wholly tender, half tearful, stole over the little man's face.

"Lassie," he whispered, and his voice was infinitely soft, "it's been a long time since I've dared look at ye. But it's not that ye're forgotten, dearie."

Then he covered his eyes with his hand as though he were blinded.

"Don't look at me that way, lass!" he cried, and fell on his knees, kissing the picture, hugging it to him and sobbing passionately.

Red Wull came up and pushed his face into his master's in sympathy; but the little man shoved him roughly away, and the dog retreated into a corner, puzzled and reproachful.

Memories swarmed back on the little man.

It was more than ten years ago now, and yet he hardly dared to think of that last evening when she had lain so white and still in the little room above.

"Put the child on the bed, Adam, my dearest," she had said in a low voice. "I'll be going in a little while now. It's the long goodbye to you—and to him."

He had done what she wished and lifted David up. The tiny boy lay still a moment, looking at this white-faced mother whom he hardly recognized.

"Mama!" he called pitifully. Then, thrusting a small, dirty hand into his pocket, he pulled out a grubby piece of candy.

"Mama, have a sweetie—one of Davie's sweeties!" and he held it out anxiously in his warm, plump palm, thinking it would be a certain cure for any disease.

"Eat it for mother," she said, smiling tenderly; and then: "Davie, my heart, I'm leaving ye."

The boy stopped sucking on the sweet, and looked at her, the corners of his mouth drooping sadly.

"Ye're not going away, mother?" he asked, his face moving. "Ye won't leave yer little boy?"

"Ay, laddie, away—far away. HE's calling me." She tried to smile; but the mother's heart was nearly breaking.

"Ye'll take yer little Davie with ye, mother!" the child begged, crawling up toward her face.

The great tears rolled freely down her pale cheeks, and McAdam, at the head of the bed, was sobbing openly.

"Oh, my child, my child, I'm sorry to leave ye!" she cried brokenly. "Lift him up for me, Adam."

He placed the child in her arms; but she was too weak to hold him. So he laid the boy on his mother's pillow; and little Davie wound his soft arms around her neck and sobbed violently.

And the two lay thus together.

Just before she died, Flora turned her head and whispered:

"Adam, my dearest, ye'll have to be mother and father both to the lad now"; and she looked at him with tender confidence in her dying eyes.

"I will! Before God, as I stand here, I will!" he declared passionately. Then she died, and there was a look of utter peace on her face.

◆ ◆ ◆

"Mother and father both!"

The little man rose to his feet and flung the photograph from him. Red Wull pounced upon it; but McAdam leapt at him as he took it in his mouth.

"Get away, ye devil!" he screamed; and, picking it up, stroked it lovingly with trembling fingers.

"Mother and father both!"

How had he fulfilled his love's last wish? How!

"Oh, God!"—and he fell on his knees at the side of the table, hugging the picture, sobbing and praying.

Red Wull crouched fearfully in the far corner of the room, and then crept whining up to where his master knelt. But McAdam paid no attention to him, and the great dog slunk away again.

There the little man knelt in the gloom of the winter afternoon, miserable and full of regret. His head, touched with gray, was bowed upon his arms; his hands clutched the picture; and he prayed aloud in gasping, unsteady tones.

"Give me grace, O God! 'Father and mother both,' ye said, Flora—and I haven't done it. But it isn't too late—say it's not, lass. Tell me there's still time, and say ye forgive me. I've tried to be patient with him many and many a time. But he has angered me, and set himself against me, and hardened me against him, and ye know how I was always quick to take offense. But I'll make it up to him—make it up to him and more. I'll humble myself before him, and that'll be hard enough. And I'll be father and mother both to him. But there's been no one to help me; and it's been painful without ye. And—oh, but lassie, I miss ye so!"

◆ ◆ ◆

It was a dreary little procession that wound its way through the drizzle from Kenmuir to the little Dale Church. At the head of it walked James Moore with a stiff, angry step, and close behind him David in his small, tight coat. Last of all, as if to guide those lagging behind in the weary road, came Owd Bob.

There was a full congregation in the tiny church now. In the Squire's pew were Cyril Gilbraith, Muriel Sylvester, and, most noticeable, Lady Eleanour. Her slender figure was simply draped in gray, with gray fur around the neck and gray fur edging her sleeves and her jacket; her veil was lifted, and you could see the soft hair around her temples, like waves breaking on white cliffs, and her eyes big with tender sympathy as she glanced toward the pew on her right.

For there were the mourners from Kenmuir: the Master, tall, grim, and gaunt; and beside him Maggie, trying to be calm, and little Andrew, a small version of his father.

Alone, in the pew behind them, sat David McAdam in his father's coat.

The back of the church was packed with farmers from the whole March Mere Estate; friends from Silverdale and Grammoch-town; and nearly every soul in Wastrel-dale, who had come to show their sympathy for the living and their reverence for the dead.

❖ ❖ ❖

At last the end came in the wet dreariness of the little church-yard, and slowly the mourners went away, until at length only the parson, the Master, and Owd Bob were left.

The parson was speaking in rough, short tones, digging nervously at the wet ground. The Master, tall and thin, his face tense and half turned away, stood listening. By his side was Owd Bob, looking at his master's face, a sad and thought-ful sympathy in his melancholy gray eyes; while close by, one of the parson's terriers was nosing curiously at the wet grass.

Suddenly, James Moore, his face still turned away, stretched out a hand. The parson stopped speaking abruptly and grasped it. Then the two men walked away quickly in opposite directions, the terrier hopping on three legs and shaking the rain off his wiry coat.

◆ ◆ ◆

David's steps sounded outside. McAdam rose from his knees. The door of the house opened, and the boy's feet shuffled in the hallway.

"David!" the little man called in a trembling voice.

He stood in the half-light, one hand on the table, the other clasping the picture. His eyes were bleary, his thin hair tousled, and he was shaking.

"David," he called again, "I've something I wish to say to ye!"

The boy burst into the room. His face was stained with tears and rain; and the new black coat was wet and slimy all down the front, and on the elbows were greenish-brown, muddy spots. For on his way home, he had flung himself down in the Stony Bottom just as he was, without caring about the wet earth and his father's coat, and, lying on his face thinking of that second mother lost to him, he had wept his heart out in a storm of grief.

Now he stood defiantly, his hand on the door.

"What do ye want?"

The little man looked from him to the picture in his hand.

"Help me, Flora—he won't..." he prayed. Then, raising his eyes, he began: "I'd like to say—I've been thinking—I think I should tell ye—it's not an easy thing for a man to say—"

He broke off short. The task he had set himself was almost more than he could carry out.

He looked at David for help. But there was no understanding at all in that white, hard face.

"O God, it's almost more than I can do!" the little man muttered; and the sweat stood out on his forehead. Again he began: "David, after I saw ye this afternoon stepping down the hill—"

Again he paused. He glanced at the coat without thinking. David misunderstood the look; misunderstood the dimness in his father's eyes; misunderstood the tremor in his voice.

"Here it is! Take yer coat!" he cried violently; and, tearing it off, flung it down at his father's feet. "Take it—and—curse ye."

He banged out of the room and ran upstairs; and, locking himself in, threw himself onto his bed and sobbed.

Red Wull made a movement to fly at the retreating figure; then turned to his master, his stump-tail vibrating with pleasure.

But little McAdam was looking at the wet coat now lying in a wet bundle at his feet.

"Curse ye," he repeated softly. "Curse ye—ye heard him, Wullie?"

A bitter smile crept across his face. He looked again at the picture now lying crushed in his hand.

"Ye can't say I didn't try; ye can't ask me to try again," he muttered, and slipped it into his pocket. "Never again, Wullie; not if the Queen were to ask it."

Then he went out into the gloom and drizzle, still smiling the same bitter smile.

◆ ◆ ◆

That night, when it came to closing-time at the Sylvester Arms, Jem Burton found a little gray-haired figure lying on the barroom floor. At the little man's head lay a great dog.

"You beast!" said the high-minded landlord of the tavern, gazing at the figure of his best customer with scorn. Then, catching sight of a photograph in the little man's hand:

"Oh, you're that kind of a man, are you, you sly fellow?" he said meanly. "Give us a look at her," and he tried to wrestle the picture out of the little man's grasp. But at the attempt, the great dog rose and bared his teeth, with such a devilish expression on his face that the big landlord quickly retreated behind the bar.

"The two of ye!" he shouted viciously, stamping his heels; "beasts both of ye!"

PART THREE
The Shepherds' Trophy

CHAPTER 9

Rivals

M c ADAM never forgave his son. After the scene on the evening of the funeral, there could be nothing else but war between them for all time. The little man had tried to humble himself, and had been rejected; and the bitterness of defeat, when by rights he should have had victory, hurt him and bothered him like a poisoned arrow in his side.

Yet his feeling of indignation was not against David, but against the Master of Kenmuir. He blamed his unhappiness on the effect and the influence that James Moore had on David, and therefore turned his anger on him. In public or in private, in the barroom or in the marketplace, he never grew tired of speaking against his enemy.

"Feel the loss of his wife, you say?" he would cry out. "Oh, indeed—as much as I feel the loss of my hair. James Moore cannot feel anything, I tell you, except, maybe, a bit of bad luck to his miserable dog."

When the two met, as they often did, McAdam always tried to trick his enemy into saying something low and mean. But James Moore, though greatly tested, never gave way. He met the little man's sneers with a silence that quieted him, looking down on his sharp-tongued neighbor with a scorn flashing from his blue-gray eyes that hurt the little man more than words.

Only once was he provoked into answering. It was in the barroom of the Dalesman's Daughter at the time of the big spring fair in Grammoch-town, when there was a large gathering of farmers and their dogs in the room.

McAdam was standing at the fireplace with Red Wull at his side.

"Ye play a noble game, don't ye, James Moore," he cried loudly across the room, "setting a son against his father, and dividing a house against itself. It's worthy of ye, with yer churchgoing and yer psalm-singing and yer godliness."

The Master looked up from the far end of the room.

"Maybe yo're not aware, McAdam," he said sternly, "that if it hadn't been for me, David would have left you years ago—and it would only have served yo' right, I'm thinking."

The little man was beaten at his own game, so he changed tactics.

"Don't shout like that, man—I have ears to hear with. Besides, ye irritate Wullie."

The Tailless Tyke had indeed walked forward from the fireplace and now stood, huge and hideous, in the very center of the room. There was distant thunder in his throat, a threatening look upon his face, a challenge in every wrinkle. And the Gray Dog stole gladly out from behind his master to take up the challenge to do battle.

Immediately there was silence; tongues stopped wagging, tankards clinking. Every man and every dog was quietly gathering around those two central figures. Every one of them had wished for revenge against the Tailless Tyke; every one of them was burning to join in, once the battle began. And the two gladiators stood looking past each other, muzzle to muzzle, each with a tiny flash of teeth glinting between his lips.

But there was to be no fight; for the twentieth time, the Master stepped in.

"Bob, lad, come in!" he called, and, bending, grasped his favorite by the neck.

McAdam laughed softly.

"Wullie, Wullie, to me!" he cried. "The look of you's enough for that gentleman."

"If they get to fighting, it won't be Bob here that I'll strike, I warn yo', McAdam," said the Master grimly.

"If ye so much as touched Wullie, do ye know what I'd do, James Moore?" asked the little man very smoothly.

"Yes—yo'd curse," the other replied, and strode out of the room amid a roar of mocking laughter at McAdam's expense.

Owd Bob had now nearly reached perfection in his art. Parson Leggy declared firmly that they had not seen a dog like him since the days of Rex, son of Rally. Among the Dalesmen, he was a hero and a favorite, his strength and skill and gentle manners winning him friends on every side. But what they liked most about him was that he was the very opposite of Red Wull.

Almost every man in that countryside held a grudge against the ferocious savage; yet not a single one dared to act on it. Once, Long Kirby the blacksmith, full of beer and courage, had tried to pay back Red Wull. Coming upon McAdam and the dog as he was driving into Grammoch-town, Long Kirby leaned over and, with his whip, thrashed the dog a terrible sword-like slash that made an angry ridge of red from the dog's hip to his shoulder; and Kirby was twenty yards down the road before the little man's shrill curse reached his ear, drowned in a hideous bellow.

Kirby stood up and whipped his colt, who, quick on his legs for such a young animal, soon settled into a steady gallop. But glancing over his shoulder, Long Kirby saw a form bounding along behind him, catching up with him as quickly as though he were walking. His face turned sickly white; he screamed; he lashed his horse; he looked back. Right beneath the tail-board of the carriage was the red devil running in the dust; while, racing a couple of hundred yards behind, on the turnpike road, was the crazed figure of McAdam.

Long Kirby struck back and front, lashing the dog with his whip and flogging his horse forward. It was no use. Leaping like a tiger, the murderous brute flew up onto the carriage. At the shock of the great body landing, the colt was thrown violently onto his side; Kirby was tossed over the hedge; and Red Wull was pinned beneath the wreckage.

McAdam was just in time to rush up and save a tragedy from happening.

"I'm tempted to stick a knife into ye, Kirby," he panted, as he bandaged the smith's broken head.

After that, you may be sure, the Dalesmen preferred to swallow his insults rather than to risk their lives; and their helplessness only fed their hatred until it blazed white hot.

The working methods of the two dogs were as different as their looks. In a word, one dog forced, while the other persuaded.

His enemies said the Tailless Tyke was rough; not even Tammas denied that he was ready and willing. His brain was as big as his body, and he used them both to good purpose. "As quick as a cat, with the heart of a lion and the temper of the devil himself," was how Parson Leggy described him.

What could be done using pure determination, Red Wull could do; but to make something happen by doing nothing— the highest of all strategies—was not his way. In situations where the most delicate handling of the sheep was required, where the slightest sign of any emotion other than calm indifference was ruinous, when the sheep were restless, when the singing of the wind filled them with a sense of looming disaster, when the air seemed charged with invisible panic, when one wrong motion would have spelled catastrophe—in those situations Owd Bob o' Kenmuir was the best.

People still tell how, when the Squire's new threshing machine went running out of control in Grammoch-town, and for some minutes the market square was a wild sea of cursing men, yelping dogs, and stampeding sheep, only one flock stood by the bullring as calm as a mill pond, watching the riot almost with indifference. And in front, sitting between them and the storm, was a quiet gray dog, his mouth stretched in a wide yawn: to yawn, at that moment, was to win, and he won.

When the worst of the uproar was over, many men glanced with a look of triumph first at that one quiet flock, and then at McAdam, as he waded through his own disorder of huddling sheep.

"And where's your Wullie now?" asked Tupper scornfully.

"Well," the little man answered with a sly smile, "at this minute he's killing your Rasper down by the pump." Which was indeed true; for big blue Rasper had interfered with the great dog as he did his duty, and was now paying the price.

❖ ❖ ❖

Spring turned into summer; and the excitement over the coming Sheep Trials, when at last the two rivals would be pitted against each other, reached a height that old Jonas Maddox could hardly remember in all his eighty years.

Almost every night, down in the Sylvester Arms, McAdam

would get into a fight with Tammas Thornton, spokesman of the Dalesmen. The two had many a long-drawn-out quarrel as to the respective merits of the red dog and the gray, and their chances of winning the Cup. In these duels, Tammas was usually defeated. His temper would get the better of his wisdom; and he would change from skeptical debater to hot-tongued defender of the gray dog.

During these contests, the other men would usually maintain a strict silence. Only when their champion was being beaten, and it was time for the strength of their voices to conquer the strength of McAdam's arguments, would they join in heartily and roar the little man down, for all the world like the gentlemen who rule the British Empire at Westminster, the seat of government in London.

Tammas was an easy target for McAdam to provoke, but David was easier. When the insults were directed at himself, the boy put up with them calmly, for he was used to them. But a poisonous dart shot against his friends at Kenmuir never failed to rouse him. And the little man showed an amazing talent for making up clever lies about James Moore.

"I hear," said he, one evening, sitting in the kitchen, sucking his twig; "I hear that James Moore is goin' to git married again."

"You're hearin' lies—or more likely telling them," David answered curtly. For he now treated his father with contemptuous indifference.

"Seven months since his wife died," the little man continued thoughtfully. "Well, I'm only surprised he's waited this long. Bury one, take another—that's James Moore."

David burst angrily out of the room.

"Goin' to ask him if it's true?" called his father after him. "Good luck to ye—and to him."

David now had a new interest at Kenmuir. He now found

Maggie endlessly fascinating as a subject of study. After her mother died, the girl had taken over the management of Kenmuir; and gallantly she played her part, whether in tenderly mothering the baby, little Anne, or in the more serious matters of household work. She did her duty, young though she was, with a surprising, old-fashioned womanliness that won many a smile of approval from her father, and caused David's eyes to open with astonishment.

And he soon discovered that Maggie, mistress of Kenmuir, was a different person from his former playmate and servant.

The happy days when his size and strength won out over her, even when he was wrong, were gone and would never return. David often missed them, especially when, in an argument, Maggie with her quick answers and teasing eyes chased him, sulky and defeated, off the battlefield. The two were always squabbling now. In the good old days, he remembered bitterly, squabbles between them were unknown. He had never allowed them; any attempt on Maggie's part to think or act independently was sternly quashed, as though they were still living in the Middle Ages. She had to follow wherever he led—"My word!" he would say.

Now she was the mistress where he had been the master; she commanded, he obeyed. As a result, they were always at war. And yet he would sit for hours in the kitchen and watch her, as she went about her business, with solemn, interested eyes, half in admiration, half in amusement. In the end, Maggie always turned on him with a little laugh that was touched with irritation.

"Haven't you got anything better to do than that—to look at me?" she asked one Saturday about a month before Cup Day.

"No, I haven't," the pert fellow answered.

"Then I wish you had. It makes me quite jumpy having you watching me that way, like a cat watching a mouse."

"Don't you trouble yourself on my account, my girl," he answered calmly.

"Your girl indeed!" she cried, tossing her head.

"Ay, or will be," he muttered.

"What's that?" she cried, springing around toward him, a flush of color on her face.

"Nothing, my lassie. You'll know as soon as I want you to, you may be sure, and no sooner."

The girl went back to her baking, half angry, half suspicious.

"I don't know what you mean, Mr. McAdam," she said.

"Don't you, Mrs. McA—"

The rest was lost in the crash of a falling plate; at which David laughed quietly, and asked if he should help pick up the pieces.

◆ ◆ ◆

That same evening, at the Sylvester Arms, an announcement was made that knocked the breath out of its hearers.

In the debate that night on the fast-approaching Dale Trials and the abilities of the red dog compared to those of the gray, McAdam on one side and Tammas, backed by Long Kirby and the rest, on the other, had pounded each other with more than usual vigor. The quarrel rose to fever heat; argument was followed by insult; and again and again, the little man was hooted into silence.

"It's easy to laugh," he cried at last, "but ye'll laugh out of the other side of yer ugly faces on Cup Day."

"Will we indeed? We'll see," came the mocking chorus of voices.

"We'll whip ye till ye're deaf, dumb, and blind, Wullie and I."

"Yo' won't!"

"We will!"

The voices were rising like the east wind in March.

"You won't, and for a very good reason too," Tammas declared loudly and solemnly.

"Give us yer reason, ye great liar," cried the little man, turning on him.

"Because—" began Jim Mason and stopped to rub his nose.

"You hold your tongue, Jim," advised Rob Saunderson.

"Because—" This time it was Tammas who paused.

"Git on with it, ye stammering stirk!" cried McAdam. "Why?"

"Because—Owd Bob isn't goin' to run."

Tammas sat back in his chair.

"What!" screamed the little man, lunging forward.

"What's that!" bellowed Long Kirby, leaping to his feet.

"Man, say it again!" shouted Rob.

"What's the crazy old bean telling us?" cried Liz Burton.

"Knock 'im on the head!" shouts Tupper.

"Strike 'im in the eye!" says Ned Hoppin.

They jostled around the old man's chair: McAdam in front; Jem Burton and Long Kirby leaning over his shoulder; Liz behind her father; Saunderson and Tubber tackling him on either side; while the rest peered and elbowed in the rear.

The announcement had fallen like a thunderbolt among them.

Tammas looked slowly up at the little mob of eager faces above him. In his expression was a mixture of pride at the sensation caused by his news and genuine sorrow over what he had told them.

"Ay, you may well pay attention, all of you. It's enough to make the dead listen. I say again: We shall not run our Bob in the Cup. And you may guess why. It isn't every man, Mr. McAdam, that would put aside his chance of the Cup, especially when it would practically be handed to him"—McAdam's tongue was in his cheek—"and a sure thing," the old man continued warmly, "out o' respect for his wife's memory."

The news was received in utter silence. The shock of the surprise, together with the bitterness of the disappointment, froze the slow tongues of his listeners.

Only one small voice broke the stillness—it was McAdam.

"Oh, what a tender-hearted man! He should get his rent reduced for such a display of the proper spirit. I'll remind Mr. Hornbut to let old Sylvester know about it."

Which he did, and would have got a beating for his trouble if Cyril Gilbraith had not thrown him out of the parsonage before the angry minister could lay hands upon him.

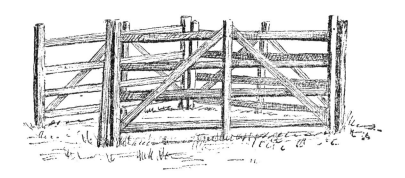

CHAPTER 10

Red Wull Wins

TAMMAS had simply told the sad truth. Owd Bob was not going to run for the cup. And this decision, which denied him something he wanted, speaks more for James Moore's love of his lost wife than many an impressive stone monument.

To the people of the Daleland, from the Black Water to the market cross in Grammoch-town, the news came with the shock of a sudden blow. They had set their hearts on the Gray Dog's success; and had felt serenely confident of his victory. But the most painful part of it was this: that now the Tailless Tyke might well win.

McAdam, on the other hand, was plunged into a fervor of delight at the news. For to win the Shepherds' Trophy was the goal of his ambition. David now meant less than nothing to the lonely little man, while Red Wull meant everything to him. And to have that name handed down through the generations, gallantly holding its place among the names of the most famous sheepdogs of all time, was his heart's desire.

As Cup Day drew near, the little man's delicate nature was strained to the highest pitch of nervousness, and he was tossed on a sea of worry. His hopes and fears ebbed and flowed with the tide of each moment. His moods were as undependable as the winds of March; and his state of mind was always changing. At one minute he paced up and down the kitchen, his face already flushed with the glow of victory, chanting the patriotic Scottish battle-song:

"Scots wha hae wi' Wallace bled!"

(Scots who have with Wallace bled!)

At the next minute, he was bent over the table, his head buried in his hands, his whole body shaking, as he cried in a choking voice: "Eh, Wullie, Wullie, they're all against us."

David found that living with his father was now like living with an unfriendly wasp. Though he pretended to be indifferent to his father's changeable moods, they tormented him almost to madness, and he fled at every moment to Kenmuir; for, as he told Maggie, "I'd rather put up with your airs and impertinence, miss, than with him, woman that he be!"

◆ ◆ ◆

At last the great day came. Fears, hopes, doubts, dismays, all scattered in the presence of the reality.

Cup Day is always a general holiday in the Daleland, and every soul crowds over to Silverdale. Shops were shut; special trains ran in to Grammoch-town; and the road leading out from the little town was a confusion of carriages, wagons, and carts of all kinds, as well as people on foot, all making their way toward the Dalesman's Daughter. And soon the paddock below that little inn was humming with the crowd of sportsmen and spectators who had come to see the battle for the Shepherd's Trophy.

There, very noticeable with its red body and yellow wheels, was the great Kenmuir wagon. Many people were gazing at the handsome young pair who stood in it, so conspicuous yet unaware, above the crowd: Maggie, looking as sweet and fresh as a mountain flower in her simple printed cotton dress; while David's fair face was all gloomy, his forehead creased.

In front of the wagon was a black cluster of Dalesmen, discussing McAdam's chances. In the center was Tammas voicing his opinions. If you had walked by, close to the group, you might have heard: "A man, did you say, Mr. Maddox? An ape, I call him"; or: "A dog? More like a hog, I tell you." Surrounding the old man were Jonas, Henry, and Our Job, Jem Burton, Rob Saunderson, Tupper, Jim Mason, Hoppin, and others; while on the edge of the group stood Sammel Todd predicting rain and McAdam's victory. Nearby, Bessie Bolstock, who was rumored to have a soft spot for David, giggled spitefully at the pair in the Kenmuir wagon, and sang:

"Let a lad alone, lass,
Let a lad a-be."

While her father, Teddy, dodged in and out among the crowd with tray and glasses: for Cup Day was the great day of the year for him.

Past the group of Dalesmen and on all sides was a mass of bobbing heads—Scots, Northerners, Yorkshiremen, Welshmen. To the right and left, a long line of carriages and carts of all kinds, from the Squire's low-bellied landau and Viscount Birdsaye's gorgeous long-bodied barouche to Liz Burton's three-legged donkey-cart with little Mrs. Burton, the twins, young Jake (who should have walked), and Monkey (ditto) packed away inside. Beyond the Silver Lea, the gaunt Scaur raised its rugged peak, and the Pass, stretching out along the side of it, shone white in the sunshine.

At the back of the carriages were booths containing games in which you threw a ball at a row of coconuts on a shelf, or tried to knock the pipe out of the mouth of a scarecrow called Aunt Sally, and shows, and stools on which the bookies sat taking bets on the dogs, and all the busy throng of such a contest. Here Master Launcelot Bilks and Jacky Sylvester were fighting; Cyril Gilbraith was offering to challenge the professional boxing man; Long Kirby was betting against Red Wull while the odds were good; and Liz Burton and young Ned Hoppin were being photographed together, while Melia Ross in the background was pretending she didn't care.

Across the stream, on the far bank, was a little cluster of men and dogs, and everyone was watching them.

The Juvenile Stakes had been run and won; Londesley's Lassie had triumphed in the Locals; and the fight for the Shepherds' Trophy was about to begin.

"You're not lookin' at me now," whispered Maggie to the silent boy by her side.

"No; and never wish to again," David answered roughly. He was looking over the heads of the crowd in front to a place where, beyond the Silver Lea, a group of shepherds and their dogs were gathered, while standing apart from the rest, by himself as always, was the bent figure of his father, and beside him the Tailless Tyke.

"Don't you want your father to win?" asked Maggie softly, following his gaze.

"I'm praying he'll be beaten," the boy answered moodily.

"Oh, Davie, how can you?" cried the girl, shocked.

"It's easy to say, 'Oh, David,'" he snapped. "But if you lived with them two"—he nodded toward the stream—"maybe you'd understand a bit....'Oh, David,' indeed! Honestly!"

"I know, lad," she said tenderly; and he grew calmer.

"He'd give his right hand for his blessed Wullie to win; I'd give my right arm to see him lose...And our Bob there all the while"—he nodded to the far left of the line, where James Moore stood with Owd Bob, Parson Leggy and the Squire.

When at last Red Wull came out to run his course, he worked with the savage dash that was always his own special way. His method was his own; but the work was admirably well done.

"Keeps right on the back of his sheep," said the parson, watching intently. "Strange thing they don't scatter!" But they didn't. There was no waiting, no coaxing; he drove them straight on with a cunning that was almost devilish. He brought his sheep along at a terrific pace, never missing a turn, never hesitating, never straying from the course. And the crowd applauded, for the crowd loves a dashing display. While little McAdam, hopping nimbly about, his face blazing with excitement, handled dog and sheep with a masterly precision that compelled the admiration even of his enemies.

"McAdam wins!" roared a bookie, giving the odds for those who had placed bets: "Twelve to one against the field!"

"He wins, dang him!" said David quietly.

"Wull wins!" said the parson, shutting his lips.

"And deserves to!" said James Moore.

"Wull wins!" softly cried the crowd.

"We don't!" said Sammel gloomily.

And in the end, Red Wull did win; and no one but Tammas, who was so fixed in his opinion, and Long Kirby, who had lost a good deal of his wife's money and a little of his own betting on the outcome, protested the fairness of the verdict.

The win was greeted with little enthusiasm. At first there was a faint cheering; but it sounded like the echo of an echo, and soon died away. To produce loud and long applause, there must be money behind it, or a few roaring fanatics to start it off and keep it going. Here, there was neither; only ugly stories, mean remarks, on all sides. And, as always happens, the hundreds who did not know McAdam or Red Wull followed the example of those who said they did.

McAdam could not help seeing the lack of enthusiasm as he pushed his way through the crowd toward the tent where the committee sat. Not a single voice honored him as the winner; not a single friendly hand patted his shoulder in congratulation. Broad backs were turned; contemptuous glances were aimed at him; spiteful remarks were fired off. Only the people who were not from the area looked curiously at the little bent figure with the glowing face, and shrank back at the size and savage appearance of the great dog at his heels.

But what did he care? His Wullie was recognized as champion, the best sheepdog of the year; and the little man was happy. They could turn their backs on him; but they could not change that; and he could afford to be indifferent. "They don't like it, lad—he, he! But they'll just have to put up wi' it. Ye've won it, Wullie—won it fair."

He elbowed his way through the crowd, heading toward the rope-guarded enclosure in front of the committee tent, around which the people were now pressing. In the door of the tent stood the secretary, various stewards, and members of the committee. In front, alone in the roped-off space, was Lady Eleanour, fragile, dainty, graceful, waiting with a smile on her face to greet the winner. And on a table beside her, alone and dignified, the Shepherds' Trophy.

There it stood, kingly and impressive; its fair white sides inscribed with many names; cradled in three shepherds' crooks; and on the top, as if to guard the Cup's contents, an exquisitely carved collie's head. The Shepherds' Trophy, the goal of his life's race, and that of many another man's.

He climbed over the rope, followed by Red Wull, and took off his hat with almost courtly respectful politeness to the fair lady before him.

As he walked up to the table on which the Cup stood, a shrill voice, easily recognizable, broke the silence.

"You'd like it better if 'twas full and you could swim in it, you and yer Wullie," the voice called out. At which the crowd giggled, and Lady Eleanour looked indignant.

The little man turned.

"I'll remember to drink yer health, Mr. Thornton, never fear, though I know ye'd rather drink your own," he said. At which the crowd giggled again; and a gray head at the back, which had hoped to go unrecognized, disappeared suddenly.

The little man stood there in the stillness, sourly smiling, his face still damp from his hard work; while the Tailless Tyke at his side defiantly faced the tightly packed ring of onlookers, a white fence of teeth faintly visible between his lips.

Lady Eleanour looked uncomfortable. Usually the lucky winner was unable to hear her little speech, as she gave the Cup away, because the applause was so deafening. Now there was utter silence. She glanced up at the crowd, but there was no response to her unspoken appeal in that forest of un-friendly faces. And her gentle heart bled for the forlorn little man before her. To make up for it, she smiled on him so sweetly that it was more than enough.

"I'm sure you deserve your success, Mr. McAdam," she said. "You and Red Wull there worked splendidly—every-body says so."

"I've heard nothin' about it," the little man answered dryly. At which someone in the crowd chuckled.

"And we all know what a grand dog he is; though"—with a reproachful smile as she glanced at Red Wull's square, short back end—"he's not very polite."

"His heart is good, your Ladyship, if his manners are not," McAdam answered, smiling.

"Liar!" came a loud voice in the silence. Lady Eleanour looked up, hot with indignation, and half rose from her seat. But McAdam merely smiled.

"Wullie, turn around and make yer bow to the lady," he said. "They'll not hurt us now we're doing well; it's when we're down that they'll flock like crows to fresh-killed carrion."

At that, Red Wull walked up to Lady Eleanour, faintly wagging his tail; and she put her hand on his huge bull head and said, "Dear old Ugly!" at which the crowd cheered in earnest.

After that, for some moments, the only sound was the gentle ripple of the good lady's voice and the little man's bitter replies.

"Why, last winter the country was full of talk about what you and Red Wull had been doing. It was always McAdam and his Red Wull have done this and that and the other. I declare I got quite tired of you both, I heard such a lot about you."

The little man, cap in hand, smiled, blushed, and looked genuinely pleased.

"And when it wasn't you, it was Mr. Moore and Owd Bob."

"Owd Bob, bless him!" called out a booming voice. "Three cheers for our Bob!"

"Hip, hip, hooray!" The cry was echoed gallantly and cast from mouth to mouth; and strangers, though they did not understand, caught the infection and cheered too; and the uproar continued for some minutes.

When it was ended, Lady Eleanour was standing up, a faint

flush on her cheeks and her eyes flashing dangerously, like a queen cornered.

"Yes," she cried, and her clear voice thrilled through the air like a trumpet. "Yes; and now three cheers for Mr. McAdam and his Red Wull! Hip, hip—"

"Hooray!" A little knot of determined individuals at the back—James Moore, Parson Leggy, Jim Mason, and you may be sure in his heart, at least, Owd Bob—responded to the call with vigor and enthusiasm. The crowd joined in; and, once started, cheered and cheered again.

"Three cheers more for Mr. McAdam!"

But the little man waved to them.

"Don't be bigger hypocrites than ye can help," he said. "You've done enough for one day, and I thank ye for it."

Then Lady Eleanour handed him the Cup.

"Mr. McAdam, I present you with the Champion Challenge Dale Cup, open to all comers. Keep it, guard it, love it as your own, and win it again if you can. Twice more and it's yours, you know, and it will stop forever beneath the shadow of the Pike. And that's the right place for it, say I—the Dale Cup for Dalesmen."

The little man took the Cup tenderly.

"It shall not leave the Estate or my house, yer Ladyship, if Wullie and I can help it," he said emphatically.

Lady Eleanour retreated into the tent, and the crowd swarmed over the ropes and around the little man, who held the Cup beneath his arm.

Long Kirby laid careless hands upon it.

"Don't touch it!" ordered McAdam.

"I shall!"

"You shan't! Wullie, keep him off." Which the great dog proceeded to do amid the laughter of the onlookers.

Among the last, James Moore was pushed past the little man by the motion of the crowd. At the sight of him, Mc-Adam's face took on an expression of intense concern.

"Man, Moore!" he cried, peering forward as though in alarm; "man, Moore, ye're green—positively verdant. Are ye in pain?" Then, catching sight of Owd Bob, he flinched back as though in horror.

"And really! So's yer dog! Yer dog that was gray is now green. Oh, good life!"—and he made as though about to fall fainting to the ground.

Then, in mocking tones: "Ah, but you shouldn't yearn for—"

"He won't have to yearn for it long, I can tell yo'," interrupted Tammas's shrill voice.

"And why not?"

"Because next year he'll win it from yo'. Our Bob'll win it, little man. Why? That's why."

The retort was greeted with a yell of applause from the sprinkling of Dalesmen in the crowd.

But McAdam swaggered away into the tent, his head up, the Cup beneath his arm, and Red Wull guarding him from behind.

"First of all ye'll have to beat Adam McAdam and his Red Wull!" he called back proudly.

CHAPTER 11

Our Bob

M<small>CADAM'S</small> pride in the great Cup that now graced his kitchen was supreme. It stood alone in the very center of the mantelpiece, just below the old gun, a bell-mouthed blunderbuss, that hung upon the wall. The only ornament in the bare room, it shone out in its silvery purity like the moon in a gloomy sky.

For once, the little man was content. Since his mother's death, David had never known such peace. It was not that his father became actively kind; rather that he forgot to be actively unkind.

"Not that I care a brass button one way or the other," the boy informed Maggie.

"Then you should," that proper little person replied.

McAdam was, indeed, a changed man. He forgot to curse James Moore; he forgot to sneer at Owd Bob; he rarely visited the Sylvester Arms, which was a loss for Jem Burton's earnings and his temper; and he was never drunk.

"Soaks himself at home, instead," suggested Tammas, who was prejudiced. But the accusation was untrue.

"Too drunk to get so far," said Long Kirby, kindly man.

"I reckon the Cup is a sort of company to him," said Jim Mason. "Maybe it's lonesomeness that drives him here so much." And maybe you were right, charitable Jim.

"We'd best make the most of it while he has it, 'cause he won't have it for long," Tammas remarked amid applause.

Even Parson Leggy admitted—rather reluctantly, indeed, for he was only human—that the little man was wonderfully changed for the better.

"But I'm afraid it may not last," he said. "We shall see what happens when Owd Bob beats him for the Cup, as he certainly will. That'll be the decisive moment."

As things were, the little man spent all his spare moments with the Cup between his knees, polishing it and singing softly to Wullie:

"I never saw a fairer,
I never lo'ed a dearer,
And neist my heart I'll wear her,
For fear my jewel tine."

(I never saw a fairer,
I never loved a dearer,
And next my heart I'll wear her,
For fear my jewel be lost.)

"There, Wullie! Look at her! Isn't she bonnie? She shines like a twinkle—a twinkle in the sky." And he would hold it out at arm's length, his head cocked sideways the better to gaze at its bright beauties.

The little man was very protective of his treasure. David could not touch it; could not smoke in the kitchen for fear the fumes would tarnish its glorious surface; and if he came too near it, he was ordered abruptly away.

"As if I wanted to touch his nasty Cup!" he complained to Maggie. "I'd rather any day touch—"

"Hands off, Mr. David, this minute!" she cried indignantly. "Impertinence, indeed!" as she tossed her head clear of the strong fingers that were fondling her pretty hair.

So it was that McAdam, on coming quietly into the kitchen one day, was consumed with angry resentment to find David actually handling the object that the little man so worshipped; and the way he was handling it added a thousand times over to the offense.

The boy was leaning idly against the mantelpiece, his fair head shoved right into the Cup, his breath dimming its shine, and his two hands, big and dirty, slowly turning it around before his eyes.

Bursting with indignation, the little man crept up behind the boy. David was reading down the long list of winners.

"There's the first of 'em," he muttered, sticking out his tongue to point to the spot: "'Andrew Moore's Rough, 178–.' And there again—'James Moore's Pinch, 179–.' And again— 'Beck, 182–.' Ah, and there's the one Tammas tells about! 'Rex, 183–,' and 'Rex, 183–.' Ay, he was a rare one, to hear them talk! If only he'd won just one more time! Ah, there's none like the Gray Dogs—they all says that, and I say so myself; none like the Gray Dogs o' Kenmuir, bless 'em! And we'll win again too—" He broke off short; his eye had traveled down to the last name on the list.

"'McAdam's Wull'!" he read with unspeakable contempt, and put his great thumb across the name as though to wipe it out. "'McAdam's Wull'! Good gracious sakes! P-h-g-h-r-r!"— and he made a motion as though to spit on the ground.

But a little shoulder was into his side, two small fists were beating at his chest, and a shrill voice was yelling: "Devil! Devil! Stand off!"—and he was tumbled headlong away from the mantelpiece and brought up abruptly against the side wall.

The precious Cup swayed on its ebony stand, the boy's hands, roughly withdrawn, almost knocking it over. But the little man's first impulse, cursing and screaming though he was, was to steady it.

"'McAdam's Wull'! I wish he was here to teach ye, ye snot-faced, ox-limbed good-for-nothing!" he cried, standing in front of the Cup, his eyes blazing.

"Ay, 'McAdam's Wull'! And why not 'McAdam's Wull'? Have ye any objection to the name?"

"I didn't know yo' was there," said David, a bit sheepishly.

"No; or ye wouldn't have said it."

"I'd have thought it, though," muttered the boy.

Luckily, however, his father did not hear. He stretched his hands up tenderly for the Cup, lifted it down, and began reverently to polish the dimmed sides with his handkerchief.

"Ye're thinkin', no doubt," he cried, casting up a vicious glance at David, "that Wullie's not good enough to have his name alongside o' them cursed Gray Dogs. Aren't ye now? Let's have the truth, for once—just for a laugh."

"Reckon he's good enough if there's none better," David replied coolly.

"And who should there be that's better? Tell me that, ye big blockhead."

David smiled.

"Eh, that would take me a long time," he said.

"And what do ye mean by that?" his father cried.

"Nay; I was only thinking that Mr. Moore's Bob will look

very fine writ there, under that one." He pointed to the vacant space below Red Wull's name.

The little man put the Cup back on its pedestal with hurried hands. The handkerchief dropped ignored to the floor; he turned and sprang furiously at the boy, who stood against the wall, still smiling; and, seizing him by the collar of his coat, shook him to and fro with fiery energy.

"So ye're hopin', prayin', no doubt, that James Moore—curse him!—will win my Cup away from me, yer own dad. I wonder ye're not ashamed to cross my door! Ye live off o' me; ye suck my blood, ye foul-mouthed leech. Wullie and me break ourselves to keep ye in house and home—and what's yer gratitude? Ye plot to rob us of our rights."

He dropped the boy's coat and stood back.

"No rights about it," said David, still keeping his temper.

"If I win, is it not my right as much as any Englishman's?"

Red Wull, who had heard the rising voices, came trotting in, scowled at David, and took his stand beside his master.

"Ay, *if* yo' win it," said David, giving meaningful emphasis to the word "if."

"And who's going to beat us?"

David looked at his father, pretending surprise.

"I tell yo' Owd Bob's running," he answered.

"And what if he is?" the other cried.

"Why, even you should know that much," the boy sneered.

The little man could not help but understand.

"So that's it!" he said. Then, in a scream, with one finger pointing to the great dog:

"And what about him? What'll my Wullie be doing meanwhile? Tell me that, and take care! Mind ye, he stands here listening!" And, indeed, the Tailless Tyke was bristling, ready for battle.

David did not like the look of things; and edged away toward the door.

"What'll Wullie be doin', ye chicken-hearted skunk?" his father cried.

"Him?" said the boy, now close to the door. "Him?" he said, with a slow contempt that made the red bristles quiver on the dog's neck. "He'll be watching, I should think—watching. What else is he fit for? I tell yo' our Bob—"

"—'Our Bob'!" screamed the little man, darting forward. "'Our Bob'! Listen to him. I'll 'our—' At him, Wullie! at him!"

But the Tailless Tyke needed no encouragement. With a harsh growl he sprang through the air, only to crash against the closing door.

The outer door banged, and in another second a mocking finger tapped on the windowpane.

"Better luck to the two o' you next time!" laughed a scornful voice; and David ran down the hill toward Kenmuir.

CHAPTER 12

How Red Wull Held the Bridge

STARTING from that hour, the flame of McAdam's jealousy blazed into a mighty fire. The winning of the Dale Cup was all he could think about. He had won it once, and would win it again despite all the Moores, all the Gray Dogs, all the undutiful sons in existence; about that, he was determined. The fact of his having tasted the joys of victory only whetted his appetite. And now he felt he could never be happy till the Cup was his own—won for good.

At home, David was hardly allowed to enter the room where the trophy stood.

"I won't have ye touching my Cup, ye dirty-fingered, ill-born good-for-nothing. Wullie and me won it—you had nothin' to do with it. Go off to James Moore and James Moore's dog."

"Ay, and shall I take the Cup with me? or will you wait till it's taken from ye?"

And so the two went on; and every day the tension came closer to the breaking-point.

In the Dale, the little man met with no sympathy. The

hearts of the Dalesmen were one and all on the side of Owd
Bob and his master.

Whereas in the old days, at the Sylvester Arms, his shrill,
wicked tongue had rarely been still, now he maintained a sullen silence; Jem Burton, at least, couldn't complain. Crouched
away in a corner, with Red Wull beside him, the little man
would sit watching and listening as the Dalesmen talked
about Owd Bob's doings, his steadiness, good judgment, and
coming victory.

Sometimes he could no longer restrain himself. Then he
would spring to his feet, and stand, a little swaying figure,
and condemn them passionately with almost pathetic outbursts of powerful language. These speeches always ended
the same way.

"Ye're all against us!" the little man would cry in a quivering voice.

"Yes, we are," Tammas would answer smugly.

"By fair means or foul, you're pleased as long as Wullie and
me are beaten. I'm surprised you don't poison him—a little
arsenic, and the way would be clear for your Bob."

"The way is clear enough without that," came from Tammas sharply.

Then a long silence, broken only by the exceedingly bitter
cry: "Eh, Wullie, Wullie, they're all against us!"

◆　◆　◆

And always the rivals—red and gray—were on the lookout
for their opportunity. But the Master, with his commanding
presence and stern eyes, was always ready for them. Toward
the end, McAdam, silent and sneering, would secretly urge
on Red Wull to the attack; until, one day in Grammoch-town,
James Moore turned on him, his blue eyes glittering. "D'you

think, you little fool," he cried in that hard voice of his, "that once they got going we would ever get either of them off alive?" This seemed to strike the little man as a new idea; for, from that moment on, he was always the first in his feverish attempts to put his small body, like a buffer, between the would-be fighters.

❖ ❖ ❖

McAdam might curse, he might threaten, but when the time came, Owd Bob won.

The styles of the rivals were clearly different: the patience, the subtle signals, combined with the splendid dash, of one dog; and the fierce, driving fury of the other.

The outcome was never in doubt. It may have been that the temper of the Tailless Tyke failed when it was tested; it may have been that his sheep were wild, as McAdam declared; certainly not, as the little man in a choking voice tried to pro-test, that they had been chosen and purposely selected to ruin his chances. What is certain is that his tactics scared them hopelessly: and he never had control of them.

As for Owd Bob, the way he dropped smoothly to a crouch-ing position on the ground, the way he drove the sheep, the way he guided them into the pen, aroused the loud-tongued admiration of both the spectators and the competitors alike. He was patient yet persistent, quiet yet firm, and he seemed to persuade the sheep under his care to go where he wanted them to go in a manner that was uniquely his own.

When, at last, the judges announced their decision, and it was known that, after a gap of half a century, the Shepherds' Trophy had once again been won by a Gray Dog of Kenmuir, there was a scene such as has rarely been witnessed on the slope behind the Dalesman's Daughter.

Great fists were pounded on mighty backs; great feet were stamped on the sun-dried banks of the Silver Lea; strong lungs were strained to their utmost capacity; and roars of "Moore!" "Owd Bob o' Kenmuir!" "The Gray Dogs!" thundered up the hillside, and echoed, thundering, back.

Even James Moore was visibly moved as he worked his way through the cheering mob; and Owd Bob, trotting alongside him in quiet dignity, seemed to wave his silvery brush in gracious response.

Master Jacky Sylvester alternately turned cartwheels and knocked the young Honorable Launcelot Bilks to the ground. Lady Eleanour, her cheeks pink with pleasure, waved her parasol and tried to quiet her son's high spirits. Parson Leggy danced a little dance quite unusual for a minister, and shook hands with the Squire till both those fine old gentlemen were purple in the face. Long Kirby picked out a small man in the crowd, and bashed his hat down over his eyes, while Tammas, Rob Saunderson, Tupper, Hoppin, Londesley, and the rest joined hands and went dashing around like a gang of brainless boys.

Of them all, however, none was so loud and wild in the mad heat of his enthusiasm as David McAdam. He stood in the Kenmuir wagon beside Maggie, easily seen above the crowd, and roared in hoarse enchantment:

"Well done, our Bob! Well done, Mr. Moore! You've knocked him! Knock him again! Owd Bob o' Kenmuir! Moore! Moore o' Kenmuir! Hip, hip...!" until the noisy young giant attracted such attention in his violent delight that Maggie had to lay her hand on his arm to quiet him.

Alone, on the far bank of the stream, stood the defeated pair.

The little man was trembling slightly; his face was still hot from his hard work; and as he listened to the applause for the man who had beaten him, there was a pitiful fixed smile on his face. In front of him stood the defeated dog, his lips wrinkling and his hackles rising, as he, too, saw and heard and understood.

"It's a grand thing to have a son who respects you and does right by you, Wullie," the little man whispered, watching David's waving figure. "He's happy—and so are they all—not so much that James Moore has won, as that you and I are beaten."

Then, breaking down for a moment:

"Eh, Wullie, Wullie! They're all against us. It's you and I alone, lad."

Again, seeing the Squire followed by Parson Leggy, Viscount Birdsaye, and others of the gentry forcing their way through the crowd to shake hands with the winner, he went on:

"It's good to be on friendly terms with high society, Wullie. Never make friends with a man beneath you in rank, nor never make an enemy of a man above ye: that's a good rule to follow, Wullie, if ye want to be a success in honest England."

He stood there, alone with his dog, watching the crowd on the far slope as it surged upward in the direction of the committee tent. Only when the dark mass of people had packed themselves in solid rows around that ring, inside which, just a year ago, he had stood in a very different situation, and was at last quiet, a wintry smile played for a moment around his lips. He laughed a joyless laugh.

"Wait a bit, Wullie—he, he! Just wait a bit." And he recited a scrap of verse from his favorite:

"The best-laid schemes o' mice and men
Gang aft agley."

(The best-laid plans of mice and men
Oft go awry.)

As he spoke, there came down to him, above the uproar, a faint cry of mingled surprise and anger. The cheering stopped suddenly. There was silence; then there burst on the stillness a hurricane of indignation.

The crowd surged forward, then turned. Every eye looked across the stream. A hundred damning fingers pointed at the lonely figure where he stood. There were hoarse yells of: "There he is! That's him! What's he done with it? Thief! Throttle him!"

The mob came lumbering down the slope like one man, thundering their curses from a thousand throats. They looked dangerous, and their anger was inflamed by the knot of angry Dalesmen who led the way. There was more than one pale, frightened face among the women at the top of the slope as they watched the crowd blundering blindly down the hill. There were more men than just Parson Leggy, the Squire, James Moore, and the local policemen in the thick of it all, trying frantically with voice and motion—yes, and stick too—to stop the advance.

It was useless; the dark wave of men rolled on, irresistible.

On the far bank stood the little man, motionless, waiting for them with a grin on his face. And a little farther in front was the Tailless Tyke, his back and neck like a newly mown wheat field, as he rumbled a loud and echoing challenge.

"Come on, gentlemen!" the little man cried. "Come on! I'll wait for ye, never fear. Ye're a thousand to one and a dog. Those are the odds ye like, you Englishmen!"

And the mob, with murder in its throat, accepted the invitation and came on.

At the moment, however, from the slope above, sounding clear above the tramp of the crowd, a great voice bellowed: "Make way! Make way! Make way for Mr. Trotter!" The advancing crowd hesitated and a path opened in the midst of it; and the secretary of the contest came bustling through.

He was a small, fat man, fussy at all times, and always in a sweat. Now his face was dark red with anger, and streaming; he motioned wildly; vague words bubbled forth, as his short legs twinkled down the slope.

The crowd paused to admire him. Someone shouted a funny remark, and the crowd laughed. For the moment, the situation was saved.

The fat secretary hurried on down the slope, paying no attention to any insult but the most important one. He bounced over the plank-bridge: and as he came closer, McAdam saw that in each hand he was waving a brick.

"Stop, man! Don't throw!" he cried, making as though to turn in sudden terror.

"What's this? What's this?" gasped the secretary, waving his arms.

"Bricks, looks like," the other answered, staying his flight.

The secretary puffed up like a pudding rising quickly in the oven.

"Where's the Cup! Champion...Challenge, I mean," he jerked out. "Mind you, sir, you're responsible, entirely responsible! Dents, damages, delays! What does it all mean, sir? These shocking creations"—he waved the bricks, and McAdam moved back quickly—"wrapped, I swear, in straw, sir, in the carrying case that was meant to hold the Cup itself! No Cup! Shameful! Dreadful! An insult to me—to the Trial—to the committee—to everyone! What does it mean, sir!" He paused to pant, his body filling and emptying like a balloon.

McAdam went up to him with one eye on the crowd, which was heaving forward again, still threatening, but now grim and silent.

"I put them there," he whispered; and moved back to watch the result of his confession.

The secretary gasped.

"You—you not only do this—amazing thing—these shocking objects"—he hurled the bricks furiously on the innocent ground—"but you dare to tell me you did it!"

The little man smiled.

"'Do wrong and hide it, do right and confess it,' that's the Englishman's motto, and mine too, usually; but this time I had my reasons."

"Reasons, sir! No reasons can justify such an extraordinary abuse of all the—of all respectable behavior. Reasons! The reasons of a madman. That says it, sir. Dishonest withholding—dishonest, I say, sir! What were your precious reasons?"

The mob, with Tammas and Long Kirby at the front of it, had now nearly reached the plank-bridge. They still looked dangerous, and there were isolated cries of:

"Duck him!"

"Throw him in!"

"And the dog, too!"

"With one of them bricks around their necks!"

"There are my reasons!" said McAdam, pointing to the forest of threatening faces. "Ye see I'm not loved by those gentlemen there, and"—in a loud whisper in the other's ear—"I thought maybe I'd be attacked on the way here."

Tammas, out in front of the crowd, now had his foot upon the first plank of the bridge.

"Ye robber! Ye thief! Wait till we lay our hands on ye, you and yer gorilla!" he called.

McAdam half turned.

"Wullie," he said quietly, "guard the bridge."

At the order, the Tailless Tyke shot gladly forward, and the leaders on the bridge as hastily moved back. The dog galloped onto the rattling plank, took up his position squarely in the center of the narrow way, and stood facing the hostile crowd like the legendary dog Cerberus guarding the gates of hell: his bull-head was thrust forward, his hackles were up, his teeth glinting, and a distant rumbling in his throat, as though daring them to come on.

"Yo' first, old lad!" said Tammas, hopping nimbly behind Long Kirby.

"Nay; the old folks should lead the way!" cried the big blacksmith, his face grayish-white. He wrenched himself around, pinned the old man by the arms, and held him by force in front of him as a protective shield. There followed an undignified struggle between the two brave men, Tammas bellowing and kicking in the grip of mortal fear.

"Jim Mason'll show us," he suggested at last.

"Nay," said honest Jim; "I'm afraid." He could say it without embarrassment; for the courage of Postie Jim was a matter that had been decided long ago.

Then Jem Burton would go first?

Nay; Jem had a loving wife and dear little kids at home.

Then Big Bell?

Big Bell would rather see himself running in the opposite direction.

A tall figure came forcing its way through the crowd, his face a little paler than usual, carrying in his hand a fearful-looking stick with a stout knob on the end.

"I'm goin'!" said David.

"No, ye're not," answered the sturdy Sammel, gripping the boy from behind with arms like the roots of an oak. "Your time'll come soon enough, by the looks of you, without hurrying it on." And the opinion of the Dalesmen was in agreement with the big man; for, as old Rob Saunderson said:

"I reckon he'd rather claw onto your throat, lad, than any o' ours."

As there was no one who stepped up to claim the honor of leading the way, Tammas came forward with a clever idea.

"Tell you what, lads, we'd better let them that don't know nothing at all about him go first. And once they're on the bridge, see, we won't let 'em off; but keep a-shovin' 'em forward. *Then* us'll follow."

By this time, there was a little bare space of green around the head of the bridge, like a fairy circle into which mortals may not step. Around this, the mob formed a thick hedge: the Dalesmen in front, pushing back like cowards and bawling to those behind to stop that shovin'; and those behind urging bravely forward, yelling jeers and insults at the front rank. "Come on! Who's afraid? Let us through to 'em, then, ye Royal Chickens!"—for they knew very well that their demand was impossible.

And as they wedged and jostled thus, there crept out from their midst as gallant a champion as ever walked over the grass. He trotted out into the ring, watched by all, and paused to gaze at the lean, weary figure on the bridge. The sun lit the sprinkling of snow-white hair on the dome of his head; one forepaw was off the ground; and he stood there, royally alert, scanning his enemy.

"The Owd One!" went up in a roar fit to split the air as the hero of the day was recognized. And the Dalesmen spontaneously took a step forward as the gray knight walked softly across the green.

"Our Bob'll fetch him!" they roared, their blood leaping to fever heat, and gripped their sticks, grimly serious and determined to follow now.

The gray champion trotted up onto the bridge, and paused

again, the long hair about his neck rising like a thick collar, and a strange glint in his eyes; and the guardian of the bridge never moved. Red and Gray stood thus, face to face: the one light-hearted yet resolute, the other motionless, his great head slowly sinking between his forelegs, hard and heavy as a rock.

There was no shouting now: it was time for action, not words. Only, above the stillness, came a sound from the bridge like the snore of a giant in his sleep, and blending in with it, a low, deep purring thunder like some monster cat well pleased.

"Wullie," came a solitary voice from the far side, "guard the bridge!"

One ear went back, one ear was still forward; the great head was low and lower between his forelegs and the glowing eyes rolled upward so that the watchers could see the murderous white.

Forward the gray dog stepped.

Then, for the second time that afternoon, a voice, stern and hard, came ringing down from the slope above over the heads of the crowd.

"Bob, lad, come back!"

"He, he! I thought that was comin'," sneered the small voice over the stream.

The gray dog heard, and paused.

"Bob, lad, come in, I say!"

At that, he swung round and marched slowly back, gallant as he had come, dignified still in the injury to his pride.

And Red Wull threw back his head and bellowed a song of victory—challenge, triumph, scorn, all blended in that bull-like, blood-chilling howl.

❖ ❖ ❖

In the meantime, McAdam and the secretary had finished their business. It had been settled that the Cup was to be delivered over to James Moore not later than the following Saturday.

"Saturday, see! At the latest!" the secretary cried as he turned and trotted off.

"Mr. Trotter," McAdam called after him, "I'm sorry, but ye must stay this side of the Lea till I've reached the foot of the Pass. If those gentlemen"—nodding toward the crowd—"should lay hands on me, why—" and he shrugged his shoulders meaningfully. "Besides, Wullie's guarding the bridge."

With that, the little man strolled off slowly; now lingering to pick a flower, now to wave a mocking hand at the furious mob, and slowly on to the foot of the Murk Muir Pass. There he turned and whistled that shrill, peculiar note.

"Wullie, Wullie, to me!" he called.

At that, with one last threat thrown at the thousand souls he had held at bay for thirty minutes, the Tailless Tyke swung about and galloped after his lord.

CHAPTER 13

The Face in the Frame

ALL FRIDAY, McAdam never left the kitchen. He sat opposite the Cup, as though in a trance; and Red Wull lay motionless at his feet.

Saturday came, and still the two never budged. Toward evening, the little man stood up, all in a tremble, and took the Cup down from the mantelpiece; then he sat down again with it in his arms.

"Eh, Wullie, Wullie, is it a dream? Have they took her from us? Eh, but it's you and I alone, lad."

He hugged it to him, crying silently, and rocking to and fro like a mother with a dying child. And Red Wull sat up on his haunches, and moved his head from side to side in sympathy.

As the dark was falling, David looked in.

At the sound of the opening door, the little man swung around noiselessly, the Cup nursed in his arms, and glared, sullen and suspicious, at the boy; yet seemed not to recognize him. In the half-light, David could see the tears running down the pinched little face.

"Upon my life, he's going mad!" was his comment as he

turned away to Kenmuir. And again the mourners were left alone.

"A few hours now, Wullie," the little man cried, "and she'll be gone. We won her, Wullie, you and I, won her fair and square: she has lit up the house for us; she has softened all things for us—and God knows we needed it; she was the only thing we had to look to and love. And now they're taking her away, and it will be night again. We've cherished her, we've cared for her, we've loved her like our own; and now she must go to strangers who know her not."

He rose to his feet, and the great dog rose with him. His voice lifted to a wail, and he swayed with the Cup in his arms till it seemed he must fall.

"Did they win her fair and square, Wullie? No; they plotted, they planned, they worked against us, every one of them, and they beat us. Ay, and now they're robbin' us—robbin' us! But they shall not have her. Ours or nobody's, Wullie! We'll destroy her rather than give her up."

He banged the Cup down on the table and rushed madly out of the room, Red Wull at his heels. In a moment he came running back, waving a great ax about his head.

"Come on, Wullie!" he cried. "'Scots wha hae…'! Now's the day and now's the hour! Come on!"

On the table before him, calm and beautiful, stood the target of his madness. The little man ran at it, swinging his murderous weapon like the stick that is used for beating the wheat on the barn floor at harvest time.

"Ours or nobody's, Wullie! Come on! 'Lay the proud usurpers low'!" He aimed a mighty blow; and the Shepherds' Trophy—the Shepherds' Trophy which had survived the hardships of a hundred years—was almost gone. It seemed to quiver as the blow fell. But the cruel steel missed, and the ax-head sank into the wood, clean and deep, like a spade in snow.

Red Wull had leapt onto the table, and his deep voice grumbled a chorus to his master's yells. The little man danced up and down, tugging and straining at the ax-handle.

"You and I, Wullie!

'Tyrants fall in every foe!
Liberty's in every blow!'"

The ax-head was as impossible to move as the Muir Pike.

"'Let us do or die!'"

The wooden shaft of the ax snapped, and the little man stumbled back. Red Wull jumped down from the table, and, in doing so, brushed against the Cup. It toppled over onto the floor, and rolled clattering away in the dust.[*] And the little man ran madly out of the house, still yelling out his war-song.

❖ ❖ ❖

When, late that night, McAdam returned home, the Cup was gone. Down on his hands and knees he traced out its path, plain to see, where it had rolled along the dusty floor. Beyond that, there was no sign of it.

At first he was too upset to speak. Then he raved around the room like an abandoned ship, Red Wull following uneasily behind. He cursed; he swore; he screamed and beat the walls with feverish hands. A stranger, passing by, might well have thought this was a private insane asylum. At last, exhausted, he sat down and cried.

"It's David, Wullie, ye can be sure of it; David that has

---

[*]You may still see the dent in the Cup's white sides to this day.

robbed his father's house. Oh, it's a great thing to have an obedient son!"—and he bowed his gray head in his hands.

David, indeed, had taken it. He had come back to the Grange while his father was out, and, lifting the Cup from its grimy resting place on the floor, had marched it away to its rightful home. For, that evening at Kenmuir, James Moore had said to him:

"David, your father has not sent the Cup. I shall come and get it tomorrow." And David knew he meant it. Therefore, in order to avoid a collision between his father and his friend— a collision whose outcome he hardly dared to imagine, knowing the unchangeable determination of the one man and the lunatic passion of the other—the boy had decided to get the Cup himself, then and there, right in the teeth, if he had to, of his father and the Tailless Tyke. And he had done it.

When he reached home that night, he marched straight into the kitchen, which was not his usual habit.

There sat his father facing the door, waiting for him, his hands on his knees. For once the little man was alone; and David, brave though he was, thanked heaven devoutly that Red Wull was somewhere else.

For a while, father and son kept silence, watching each other like two duelers with swords in their hands.

"It was you as took my Cup?" asked the little man at last, leaning forward in his chair.

"It was me as took Mr. Moore's Cup," the boy answered. "I thought you must have been finished with it—I found it all bashed upon the floor."

"You took it—no doubt told to do so by James Moore."

David shook his head.

"Ay, by James Moore," his father went on. "He dared not come himself for the stolen goods that he won so dishonestly, so he sent the son to rob the father. The coward!"—and his whole body shook with passion. "I'd 'ave thought James Moore would 'ave been enough of a man to come himself for what he wanted. Now I see I did him a wrong—I misjudged him. I knew he was a hypocrite; one of yer remarkable good men; a man as looks to be one thing, says another, and does a third; and now I know he's a coward. He's afraid o' me, such as I am, five foot two in my socks." He rose from his chair and drew himself up to his full height.

"Mr. Moore had nothing to do with it," David persisted.

"Ye're lying. James Moore got you to do it."

"I tell you he did not."

"Ye'd have been willing enough without him, if ye'd thought of it, I admit. But ye don't have brains enough for that. All there is of ye has gone to make yer great body. However, that doesn't matter. I'll settle with James Moore another time. I'll settle with you now, David McAdam.

He paused, and looked the boy over from head to foot.

"So, ye're not only an idler! A good-for-nothing! A liar!"—he spat the words out. "Ye're—God help ye—a thief!"

"I'm no thief!" the boy answered hotly. "I only gave to the man what my father—shame on him!—wrongfully kept from him."

"Wrongfully?" cried the little man, moving forward with burning face.

"So you'd say it was an honorable thing, keeping what was not yours to keep! Holding back his rights from a man! Ay, if anyone's the thief, it's not me: it's you, I say, you!"—and he looked his father in the face with flashing eyes.

"I'm the thief, am I?" cried the other, who could hardly make himself understood, he was in such a state of emotion. "Though ye're three times my size, I'll teach my son to speak to me that way."

The old strap, now long unused, hung in the chimney corner. As he spoke, the little man sprang back, ripped it from the wall, and, almost before David realized what he was up to, had brought it down with a savage slash across his son's shoulders; and as he struck, he whistled a shrill, commanding note:

"Wullie, Wullie, to me!"

David felt the blow through his coat like a bar of hot iron laid across his back. His passion boiled inside him; every vein throbbed; every nerve quivered. In a minute he would avenge, once and for all, the wrong his father had done him for so many years; at the moment, however, there was urgent business on hand. For outside he could hear the quick patter of feet hard-galloping, and the scurry of a huge creature racing madly to a call.

With a bound he sprang at the open door; and again the strap came lashing down, and a wild voice:

"Quick, Wullie! For God's sake, quick!"

David slammed the door shut. It closed with a rasping click; and at the same moment a great body from outside thundered against it with terrific violence, and a deep voice roared like the sea when denied its prey.

"Too late, again!" said David, breathing hard; and he slid the door's bolt into its socket with a clang. Then he turned to his father.

"Now," he said, "man to man!"

"Ay," cried the other, "father to son!"

The little man half turned and leapt at the old gun hanging on the wall. He missed it, turned again, and struck with the strap full at the other's face. David caught the falling arm at the wrist, hitting it aside with such tremendous force that the bone nearly snapped. Then he struck his father a terrible blow on the chest, and the little man staggered back, gasping, into the corner; while the strap dropped from his numbed fingers.

Outside, Red Wull whined and scratched; but the two men paid no attention.

David stepped forward; there was murder in his face. The little man saw it: his time had come; but even his bitterest enemy never doubted Adam McAdam's courage.

He stood huddled in the corner, his hair and clothes rumpled, nursing one arm with the other, entirely unafraid.

"Remember, David," he said, quite calm, "it will be called murder, not manslaughter."

"Then murder it will be," the boy answered, in a thick, low voice, and came across the room.

Outside, Red Wull banged and clawed high up on the door with powerless paws.

The little man suddenly slipped his hand in his pocket, pulled something out, and flung it. The thing pattered against his son's face like a raindrop on a charging bull, and David only smiled as he came on. It dropped softly on the table at his side; he looked down and—it was the face of his mother which gazed up at him!

"Mother!" he blurted out, a sob in his voice, and stopped short. "Mother! My God, ye saved him—and me!"

He stood there, utterly beside himself, shaking and weeping quietly.

It was some minutes before he pulled himself together; then he walked to the wall, took down a pair of heavy shears, and seated himself at the table, still trembling. Near him lay the miniature photograph, all torn and crumpled, and beside it the deep-buried ax-head.

He picked up the strap and began cutting it into little pieces.

"There! and there! and there!" he said with each snip. "If ye hit me again there may be no mother to save ye."

McAdam stood huddling in the corner. He shook like an aspen leaf; his eyes blazed in his white face; and he still nursed one arm with the other.

"Honor yer father," he quoted in a small, low voice.

PART FOUR

The Black Killer

CHAPTER 14

A Mad Man

TAMMAS is on his feet in the taproom of the Arms, waving a pewter mug in the air.

"Gen'lemen!" he cries, his old face flushed; "I'll give you a toast. Stand up!"

The knot of Dalesmen around the fire rises like one man. Old Tammas waves his mug before him, careless of the good ale that drips onto the floor.

"To the best sheepdog in the North—Owd Bob o' Kenmuir!" he cries. In an instant there is an uproar: the merry applause of clinking pewters; the stamping of feet; the rattle of sticks. Rob Saunderson and old Jonas are cheering with the best; Tupper and Ned Hoppin are bellowing in each other's ears; Long Kirby and Jem Burton are thumping each other on the back; even Sammel Todd and Sexton Ross are roused from their usual melancholy.

"Here's to th' Owd One! Here's to our Bob!" yell powerful voices; while Rob Saunderson has jumped onto a chair.

"With the best sheepdog in the North I give you the

Shepherds' Trophy!—won forever, as we know it will be!" he cries. Instantly the uproar grows twice as loud.

"The Dale Cup and th' Owd One! The Trophy and our Bob! Hip, hip, for the gray dogs! Hip, hip, for the best sheepdog as ever was or will be! Hooray, hooray!"

Some minutes pass before the noise dies down; and slowly the enthusiasts go back to their seats with hoarse throats and red faces.

"Gentlemen all!"

A little man, ignored until now, is standing up at the back of the room. His face is aflame, and his hands twitch from time to time uncontrollably; and, in front of him, with hackles up and eyes gleaming, is a huge, bull-like dog.

"Now," cries the little man, "I dare ye to repeat that lie!"

"Lie!" screams Tammas; "lie! I'll give him lie! Lemme at him, I say!"

The old man in his fury is halfway over the surrounding ring of chairs before Jim Mason on the one hand and Jonas Maddox on the other can pull him back.

"Come, Mr. Thornton," soothes the eighty-year-old, "let him be. You surely ain't angered by the likes o' him!"—and he jerks his head with contempt toward the solitary figure behind him.

Tammas unwillingly returns to his seat.

The little man in the far corner of the room remains silent, waiting for his challenge to be taken up. He waits in vain. And as he looks at the collection of broad, unfeeling backs turned on him, he smiles bitterly.

"They don't dare, Wullie, not a single man, out of them all!" he cries. "They're one—two—three—four—eleven to one, Wullie, and yet they dare not. Eleven of them, and every man a coward! Long Kirby—Thornton—Tupper—Tod—Hoppin—Ross—Burton—and the rest, and not one that isn't bigger than me, and yet— Well, we might have known it. We should have known Englishmen by now. They're always the same and always have been. They tell lies, black lies—"

Once again Tammas is half out of his chair, and he is held back only by force, by the men on either side of him.

"—and then they haven't the courage to stand by their lies. Ye're English, every man o' ye, down to the marrow of yer bones."

The little man's voice rises as he speaks. He seizes the large pewter mug from the table at his side.

"Englishmen!" he cries, waving it before him. "Here's a toast for you! To the best sheepdog that ever penned a flock— Adam McAdam's Red Wull!"

He pauses, the pewter at his lips, and looks at his audience with flashing eyes. There is no response from them.

"Wullie, here's to you!" he cries. "Luck and life to ye, my trusty mate! Death and defeat to yer enemies!

'The world's wrack we share o't,
The warstle and the care o't.'"

He raises the mug and drains it to its last drop.

Then, standing up straight, he addresses his audience once more:

"And now I'll warn ye once and for all, and ye may tell James Moore I said it: He may plot against us, Wullie and me; he may threaten us; he may win the Cup outright for his great favorite; but there was never yet a man or dog that harmed Adam McAdam and his Red Wull but in the end he wished his mother hadn't given birth to him."

A little later, he walks out of the inn, the Tailless Tyke at his heels.

After he is gone, it is Rob Saunderson who says: "The little man's crazy; he'll stop at nothing"; and Tammas who answers:

"Nay; not even murder."

◆ ◆ ◆

The little man had aged a good deal lately. His hair was completely white, his eyes unnaturally bright, and his hands were never quiet, as though he were in constant pain. He looked like the very picture of disease.

After Owd Bob's second victory, he had become gloomy and untalkative. At home, he often sat silent for hours at a time, drinking and glaring at the place where the Cup had been. Sometimes he talked in a low, eerie voice to Red Wull; and twice, David, turning around suddenly, had caught his father glowering stealthily at him with an expression on his face that chilled the boy's blood. The two never spoke now; and to David, this silent, deadly enmity seemed far worse than the old-time constant warfare.

It was the same at the Sylvester Arms. The little man sat alone with Red Wull, exchanging words with no man, drinking steadily, brooding over the wrongs done to him, only now and again galvanized into sudden action.

Other people besides Tammas Thornton came to the conclusion that McAdam would stop at nothing to hurt James Moore and the gray dog. They said that drink and disappointment had affected his mind; that he was mad and dangerous. And on New Year's day, matters seemed to be coming to a crisis; for it was reported that in the gloom of a snowy evening he had drawn a knife on the Master in the High Street, but had slipped before he could accomplish his deadly purpose.

Of all of them, David was most haunted with an ever-present anxiety as to the little man's intentions. The boy even went so far as to warn his friend against his father. But the Master only smiled grimly.

"Thank ye, lad," he said. "But I reckon we can fend for ourselves, Bob and I. Eh, Owd One?"

Anxious as David might be, he was not above taking unkind advantage of this state of constant worry to work on Maggie's fears.

One evening, as he was walking her home from church, just before they reached the little grove of larch trees, he took a sudden step back and exclaimed with horror:

"Oh God! What's that?"

"What, Davie?" cried the girl, shrinking up against him and trembling.

"Couldn't say for sure. It might be something, or then again it might be nothing. But you hold on to my arm, and I'll hold you around your waist."

Maggie objected.

"Can you see anything?" she asked, still nervous.

"Behind the hedge."

"Where?"

"There!"—pointing vaguely.

"I can't see anything."

"Why, there, lass. Can't yo' see it? Then put your head next to mine—like that—closer—closer." Then, in a complaining tone of voice: "Whatever is the matter with yo', girl? You act as though I were a leper."

But the girl was walking away with her head as high as the snow-capped Pike.

"So long as I live, David McAdam," she cried, "I'll never go to church with you again!"

"Ohhh, but you will, though—once," he answered quietly.

Maggie whisked around in a flash, superbly indignant.

"What d'yo' mean, sir?"

"You know what I mean, lass," he replied sheepishly, shuffling before her queenly anger.

She looked him up and down, and down and up again.

"I'll never speak to you again, Mr. McAdam," she cried; "not if it was every so. . . . Nay, I'll walk home by myself, thank you. I'll have nothing to do with you."

So the two must return to Kenmuir, one behind the other, like a lady and her footman.

David's boldness had, more than once already, nearly caused a break between the two of them. And what had happened behind the hedge was the limit of his insolence. That had been intolerable, and Maggie, by her behavior, let him know it.

David put up with the girl's new attitude for exactly twelve minutes by the kitchen clock. Then he said to himself: "Sulk in front of me, indeed! I'll teach her!" and he marched out the door, "Never to come through it again, my word!"

Afterward, however, he gave in so far as to go on with his visits as before; but he made it clear that he came only to see the Master and to hear about Owd Bob's doings. On these visits he loved best of all to sit on the windowsill outside the kitchen, and talk and joke with Tammas and the men in the yard, pretending to be uncomfortable and shy if the name of Bessie Bolstock was mentioned. And after sitting in this way for some time, he would half turn, look over his shoulder, and remark in an indifferent tone of voice to the girl inside: "Oh, good evening! I forgot you"—and then go on with his conversation. While the girl inside, her face a little pinker, her lips a little tighter, and her chin a little higher, would go about her business, pretending neither to hear nor care.

The suspicion that McAdam was planning some dark mischief against James Moore was somewhat confirmed in that, several times in the cold, dusky January afternoons, a sly little figure was reported to have been seen lurking among the farm buildings of Kenmuir.

Once, Sammel Todd caught the little man skulking in the woodshed. Sammel picked him up bodily and carried him down the slope to the Wastrel, shaking him gently as he went.

Across the stream he set him down on his feet.

"If I catches you prowling around the farm again, little man," he scolded, holding up a threatening finger, "I'll take you and drop you in the Sheep wash, I warn you fair. I'd have done it now if you'd been a bigger and younger man. But there!—you're such a scrappety little bit of a person. Now, run away home." And the little man crept silently away.

For a time he did not return to the farm. Then, one evening when it was almost dark, James Moore, walking around to check the outbuildings, felt Owd Bob stiffen against his side.

"What's up, lad?" he whispered, stopping; and, laying his hand on the dog's neck, felt a ruff of rising hair beneath it.

"Steady, lad, steady," he whispered; "what is it?" He peered forward into the gloom; and after a time made out a familiar little figure huddled in the gap between two haystacks.

"It's you, isn't it, McAdam?" he said, and, bending, seized a lock of Owd Bob's coat in an iron grip.

Then, in a great voice, moved to rare anger: "Out of here before I do you harm, you miserable spying creature!" he roared. "You wait till dark comes to hide you, you coward, before you dare come crawling around my house, frightening the women-folk and up to your devilish deeds. If you have anything to say to me, come like a man in the open day. Now get off with you, before I lay hands on you!"

He stood there in the dusk, tall and strong, a terrible figure, one hand pointing to the gate, the other still grasping the gray dog.

The little man scurried away in the half-light, and out of the yard.

On the plank-bridge he turned and shook his fist at the darkening house.

"Curse you, James Moore!" he sobbed, "I'll get even with you yet."

CHAPTER 15

Death on the Marches

ON TOP of this, there was an attempt to poison the Owd One—or at any rate there was no other way of explaining what happened.

In the dead of the night, on a night that would not soon be forgotten, James Moore was waked by a low moaning beneath his room. He leapt out of bed and ran to the window to see his favorite, the Owd One, with his dark head down, the proud tail for once lowered, the supple legs wooden, heavy, unnatural—altogether pitiful.

In a moment he was downstairs and out to help his friend. "Whatever is it, Owd One?" he cried in anguish.

At the sound of that dear voice the dog tried to struggle to him, could not, and fell, whimpering.

In a second the Master was by his side, examining him tenderly, and crying for Sammel, who slept above the stables.

There was every symptom of foul play: the tongue was swollen and almost black; the breathing difficult; the body twitched horribly; and the soft gray eyes all bloodshot and straining in agony.

With the help of Sammel and Maggie, first pouring medicine down his throat and then giving him a stimulant to speed up his heart rate, the Master managed to keep him alive for the moment. And soon Jim Mason and Parson Leggy, hurriedly summoned, came running as fast as they could to the rescue.

Prompt and extreme action saved the victim—but only just. For a time, the best sheepdog in the North was pawing at the Gate of Death. In the end, as the gray dawn broke, the danger passed.

The attempt to strike out at him, if that was what it was, aroused passionate indignation in everyone for miles around. It seemed like the climax of the excitement that had been brewing for so long.

There was no sign of the culprit; there wasn't a clue that might lead them to the criminal, so cleverly had he carried out his foul deed. But though there was no proof, there was also no doubt in anyone's mind about who had done it.

At the Sylvester Arms, Long Kirby asked McAdam directly for his explanation of the matter.

"How do I account for it?" the little man exclaimed. "I don't account for it at all."

"Then how did it happen?" asked Tammas sharply.

"I don't believe it happened at all," the little man replied. "I believe James Moore is lying—as he always does." Whereupon they immediately hurled him out the door; for Red Wull was not with him, for once.

Now, that afternoon will be remembered for three reasons. First, because, as has been said, McAdam was alone. Second, because, a few minutes after he was thrown out, the window of the taproom was opened suddenly from outside, and the little man looked in. He did not say a word, but those dim, smoldering eyes of his wandered from face to face, resting for a second on each, as if to burn them into his memory. "I'll remember ye, gentleman," he said at last quietly, shut the window, and was gone.

Third, for a reason that will now be told.

Though ten days had passed since the attempt on his life, the gray dog was still not his old self. He had attacks of shivering; his liveliness seemed to have drained away; he easily became tired, and, courageous dog that he was, he would never admit it. At last, on this day, James Moore, leaving the dog behind, had gone over to Grammoch-town to ask the advice of Dingley, the vet. On his way home, he met Jim Mason accompanied by his new dog Gyp, in no way the equal of the faithful Betsy, at the Dalesman's Daughter. Together they started on the long tramp home over the Marches. And that journey should be marked with a red stone to show the special place it has in this story.

All day long, the hills had been bathed in a dense fog. All day long, there had been a steady drizzle along with it; and in the distance, the wind had moaned, threatening a storm. The darkness of the day was deepened by the gloom of the falling night as the three began climbing up the Murk Muir Pass. By the time they came out into the Devil's Bowl, it was altogether black and blind. But the threatening wind had gone, leaving utter stillness; and they could hear the splash of an otter on the far side of the Lone Tarn as they walked around the edge of that dismal lake. When, after some time, they had climbed the last steep rise up to the Marches, a breath of soft air struck them lightly, and the curtain of fog began drifting away.

The two men walked steadily on through the heather with that long stride which is so natural to the people of the moors and the highlands. They talked only a little, for they were quiet by nature: a word or two about sheep and the coming season, when the lambs would be born; after that, the approaching Trials; the Shepherds' Trophy; Owd Bob and the attempt on his life; and from that to McAdam and the Tailless Tyke.

"D'you believe McAdam had a hand in it?" the postman was asking.

"Nay; there's no proof."

"Except that he's wild to get rid of the Owd One before Cup Day."

"Him or me—it makes no difference." For a dog is not allowed to compete for the Trophy if it has changed owners during the six months before the competition. And this is true even if the change is only from father to son after the death of the father.

Jim looked curiously at his companion.

"D'you think it's come to that?" he asked.

"What?"

"Why—murder."

"Not if I can help it," the other answered grimly.

The fog had cleared away by now, and the moon was up. To their right, at the top of a rise some two hundred yards away, a small grove of trees stood out black against the sky. As they passed it, a blackbird flew up screaming, and a pair of wood pigeons winged noisily away.

"Hullo! Listen to that yammering!" muttered Jim, stopping; "and at this time of night, too!"

Some rabbits, playing in the moonlight on the outskirts of the woods, sat up, listened, and hopped back into the safety of the trees. At the same moment, a big hill-fox glided out of the underbrush. He stole a step forward and halted, listening with one ear back and one paw raised; then ran silently away in the gloom, passing close to the two men and yet not noticing them.

"What's up, I wonder?" said the postman thoughtfully.

"The fox started them clackering, I suppose," said the Master.

"Not him; he was scared out of his skin," the other answered. Then, in tones of quiet excitement, with his hands on James Moore's arm: "And look, there's my Gyp telling us to come on!"

There, indeed, at the top of the rise beside the trees, was the little mongrel, now looking back at his master, now creeping stealthily forward.

"My word! There's something wrong yonder!" cried Jim, and jerked the mailbags off his shoulder. "Come on, Master!"—and he set off running toward the dog; while James Moore, himself excited now, followed with the nimbleness of a younger man.

Some twenty yards from the lower edge of the grove, on the far side of the ridge, a tiny brook babbled through its bed of peat moss. The two men, as they came over the top of the rise, saw a flock of black-faced mountain sheep clustered in the dip between the woods and the stream. They stood pressed close together facing half toward the woods, half toward the men, their heads up, their eyes glaring, handsome as sheep look only when alarmed.

At the top of the ridge, the two men came to stop beside Gyp. The postman stood with his head a little forward, listening hard. Then he dropped down in the heather like a dead man, pulling the other with him.

"Down, man!" he whispered, clutching at Gyp with his other hand.

"What is it, Jim?" asked the Master, now thoroughly on the alert.

"Something's moving in the woods," the other whispered, listening with ears as sharp as a weasel's.

So they lay without moving for a while; but no sound came from the grove of trees.

"Maybe it was nothing," the postman admitted finally, peering cautiously around. "And yet I thought—I don't really know what I thought."

Then, getting up on his knees suddenly with a hoarse cry of terror: "Save us! What's that over there?"

Then for the first time the Master raised his head and saw, lying in the gloom between them and the dense ranks of sheep, a still, white heap.

James Moore was a man of action, not words.

"Enough waiting!" he said, and sprang forward, his heart pounding.

The sheep stamped and shuffled as he came, and yet did not scatter.

"Ah, thanks be!" he cried, dropping beside the motionless body; "It's only a sheep." As he spoke, his hands wandered skillfully over the body. "But what's this?" he called. "She was as fit as I am. Look at her fleece—crisp, close, strong; feel the flesh—firm as a rock. And no bones broken, not a scratch on her body as small as a pin could make. She's as healthy as a man—yet dead as mutton!"

Jim, still trembling from the horror of his fear, came up and kneeled beside his friend. "Ah, but there's been something wicked going on here!" he said; "I think those sheep have been badly scared, and not so long ago."

"Sheep-murder, sure enough!" the other answered. "Not the work of any fox—this is a full-grown, twice-sheared ewe that could almost knock an ox down."

Jim's hands traveled from the body to the dead creature's throat. He cried out.

"By gob, Master! Look you there!" He held his hand up in the moonlight, and it dripped red. "And warm still! Warm!"

"Tear some bracken, Jim!" ordered the other, "and set it alight. We must see to this."

The postman did as asked. For a moment the fern smoldered and smoked, then the flame ran crackling along and shot up in the darkness, weirdly lighting the scene: to the right, the low woods, a block of solid blackness against the sky; in front, the wall of sheep, staring out of the gloom with bright eyes; and in the center, that motionless white body, with the kneeling men and the mongrel sniffing hesitantly around.

The men examined the victim carefully. The throat, and only the throat, had been hideously torn apart; from the raw wounds, the flesh hung in ugly shreds; on the ground all around were pitiful little dabs of wool, apparently wrenched off in the struggle; and, crawling among the roots of the ferns, a snake-like track of red led down to the stream.

"The work of a dog, no question about that," said Jim at last, after a close inspection.

"Ay," declared the Master with slow emphasis, "and a sheepdog, too, and an experienced one, or I'm no shepherd."

The postman looked up.

"Why's that?" he asked, puzzled.

"Because," the Master answered, "the one that did this killed for blood—and for blood only. If it had been any other dog—greyhound, bull, terrier, or even a young sheepdog—d'you think he'd have stopped after one? Not he; he'd have gone through them, and be chasing them, most likely, nipping them, pulling them down, till he'd maybe killed half o' them. But the one that did this killed for blood, I say. He got it—killed just this one, and never touched the others, d'you see, Jim?"

The postman whistled, long and low.

"It's just what old Wrottesley used to tell about," he said. "I never more than half believed him then—I do now, though. D'you remember what the old lad used to tell, Master?"

James Moore nodded and spoke.

"That's it. I've never seen anything like it before, myself, but I heard my granddad talk about it many times. An old dog'll get a craving for sheep's blood, just the same as a man does for drink; he creeps out at night, runs far away, hunts his sheep, pulls it down, and satisfies the craving. And he never kills more than just that one, they say, for he knows the value of sheep same as you and me. He has his gallop, satisfies his thirst, and then he makes off for home again, maybe twenty miles away, and no one suspects a thing in the morning. And on it goes, till he comes to a bloody death, the murdering traitor."

"If he does!" said Jim.

"And he does, they say, almost always. For he gets bolder and bolder the longer he's not caught, until one fine night a bullet pierces a hole in him. And some man has the surprise of his life when they bring his best dog home in the morning, dead, with the sheep's wool still sticking in his mouth."

The postman whistled again.

"It's what old Wrottesley would tell exactly. And he'd say, if you remember, Master, that the dog would never kill his own master's sheep—like he had a conscience."

"Ay, I've heard that," said the Master. "Strange, too, with him being such a bad creature!"

Jim Mason stood up slowly.

"Truly," he said, "I wish the Owd One was here. Maybe he'd show us something!"

"I wish he was, pore old lad!" said the Master.

As he spoke, there was a crash in the woods above them; it sounded as though some big body were bursting furiously through the underbrush.

The two men rushed to the top of the rise. In the darkness they could see nothing; but, standing still and holding their breaths, they could hear the faint sound, growing fainter, of some creature galloping away over the wet moors.

"That's him! That's no fox, I'll swear. And a mighty big one, too—just listen to him!" cried Jim. Then, to Gyp, who had rushed off in hot pursuit: "Come back, you chunk-head. What use are you against a galloping hippopotamus?"

Gradually the sounds died away, and vanished entirely.

"That's him, the devil!" said the Master at last.

"Nay; the devil has a tail, they do say," replied Jim thoughtfully. For already the light of suspicion was pointing its red glare.

"Now I suppose we're in for bloody times among the sheep, for a while," said the Master, as Jim picked up his bags of letters.

"Better a sheep than a man," answered the postman, again.

CHAPTER 16

The Black Killer

THAT, as James Moore had predicted, was only the first of a long series of such solitary crimes.

Those who have not lived in a lonely place like the countryside around the Muir Pike, where sheep are the most important thing and every other man is in the sheep-herding profession, can barely imagine what a sensation this caused. In marketplace, tavern, or cottage, the subject of conversation was always the latest sheep-murder and the yet-undiscovered criminal.

Sometimes there would be a quiet spell, and the shepherds would begin to breathe more freely. Then there would come a stormy night, when the skies were veiled in the cloak of crime, and the wind moaned, rising and falling over ponds and frontier lands, and another victim would be added to the growing list.

It was always black nights like these, nights of wind and weather, when no one roamed outdoors, that the murderer chose for his bloody work; and that was how he became known from the Red Screes to the Muir Pike as the Black

Killer. In the Daleland they still call a wild, wet night "A Black Killer's Night"; for they say: "His ghost'll be out tonight."

There was hardly a farm in the countryside that had not been marked with the seal of blood. Kenmuir escaped, and the Grange; Rob Saunderson at the Holt, and Tupper at Swinsthwaite; and they were about the only lucky ones.

As for Kenmuir, Tammas declared with a certain grim pride: "He knows better'n to come where the Owd One be." At which McAdam was overcome by a fit of private laughter, rubbing his knees and cackling insanely for a half hour afterward. And as for the luck of the Grange—well, there was a reason for that, too, so the Dalesmen said.

Though the area of crime stretched from the Black Water to Grammoch-town, twenty or so miles, there was never a sign of the criminal. The Killer did his bloody work with a thoroughness and a devilish cunning that made it impossible to find him out.

It was obvious that each murder was the work of the same creature. Each was committed in the same way: one sheep killed, its throat torn to red ribbons, and the others untouched.

Following Parson Leggy's suggestion, the Squire brought in a bloodhound to track the Killer to his doom. Starting from a fresh-killed carcass at the One Tree Knowe, the hound followed the scent some distance in the direction of the Muir Pike; then was stopped by a little bustling brook, and never found it again. Afterward he became impossible to manage, and was of no further use. Then there was talk of asking Tommy Dobson and his pack of hounds to come over from Eskdale, but nothing came of that. The Master of the Border Hunt lent a couple of foxhounds, who did nothing; and there were a hundred other attempts and just as many failures. Jim Mason set a clever trap or two and caught his own bob-tailed tortoise-shell cat, along with a terrible scolding from his wife;

Ned Hoppin sat up with a gun for two nights over a newly slain victim and Londesley of the Home Farm poisoned a carcass. But the Killer never returned to the kill, and went about in the midst of them all, carrying on his shameful business and laughing to himself all the while.

Meanwhile, the Dalesmen raged and swore vengeance; their helplessness, their lack of success in finding him, and the loss of their sheep heated their anger to madness. And the most bitter part of it all was this—that though they could not unmask him, they were almost sure who the culprit was.

Many a time was the Black Killer named by hushed voices in secret meetings; many a time did Long Kirby, as he stood in the Border Ram and watched McAdam and the Terror walk down the main street, nudge Jim Mason and whisper:

"There's the Killer—may his grave be a restless one!" To which practical Jim always made the same answer:

"Ay, there's the Killer; but where's the proof?"

And that was the main problem. There was hardly a man for miles around who doubted that the Tailless Tyke was guilty; but, as Jim said, where was the proof? They could only point to his well-deserved nickname; his evil reputation; and say that, magnificent sheepdog though he was, he was known to be rough with the sheep even in his work. Lastly, they would remark, with a meaningful look, that the Grange was one of the few farms that had so far escaped the menace. For along with their belief that the Black Killer was a sheepdog, they were sure that he would feel it a point of honor to spare his own master's flock.

They may, indeed, have been prejudiced in their opinion. For each had his own private grudge against the Terror; and almost every man some mark on his own body, or on his clothes, or on the body of his dog, left by that huge savage.

Proof?

"Why, he nearly killed my Lassie!" cries Londesley.

"And he did kill the Wexer!"

"And Wan Tromp!"

"And just look at my poor old Venus!" says John Swan, and shows his lovely fighter, so battered you could hardly recognize her, but a fighter still.

"That's Red Wull—may his end be bloody!"

"And he did such harm to my Rasper he couldn't move for nearly three weeks!" continues Tupper, pointing to the scars, not yet healed, on the neck of his big bob-tailed sheepdog. "See this here—his work."

"And look here!" cries Saunderson, showing a ragged wound on Shep's throat; "That's the Terror—black be his fate!"

"Ay," says Long Kirby, swearing; "our tykes love him nearly as much as we do."

"Yes," says Tammas. "Just you watch!"

The old man slips out of the taproom; and in another moment, from the road outside comes a heavy, regular pat-pat-pat, as though some big creature is coming near, and, blending with the sound, little shuffling footsteps.

In an instant, every dog in the room has risen to his feet and stands staring at the door with gloomy, glowing eyes; lips wrinkling, bristles rising, throats rumbling.

An unsteady hand fumbles at the door; a shrill, thin voice calls, "Wullie, come here!" and the dogs move away, surly, to either side of the fireplace, tails down, ears back, still grumbling; showing both fear and passion.

Then the door opens; Tammas enters, grinning; and each, after studying him for a moment, returns to lie down where he was before, in front of the fire.

◆ ◆ ◆

Meanwhile, a change had come over McAdam, who seemed unaware of these suspicions. Whether it was because for some time now he had been hearing less about the best sheepdog in the North, or for some other, more mysterious reason, the fact was that he became his old self again. He talked on and on as cheerfully and bitterly as ever; and hardly an evening went by when he did not move Tammas almost to blows with his hints and his sly, sarcastic remarks.

One evening at the Sylvester Arms, old Jonas Maddox asked him who he thought the Killer might be.

"I have my suspicions, Mr. Maddox; I have my suspicions," the little man answered, wagging his head knowingly and giggling. But they could not get more than that from him. A week later, however, he was asked:

"And what are you thinking about this Black Killer, Mr. McAdam?" And this time he answered earnestly:

"Why *black*? Why *black* more than white—or *gray*, shall we say?" Luckily for him, however, the Dalesmen are as slow to understand as they are slow to speak.

David, too, noticed the difference in his father, who nagged at him now with all the old spirit. At first he was glad of the change, for he preferred this open, direct warfare to the quiet hatred of earlier times. But soon he almost wished the earlier times back again; for the older he grew, the more difficult it was for him to stay calm during the constant quarreling.

There was one reason he was truly pleased with the changed situation; he believed that, for now at least, his father had given up any evil plans he might have cherished against James Moore; those sneaking night visits to Kenmuir had, he hoped, come to an end.

Yet Maggie Moore, if she had been on speaking terms with

him, could have told him this was not so. For, one night, when she was alone in the kitchen, she had looked up suddenly and had seen, to her horror, a dim, moonlike face glued against the windowpane. In the first mad panic of the moment she almost screamed, and she dropped her work; then— true Moore that she was—she controlled herself and sat pretending to work on, yet still watching all the while.

It was McAdam, she knew: the face pale in its framework of black; the hair lying damp and dark on his forehead; and the white eyelids blinking, slow, regular, horrible. She thought of the stories she had heard of his sworn vengeance on her father, and her heart stood still, though she never moved. At last, with a gasp of relief, she saw that the eyes were not directed at her. Cautiously following their gaze, she saw that they rested on the Shepherds' Trophy; and they remained fixed on the Cup and motionless, while she sat still and watched.

An hour, it seemed to her, went by before those eyes shifted their direction and wandered around the room. For a second they rested on her; then the face drew back into the night.

Maggie told no one what she had seen. Knowing very well how terrible her father was when angry, she judged it wiser to keep silence. While as for David McAdam, she would never speak to him again!

And not for a moment did that young man suspect where his father was coming from when, on that night, McAdam returned to the Grange, chuckling to himself. Lately, David had been growing used to these fits of silent humor that seemed to have no obvious cause; and when his father began giggling and muttering to Red Wull, at first he paid no attention.

"He, he! Wullie. Perhaps we'll beat him yet. There's many a slip twixt Cup and lip—eh, Wullie, he, he!" And he talked about the wicked and how they would come to a bad end, always concluding with the same words: "He, he! Wullie. Perhaps we'll beat him yet."

He continued on this subject until David lost his patience and asked roughly:

"Who is it you're mumbling about? Who is it you'll beat, you and yer Wullie?"

The boy's tone was as scornful as his words. He had long ago put aside any hint of respect for his father.

McAdam only rubbed his knees and giggled.

"Just listen to the dear lad, Wullie! Listen how pleasantly he speaks to his old dad!" Then, turning on his son, and grinning at him: "Who is it, ye ask? Who else should it be but the Black Killer? Who else would I be wishing to hurt?"

"The Black Killer!" echoed the boy, and looked at his father in amazement.

Now David was almost the only man in Wastrel-dale who declared that Red Wull was not the Killer. "Nay," he said once; "he'd kill me, given half a chance, but a sheep—no." Yet, though this was his own opinion, he knew very well what others were saying, and was therefore astonished by his father's remark.

"The Black Killer, is it? What d'you know about the Killer?" he asked.

"Why do they call him *black*, I'd like to know? Why *black*?" the little man asked, leaning forward in his chair.

Now David, when he was in the village, might deny that Red Wull had anything to do with the crimes, but when he was at home he liked to drop clever hints that Red Wull was indeed involved in them.

"What color would you like him to have, then?" he asked. "Red, yellow, muck-dirt?"—and he stared meaningfully at the Tailless Tyke, who was lying at his master's feet. The little man stopped rubbing his knees and looked at the boy. David shifted uneasily beneath that dim, steady gaze.

"Well?" he said at last gruffly.

The little man giggled, and his two thin hands went back to what they had been doing before.

"Maybe his poor old fool of a dad knows more than the dear lad thinks, ay, or wishes—eh, Wullie, he, he!"

"Then what is it you do know, or think you know?" David asked, irritated.

The little man nodded and chuckled.

"Nothing at all, laddie, nothing worth mentioning. Only perhaps the Killer'll be caught before too long."

David smiled in disbelief, wagging his head doubtfully.

"You'll catch him yourself, I suppose, you and yer Wullie? Take a chair out on the Marches, whistle a while, and when the Killer comes, why! put a pinch of salt on his tail—if he has one."

At the last words, heavily emphasized by David, the little man stopped his rubbing as though he'd been shot.

"What d'ye mean by that?" he asked softly.

"What d'yo' think?" the boy replied.

"I don't know for sure," the little man answered; "and it's perhaps just as well for you, dear lad"—in a falsely loving tone—"that I don't." He began rubbing and giggling again. "It's a grand thing, Wullie, to have a dutiful son; a sharp lad who has no silly sense of shame about sharpening his wits at his old dad's expense. And yet, despite our comical lad there, perhaps we will have a hand in catching the Killer, you and I, Wullie—he, he!" And the great dog at his feet wagged his stump of a tail in reply.

David rose from his chair and walked across the room to where his father sat.

"If you know such a mighty heap of things," he shouted, "maybe you'll just tell me what you do know!"

McAdam stopped stroking Red Wull's massive head, and looked up.

"Tell ye? Ay, who should I tell if not my dear David? Tell? Ay, I'll tell ye this"—with a sudden snarl of bitterness—"that you'd be the very last person I would tell."

CHAPTER 17

A Mad Dog

DAVID and Maggie, meanwhile, were drifting farther and farther apart. He now thought the girl took too much responsibility for the household; that she went too far in playing the part of woman and mother. Once, on a Sunday, he caught her drilling Andrew in his Bible verses. He watched the two of them through a crack in the door, and listened, laughing to himself, to her simple teaching. At last his laughter grew so loud that she looked up, saw him, rose immediately to her feet, crossed the room, and shut the door, rebuking him with such sweet dignity that he crept away feeling decently ashamed, for once. And the incident only added to his anger.

And so he was rarely at Kenmuir, and more often at home, quarreling with his father.

Since the day, two years before, when the boy had helped to take the Cup away from him, father and son had been as though charged with electricity, contact between them might result at any moment in a shock and a flash. This was the result not of a single moment but of years.

Lately the contest had become distinctly fiercer; for McAdam noticed that his son was at home more often, and commented on the fact in his usual spirit of playful mockery.

"What's come over ye, David?" he asked one day. "Yer old dad's in danger of feeling flattered at your graciousness. Is it that James Moore won't have you at Kenmuir anymore, afraid ye'll steal the Cup from him, as ye stole it from me? Or what is it?"

"I thought I could maybe keep an eye on the Killer if I stayed here," David answered, gazing at Red Wull.

"Ye'd do better at Kenmuir—eh, Wullie!" the little man replied.

"Nay," the other answered, "he'll not go to Kenmuir. There's the Owd One to see to him there at night."

The little man whipped around.

"Are ye so sure he is there at night, my lad?" he asked with slow meaningfulness.

"He was there when someone—I didn't say who, though I have my thoughts—tried to poison him," sneered the boy, mimicking his father's manner.

McAdam shook his head.

"If he was poisoned, and now I think maybe he was, he didn't pick it up at Kenmuir, I tell ye that," he said, and marched out of the room.

In the meantime, the Black Killer went on with his bloody business unrestrained. The public, always greedy for a new sensation, took up the subject. In several of the larger daily newspapers, articles on the "Agrarian Outrages" appeared, followed by numerous letters from readers. There were sharp differences of opinion; each correspondent had his own theory and his own solution of the problem; and each grew indignant as his were rejected in favor of another's.

The Terror had already lasted two months when lambing time came and matters became still more serious.

It was bad enough to lose one sheep, often the finest in the pack; but in order to kill one, the Killer hunted the whole flock, and scared the woolly mothers-about-to-be almost out of their fleeces. This was ruinous for the small farmers and difficult even for the bigger ones.

Such a dismal season had never been known before; the curses were loud, the vows of revenge were deep. Many a shepherd at that time patrolled all night long with his dogs, only to find in the morning that the Killer had given him the slip and brought destruction to some distant part of his flock.

It was heartbreaking work; especially since the proof seemed as far off as ever, while there was still the same positive certainty as to the identity of the criminal.

Long Kirby, indeed, grew quite daring, and went so far as to say, once, to the little man: "And d'you think the Killer is a sheepdog, McAdam?"

"I do," the little man replied firmly.

"And that he'll spare his own sheep?"

"Never a doubt of it."

"Then," said the smith with a nervous chuckle, "it must be either you or Tupper or Saunderson."

The little man leaned forward and tapped the other man on the arm.

"Or Kenmuir, my friend," he said. "Ye've forgot Kenmuir."

"So I have," laughed the smith, "so I have."

"Then don't forget it a second time," the other continued, still tapping. "I'd remember Kenmuir, d'ye see, Kirby?"

◆ ◆ ◆

It was about the middle of the lambing time, when the Killer was working his worst, that the Dalesmen had a shocking glimpse of Adam McAdam as he might be, if he were ever wounded through his Wullie.

It came about this way: It was market day in Grammoch-town, and in the Border Ram old Rob Saunderson was the center of interest. For on the previous night Rob, who till then had escaped harm, had lost a sheep to the Killer; and—far worse—his flock of Herwicks, many carrying lambs, had been made to gallop, with disastrous results.

The old man, with tears in his eyes, was telling how on four nights that week he had been up with Shep to stand guard; and on the fifth, worn out from working day and night, he had fallen asleep at his watch. He had slept only a little while; yet when he woke at dawn and hurried to make the rounds, he soon came upon a slaughtered sheep and the pitiful remains of his flock. Remains, indeed! For on all sides of him were cold little lambs and their mothers, dead and dying of exhaustion and their premature labor—a slaughter of the innocents.

The Dalesmen were clustered around the old shepherd, listening with darkly threatening faces, when a dark gray head peered in at the door and two sad eyes rested for a moment on the speaker.

"Talk o' the devil!" muttered McAdam, but no man heard him. For Red Wull, too, had seen that sad face, and, rising from his master's feet, had leaped with a roar at his enemy, knocking over Jim Mason like a bowling pin in the fury of his charge.

In a second, every dog in the room, from the battered Venus to Tupper's big Rasper, was on his feet, bristling to attack the tyrant and take revenge for past injuries, if the gray dog would only lead the way.

It was not to be, however. For Long Kirby was standing at

the door with a cup of hot coffee in his hand. Barely had he greeted the gray dog with—

"Hullo, Owd One!" when hoarse yells of "Watch out, lad! The Terror!" mingled with Red Wull's roar.

Half turning, he saw the great dog leaping to the attack. Right away he flung the boiling contents of his cup full in that raging face. The burning liquid splashed against the huge bull-head. Blinding, bubbling, burning, it did its evil work well; nothing escaped that merciless stream. With a cry of agony, half bellow, half howl, Red Wull stopped short in his charge. From outside, the door was banged shut; and again the duel was postponed. While inside the taproom a huddle of men and dogs were left alone with a madman and a madder brute.

Blind, crazed, in pain, the Tailless Tyke thundered around the little room gnashing his teeth, snapping, overturning one thing after another: men, tables, chairs were tipped off their legs as though they were little toys. He spun around like a monstrous top; he banged his tortured head against the wall; he burrowed into the hard floor. And all the while McAdam trotted after him, laying hands upon him only to be flung aside as a terrier flings a rat. Now up, now down again, now tossed into a corner, now dragged along the floor, yet always following on and crying to him in pleading tones, "Wullie, Wullie, let me come to ye! Let yer man help ye!" and then, with a scream and a murderous glance, "By God, Kirby, I'll deal with you later!"

The uproar was like hell let loose. You could hear the noise of curses and blows, as the men fought to get to the door, a half mile away. And above it the horrible bellowing and the screaming of that shrill voice.

Long Kirby was the first man out of that murder-hole; and after him the others toppled one by one—men and dogs

jostling one another in the violent excitement of their fear.
Big Bell, Londesley, Tupper, Hoppin, Teddy Bolstock, white-
faced and trembling; and they pulled old Saunderson out by
his heels. Then the door was shut with a clang, and the little
man and mad dog were left alone.

In the street outside, a wide-eyed crowd had already gathered, attracted by the uproar; while at the door was James
Moore, thinking to go in. "Maybe I could give the little man
a hand," he said; but they held him back by force.

Inside was chaos: banging as though on the doors of hell;
the bellowing of that great voice; the patter of little feet; the
slithering of a body on the floor; and always that shrill, pleading prayer, "Wullie, Wullie, let me come to ye!" and, in a
scream, "By God, Kirby, I'll be dealin' with ye soon!"

It was Jim Mason who turned to the smith at last and whispered, "Kirby, lad, you'd best get out of here."

The big man obeyed and ran. The stamp, stamp of his feet
on the hard road rang above the turmoil. As the long legs
vanished around the corner and the sound of the running
steps died away, the listening crowd was seized with panic.

A woman shrieked; a girl fainted; and in two minutes, the
street was as empty of people as the plains of Russia in winter: here a white face at a window; there a door half open;
and peering around a far corner a frightened boy. Only one
man refused to run. Alone, James Moore walked with long
strides down the center of the road, slow and calm, Owd Bob
trotting at his heels.

❖ ❖ ❖

It was a long half hour before the door of the inn burst open
and McAdam came running out, flinging the door behind
him.

He rushed into the middle of the road; his sleeves were rolled at the wrist like a surgeon's; and in his right hand was a black-handled jack-knife.

"Now, by God!" he cried in a terrible voice, "where is he?"

He looked up and down the road, darting his fiery glances everywhere; and his face was whiter than his hair.

Then he turned and hunted madly down the whole length of the main street, nosing like a weasel in every corner, stabbing at the air as he went, and screaming, "By God, Kirby, wait till I get ye!"

CHAPTER 18

How the Killer Was Nearly Caught

NO FURTHER harm came of the incident; but it served as a lesson for the Dalesmen.

Although, in fact, it may have been a coincidence, during the two weeks following Kirby's deed, there was a quiet period in which no crimes were committed. Then, as though to make up for that, came seven days which are still remembered in the Daleland as the Bloody Week.

On the Sunday, the Squire lost a Cheviot ewe, killed only a hundred yards from the Manor wall. On the Monday, a farm on the Black Water was marked with the red cross. On Tuesday—a black night—Tupper at Swinsthwaite came upon the murderer at his work; he fired into the darkness without striking anything; and the Killer escaped with a scare. On the following night, Viscount Birdsaye lost a shearling ram for which he was said to have paid a great sum of money. Thursday was the one blank night of the week. On Friday, Tupper was again visited and punished heavily, as though in revenge for that shot.

On the Saturday afternoon, a big meeting was held at the

Manor to discuss what could be done. The Squire presided over it; many gentlemen and officials of the court of law were present, and every farmer in the countryside.

To start things off, the Special Commissioner read a pointless letter from the Board of Agriculture. After him, Viscount Birdsaye stood up and proposed that instead of the £5 suggested by the Police, a reward should be offered that was more in keeping with the seriousness of the case, and he backed up his proposal with a check for £25. Several others spoke, and, last of all, Parson Leggy got to his feet.

He gave a short history of the crimes; repeated his belief that a sheepdog was the criminal; declared that nothing had happened to change his mind; and ended by offering a solution for them to consider. It was so simple, he said, that they might laugh; but, if their suspicion was correct, it would work to prevent, if not cure, and it would at least give them time to turn around. He paused.

"My suggestion is: That every one of you who owns a sheepdog ties him up at night."

The farmers were given half an hour to consider the suggestion, and they gathered in small groups to talk it over. Many of them looked at McAdam; but that little man seemed not to notice.

"Well, Mr. Saunderson," he was saying in a shrill tone of voice, "and will ye tie Shep?"

"What d'you think?" asked Rob, staring at the man at whom the solution was aimed.

"Why, it's this way, I'm thinking," the little man answered. "If ye think Shep's the guilty one, I *would*, by all manner of means—or shootin' would be better, maybe. If not, why"—he shrugged his shoulders meaningfully; and having revealed his thoughts and made his point, the little man left the meeting.

James Moore stayed to see the Parson's suggestion voted

down by a large majority, and then he too left the hall. He had predicted the result, and, before the meeting, had warned the Parson how it would be.

"Tie up!" he cried almost indignantly, as Owd Bob came galloping up to his whistle; "I can't see myself chaining you, owd lad, like any murderer. Why it's you has kept the Killer off Kenmuir so far, I'll bet."

At the lodge-gate was McAdam, for once without his companion, playing with the lodge-keeper's child; for the little man loved all children but his own, and was loved by them. As the Master came near, he looked up.

"Well, Moore," he called, "and are you goin' to tie yer dog?"

"I will if you'll tie yours," the Master answered grimly.

"Na," the little man answered, "it's Wullie that frightens the Killer off the Grange. That's why I've left him there now."

"It's the same with me," the Master said. "He's not come to Kenmuir yet, and he won't, so long as the Owd One's loose, I think."

"Loose or tied, as far as that goes," the little man responded, "Kenmuir will escape." He made the statement firmly, smacking his lips.

The Master frowned.

"Why is that?" he asked.

"Haven't ye heard what they're saying?" the little man asked with raised eyebrows.

"Nay; what?"

"Why, that the very reputation of the best sheepdog in the North should keep him off. And I guess they're right," and he laughed shrilly as he spoke.

The Master walked on, puzzled.

"Which way are ye goin' home?" McAdam called after him. "Because," with a polite smile, "I'll take t'other."

"I'm off by the Windy Brae," the Master answered, striding on. "Squire asked me to leave a note with his shepherd on the other side of the Chair." So he headed away to the left, making for home by the route along the Silver Mere.

The well-named Windy Brae is a long stretch of almost unbroken moorland; sloping gently down in mile after mile of heather from the Mere Marches at the top to the edge of the shimmering Silver Mere below. In all that waste of moorland, the only break is the quaint-shaped Giant's Chair, a puzzle for geologists, looking as though it had been plumped down by accident in the heathery wilderness. The ground rises suddenly from the smooth slope of the Brae; up it goes, growing ever steeper, until at last it runs abruptly into a sheer curtain of rock—the Fall—which rises perpendicular some forty feet, on the top of which rests that tiny grassy bowl—not twenty yards across—they call the Scoop.

The Scoop forms the seat of the Chair and rests on its collar of rock, cool and green and unworldly, like wine in a metal cup; the front is the forty-foot Fall; behind, rising sheer again, the wall of rock which makes the back of the Chair. It is impossible to reach from above; the only way to enter that little hollow is by two narrow sheep-tracks which crawl dangerously up between the sheer wall on the one hand and the sheer Fall on the other, entering it at opposite sides.

It stands out clearly from the gradual slope, that strange rise of ground; yet as the Master and Owd Bob came out onto the Brae it was already invisible in the darkening night.

Through the heather the two walked on at an easy pace, the Master thinking now with a smile of David and Maggie; wondering what McAdam had meant; meditating with a frown on the Killer; puzzling over his identity—for he was half convinced, like David, that Red Wull was innocent; and thanking his stars that so far Kenmuir had escaped, a piece of

luck he felt was due entirely to the watchfulness of the Owd
One, who, sleeping in the front entryway, slipped out at all
hours and went around to every part of the farm, protecting
it from danger. And at the thought, he looked down toward
the dark head which should be traveling along by his knee;
yet he could not see it, so thick was the dark cover of the
night.

So he brushed his way along, and the night grew blacker
and blacker; until, from the rising of the ground beneath his
feet, he knew he was going around the Giant's Chair.

Now, as he walked quickly along the foot of the rise, there
suddenly burst on his ear the patter of many galloping feet.
He turned, and at that second, a wave of sheep almost knocked
him down. The night was velvet-black, and they ran furiously
by, yet he could dimly make out, driving them at their backs,
a vague hound-like form.

"The Killer, by thunder!" he exclaimed, and, startled
though he was, struck down toward that last pursuing shape,
missing and almost falling.

"Bob, lad!" he cried, "follow on!" and he swung around;
but in the darkness could not see if the gray dog had obeyed.

The chase swept on into the night, and, far above him on
the hillside, he could now hear the rattle of the flying feet. He
started fiercely after them, and then, realizing how useless it
would be to follow when it was so dark that he could not
even see his hand before his face, came to a stop. So he stood
without moving, listening and peering into the blackness,
hoping the Owd One was on the villain's heels.

He prayed for the moon; and, as though in answer, the
lantern of the night shone out and lit the grim face of the
Chair above him. He shot a glance at his feet; and thanked
heaven to see that the gray dog was not beside him.

Then he looked up. The flock had broken apart, and the

sheep were scattered over the steep hillside, still galloping madly. In the wild flight, one pair of darting figures caught and held his gaze: the foremost dodging, twisting, speeding upward, the one in back hard on the leader's heels, swift, relentless, never changing. He looked for a third pursuing form; but he could not see it.

"He must have missed him in the dark," the Master muttered, the sweat standing on his forehead as he strained his eyes upward.

Higher and higher sped those two dark specks, far higher than the scattered remnants of the flock. Up and up, until suddenly the sheer Fall dropped its barrier in the path of the fugitive. Away she ran, moving swiftly and easily along the foot of the rock wall; came to the familiar track leading to the Scoop, and turned up it, bleating pitifully, nearly exhausted, the Killer close behind her now.

"He'll strike her down in the Scoop!" cried the Master hoarsely, following with fascinated eyes. "Owd Un! Owd Un! Wherever have you got to?" he called in agony; but no Owd One answered.

As they reached the summit, just as he had predicted, the two black dots became one; and down they rolled together into the hollow of the Scoop, out of the Master's sight. At the same instant the moon, as though unwilling to watch the last act of the bloody play, veiled her face.

It was his chance. "Now!"—and up the hillside he sped like a young man, preparing for the struggle. The slope grew steep and steeper; but on and on he went in the darkness, gasping painfully, yet running still, until the face of the Fall blocked his way too.

There he paused a moment, and whistled a low call. If he could send the old dog up the one path to the Scoop, while he took the other, the murderer's road to safety would be blocked.

He waited, expectant; but no cold muzzle was shoved into his hand. Again he whistled. A pebble from above dropped almost on him, as if the criminal up there had moved to the brink of the Fall to listen; and he did not dare to continue.

He waited till all was still again, then crept, cat-like, along the foot of the rock, and came, at last, to the track up which the Killer and the victim had fled a while before. Up that rough path he crawled on hands and knees. The sweat rolled off his face; one elbow brushed the rock again and again; one hand plunged now and then into that bare emptiness on the other side.

He prayed that the moon might reappear soon; that his feet might be saved from falling, where one slip might well mean death, certain destruction of any chance of success. He cursed his luck that the Owd One had somehow missed him in the dark; for now he must trust to chance, his own great strength, and his good oaken stick. And as he climbed, he formed his plan: to rush in on the Killer as he still gorged, and wrestle with him. If in the darkness he missed—and in that small hollow the possibility was not likely—the murderer might still, in the panic of the moment, forget the one path to safety and leap over the Fall to his death.

At last he reached the summit and pause to take a breath. The black emptiness before him was the Scoop, and in the center of it—no more than ten yards away—must be lying the Killer and the killed.

He crouched against the wet rock face and listened. In that dark silence, suspended between heaven and earth, he seemed a million miles away from any living soul.

No sound, and yet the murderer must be there. Yes, there was the clatter of a dislodged stone; and again, the tread of cautious feet.

The Killer was moving; alarmed; was off.

Quick!

He rose to his full height; gathered himself, and leapt.

Something knocked against him as he sprang; something wrestled madly with him; something tore itself away from beneath him; and in a moment he heard the thud of a body striking the ground far below, and the sliding and pattering of some creature speeding furiously down the hillside and away.

"Who the blazes?" he roared.

"What the devil?" screamed a little voice.

The moon shone out.

"Moore!"

"McAdam!"

And there they were, still struggling over the body of a dead sheep.

In a second they had separated and rushed to the edge of the Fall. In the quiet, they could still hear the scrambling hurry of the villain far below them. Nothing was to be seen, however, but a crowd of startled sheep on the hillside, silent witnesses of the murderer's escape.

The two men turned and looked at each other; the one grim, the other mocking: both rumpled and tousled and suspicious.

"Well?"

"Well?"

A pause and careful examination.

"There's blood on your coat."

"And on yours."

Together they walked back into the little moonlit hollow. There lay the murdered sheep in a pool of blood. It was easy to see where the marks on their coats came from. McAdam touched the victim's head with his foot. The movement revealed its throat. With a shudder he replaced it where it had been.

The two men stood back and gazed at each other.

"What are you doing here?"

"After the Killer. And you?"

"After the Killer?"

"How did you come?"

"Up this path," pointing to the one behind him. "And you?"

"Up this one."

Silence; then again:

"I'd have had him but for yo'."

"I did have him, but ye tore me off."

A pause again.

"Where's yer gray dog?" This time the challenge was unmistakable.

"I sent him after the Killer. Where's your Red Wull?"

"At home, as I told ye before."

"You mean you left him there?"

McAdam's fingers twitched.

"He's where I left him."

James Moore shrugged his shoulders. And the other began:

"When did yer dog leave ye?"

"When the Killer came past."

"Ye mean ye missed him then?"

"I say what I mean."

"Ye say he went after the Killer. Now the Killer was here," pointing to the dead sheep. "Was your dog here, too?"

"If he had been, he'd be here still."

"Unless he went over the Fall!"

"That was the Killer, you fool."

"Or your dog."

"There was only *one* beneath me. I felt him."

"Just so," said McAdam, and laughed. The other man frowned.

"And that was a big one," he said slowly. The little man stopped his cackling.

"There you lie," he said, smoothly. "He was small."

They looked each other full in the eyes.

"That's a matter of opinion," said the Master.

"It's a matter of fact," said the other.

The two stared at each other, silent and grim, each trying to read the other's soul; then they turned again to the edge of the Fall. Down below them, plain to see, was the mark and the line in the gravel showing the Killer's line of retreat. They looked at each other again, and then each departed the way he had come, to give his version of the story.

"Between us, we messed it up," said the Master. "If the Owd Un had stayed with me, I would have had him."

And—

"I tell ye I did have him, but James Moore pulled me off. Strange, too, his dog not bein' with him!"

CHAPTER 19

Lad and Lass

THIS ENCOUNTER in the Scoop created a great sensation in the Daleland. It encouraged the Dalesmen to new activity. James Moore and McAdam were questioned and questioned again as to the smallest details of the incident. All around the countryside, huge notices were put up offering a reward of £100 for the capture of the criminal, dead or alive. And the watchers were so vigilant that in a single week they caught a donkey, an old woman, and two amateur detectives.

In Wastrel-dale, the near escape of the Killer, the collision between James Moore and McAdam, and the failure of Owd Bob, who was not used to failing, provoked intense excitement, along with a certain anxiety about their favorite dog.

For when the Master had reached home that night, he had found the old dog already there, and he must have wrenched his foot in the pursuit or run a thorn into it, for he was very lame. At which, when it was reported in the Sylvester Arms, McAdam winked at Red Wull and muttered, "Ah, forty feet down—that's an ugly tumble."

A week later, the little man stopped in at Kenmuir. As he

entered the yard, David was standing outside the kitchen window, looking very glum and miserable. On seeing his father, however, the boy started forward, all alert.

"What d'you want here?" he cried roughly.

"Same as you, dear lad," the little man laughed, advancing. "I come on a visit."

"Your visits to Kenmuir are usually paid by night, so I've heard," David sneered.

The little man pretended not to hear.

"So they don't allow ye indoors with the Cup," he laughed. "They know yer little ways then, David."

"Nay, I'm not wanted in there," David answered bitterly, but not so loud that his father could hear. Maggie, inside the kitchen, heard, however, but paid no attention; for she had hardened her heart against the boy, who, though he never spoke to her, had lately made himself as unpleasant in a thousand little ways as only David McAdam could.

At that moment, the Master came stalking into the yard, Owd Bob ahead of him; and when the old dog recognized the visitor, he bristled spontaneously.

At the sight of the Master, McAdam hurried forward.

"I came only to ask after the tyke," he said. "Is he gettin' over his lameness?"

James Moore looked surprised; then his stern face relaxed into a friendly smile. Such generous anxiety about the welfare of Red Wull's rival was a completely new quality in the little man.

"It's kind of you, McAdam," he said, "to come and ask."

"Is the thorn out?" asked the little man with eager interest, shooting his head forward to stare closely at the other.

"It came out last night after we put warm compresses on it," the Master answered, returning the other's gaze, calm and steady.

"I'm glad of that," said the little man, still staring. But his yellow, grinning face said as plain as words, "What a liar ye are, James Moore."

◆ ◆ ◆

The days passed on. His father's scornful and provoking remarks, becoming more and more bitter, drove David almost mad.

He longed to make up with Maggie; he longed for that tender sympathy which she had always shown him when his troubles with his father were a heavy burden to him. Their quarrel had continued for months now, and he was quite tired of it, and utterly ashamed. For, at least, he had the good grace to admit that no one was to blame but himself; and that it had been nourished only by his ugly pride.

At last he could not stand it any longer, and resolved to go to Maggie and ask for her forgiveness. It would be a painful ordeal for him; always unwilling to admit he was wrong, even to himself, how much harder it would be to confess it to this little slip of a girl. For a while, he thought it was almost more than he could do. Yet, like his father, once he had decided upon a course of action, nothing could turn him aside from it. So, after a week of doubts and resolutions, of cowardice and courage, he pulled himself together and set off.

It took him an hour to go from the Grange to the bridge over the Wastrel—a distance that usually required only a quarter of an hour. Now, as he walked on up the slope from the stream, very slowly, encouraging himself in his repentance, he was aware of a strange disturbance in the yard above him: the noisy cackling of hens, the snorting of pigs disturbed, and above the rest the cry of a little child ringing out in shrill anxiety.

He began to run, and hurried up the slope as fast as his long legs would carry him. As he pulled himself up over the gate, he saw the figure of Wee Anne, dressed in white, running away with unsteady, toddling steps, her fair hair streaming out behind, and one bare arm striking wildly back at a great pursuing sow.

David shouted as he cleared the gate, but the animal paid no attention and was almost touching the little girl when Owd Bob came galloping around the corner and in a second had flashed between pursuer and pursued. So close were the two that as he swung round at the startled sow, his tail brushed the baby to the ground; and there she lay kicking her fat legs to heaven and calling on all her gods.

David, leaving the old dog to hold the warrior pig, ran around to her; but someone else had got there before him. The whole incident had barely taken a minute's time; and Maggie, rushing from the kitchen, now had the child in her arms and was hurrying back with her to the house.

"Eh, my pet, are you hurted, dearie?" David could hear her asking with tears in her voice, as he crossed the yard and settled in the doorway.

"Well," he said, in teasing tones, "you're a fine one to be left in charge of our Annie!"

It was a sore subject with the girl, and well he knew it. Wee Anne, that mischievous golden-haired child, was forever avoiding her sister-mother's eye and putting herself in danger. More than once she had been saved from serious harm only by the watchful devotion of Owd Bob, who always found time, despite his many labors, to keep a guardian eye on his well-loved lassie. In the previous winter, she had been lost on a bitter night on the Muir Pike; once she had climbed into a field with the Highland bull and barely escaped with her life, while the gray dog kept the great creature at a distance; only a little while before, she had been rescued from drowning by the Tailless Tyke; there had been many other mishaps; and now the present one. But the girl paid no attention to her tormentor in her joy at finding the child unhurt.

"There! You ain't so much as scratched, my precious, are you?" she cried. "Run out again, then," and the baby toddled joyfully away.

Maggie rose to her feet and stood with her face turned away. David's eyes rested lovingly upon her, admiring the position of her neat head with its thick cap of pretty brown hair; her slim figure, and her slender ankles peeping modestly from below the hem of her print dress.

"My word! If your dad should hear tell how his Anne—" he broke off into a long-drawn-out whistle.

Maggie kept silent; but her lips trembled, and the flush deepened on her cheek.

"I'm afraid I'll have to tell him," the boy went on. "It's my duty."

"You may tell whoever you like whatever you like," the girl replied coldly; but there was a tremor in her voice.

"First you throws her in the stream," David went on pitilessly; "then you chucks her to the pig, and if it hadn't been for me—"

"You, indeed!" she broke in scornfully. "You! 'Twas Owd Bob rescued her. You'd nothing to do with it, except to look on—which is about all you're fit for."

"I tell you," David went on stubbornly, "if it hadn't been for me, you wouldn't have no sister by now. She'd be lying still, she would, poor little lass, cold as ice, poor mite, with no breath in her. And when your dad come home, there'd be no Wee Anne to run to him, and climb on his knee, and yammer to him, and beat his face. And he'd say, 'What's gotten to our Annie, as I left with you?' And then you'd have to tell him, 'I never bothered about her, dad; soon as your back was turned, I—'"

The girl sat down, buried her face in her apron, and gave in, as she almost never did, to a fit of weeping.

"You're the cruelest man as ever was, David McAdam," she sobbed, rocking to and fro.

He was at her side in a moment, tenderly bending over her.

"Eh, Maggie, I'm sorry, lass—"

She wrenched away from under his hands.

"I hate you," she cried fiercely.

He gently took her hands away from her tear-stained face.

"I was only teasing, Maggie," he pleaded; "say you forgive me."

"I don't," she cried, struggling. "I think you're the most hateful lad as ever lived."

The moment had come; it was a time for heroic measures.

"No, ye don't, lass," he protested; and, releasing her wrists, lifted the little drooping face, wet as it was, like the earth after a spring shower, and, holding it between his two big hands, kissed it twice.

"You coward!" she cried, a flood of warm red covering her cheeks; and she struggled uselessly to free herself.

"You used to let me," he reminded her, sounding injured.

"I never did!" she cried, more indignant than truthful.

"Yes, you did, when we were little; that is, you was always in favor of kissing and I was always against it. And now," with wholehearted bitterness, "I can't so much as peek at you over a stone wall."

However that might be, he was peeking at her from very close up now; and in that position—for he still held her firmly —she could not help but peek back. He looked so handsome

—humble, for once; remorseful yet reproachful; his own eyes a little moist; and yet his usual bold self—that despite herself, her anger died down a little.

"Say you forgive me and I'll let you go."

"I don't, and never shall," she answered firmly; but in her heart she was less convinced.

"Yes you do, lass," he pleaded, and kissed her again.

She struggled faintly.

"How can you?" she cried through her tears. But he was not going to be moved.

"Will you now?" he asked.

She remained silent, and he kissed her again.

"Impudence!" she cried.

"Ay," he said, closing her mouth.

"I wonder at ye, Davie!" she said, surrendering.

◆ ◆ ◆

After that, Maggie had to give in; and it was understood, though nothing definite had been said, that the boy and girl were courting. And in the Dale the unanimous opinion was that the young couple would make "a fine pair, surely."

McAdam was the last person to hear the news, long after it had been common knowledge in the village. It was in the Sylvester Arms that he first heard it, and right away he fell into one of those foaming fits of madness that often came over him.

"The daughter of Moore of Kenmuir, you say? Such a daughter of such a man! The daughter of the one man in the world that's harmed me above all the rest! I wouldn't have believed it if you hadn't told me. Oh, David, David! I'd not have thought it even of you, ill son as you've always been to me. I think he might have waited till his old dad was gone, and he'd not have had to wait long now." Then the little man sat down and burst into tears. Gradually, however, he resigned himself, and the more easily when he realized that David, by this act, had revealed a fresh wound into which he might plunge his sharp arrows. And he took full advantage of his new opportunities. Often and often David had the greatest trouble restraining himself.

"Is it true what they're saying—that Maggie Moore's not quite the decent lass she ought to be?" the little man asked one evening with anxious interest.

"They're not saying so, and if they were, 'twould be a lie," the boy answered angrily.

McAdam leaned back in his chair and nodded his head.

"Ay, they told me that if any man knew, it would be David McAdam."

David walked across the room.

"No—no more of that," he shouted. "You ought to be ashamed, an old man like you, to speak that way of a lass." The little man edged close up to his son, and looked into the fair, flushed face towering above him.

"David," he said in smooth, soft tones, "I'm astonished ye didn't strike yer old dad." He stood with his hands clasped behind his back as if daring the young giant to raise a finger against him. "You might now," he went on smoothly. "Ye must be six inches taller, and a good four stone heavier. However, maybe you're wise to wait. Another year or two and I'll be an old man, as ye say, and weaker, and Wullie here'll be getting on, while you'll be in the prime of yer strength. Then I think ye might hit me with safety to yer own body and honor to yerself."

He took a step back, smiling.

"Father," said David, hoarsely, "one day you'll drive me too far."

CHAPTER 20

The Snapping of the String

THE SPRING was passing, marked throughout by the bloody trail of the Killer. The adventure in the Scoop scared him for a while into harmlessness; then he went back to his game with all the more energy. It seemed likely that he would torment the district till some lucky accident put an end to him, since there was no way to stop him.

Every night in the Sylvester Arms and elsewhere you could still hear the declaration, made with the same certainty as in earlier days, "It's the Terror, I tell you!" and that irritating, predictable reply: "Ay; but where's the proof?" While often, at the same moment, in a house not far away, a lonely little man was sitting before a fire that had burned down low, rocking to and fro, biting his nails, and muttering to the great dog whose head lay between his knees: "If only we had the proof, Wullie! If only we had the proof! I'd give my right hand off my arm if we had the proof tomorrow."

Long Kirby, who was always in favor of war when someone else was to do the fighting, suggested that David be asked, in the name of the Dalesmen, to tell McAdam that he must make an end to Red Wull. But Jim Mason would reject the suggestion, remarking truly enough that there was too much bad feeling already between father and son; while Tammas proposed with a sneer that the blacksmith should do the deed himself.

Whether it was this remark of Tammas's that stung the big man into action, or whether it was that the fierceness of his hatred gave him unusual courage, in any case, a few days later, McAdam caught him lurking in the granary of the Grange.

The little man may not have guessed his murderous intention; yet the smith's white-faced terror, as he crouched away in the darkest corner, could hardly avoid being noticed; although—and Kirby may thank his stars for it—the treacherous gleam of a gun barrel, not very well hidden behind him, was not observed.

"Hullo, Kirby!" said McAdam in a friendly way, "ye'll stay the night with me?" And the next thing the big man heard was a laugh on the far side of the door, lost in the clank of padlock and rattle of chain. Then—through a crack— "Goodnight to ye. Hope ye'll be comfy." And there he stayed that night, the following day, and the next night—thirty-six hours in all, with rutabaga roots to satisfy his hunger and the dew off the thatch for his thirst.

Meanwhile, the struggle between David and his father seemed to be coming to a climax. The little man's tongue wagged more bitterly than ever; now it was never quiet— searching out sores, stinging, piercing.

Worst of all, he was continually dropping hints about Maggie, hints which seemed innocent enough, yet which contained a world of subtle meaning. When David came home from Kenmuir at night, the little man would greet him with a grin and a wink and ask the simple question, "And was she

kind, David—eh, eh?"; and this would make the boy's blood
boil inside him.

And the more effective the little man saw that his shots
were, the more he continued to fire them off. And David paid
him back with the same kind. It was a war in which injury
was met with more injury, turn and turn about. There was no
peace; there were no truces in which the opponents could
bury their dead before beginning to kill again. And every day
brought them closer to that final struggle, whose outcome
neither of them wanted to imagine.

◆ ◆ ◆

There came a Saturday, toward the end of the spring, that
would be remembered for a long time in the Dale by more
people than David.

For that young man, the day started in a most dramatic way.
Rising before the sun was up, and going to the window, the
first thing he saw in the misty dawn was the gigantic bony
figure of Red Wull, bounding up the hill from the Stony Bottom; and in an instant his faith was shaken to its foundation.

The dog was traveling up at a long, lolling trot; and as he
drew rapidly near the house, David saw that his sides were all
splashed with red mud, his tongue out, and the foam dripping from his jaws, as though he had come far and fast.

He crept up to the house, leapt onto the sill of the unused
back-kitchen, some five feet from the ground, pushed with
his paw at the rickety old hatch, which was its only covering;
and, in a second, the boy, straining out of the window the
better to see, heard the rattle of the boards as the dog dropped
down inside the house.

For the moment, excited as he was, David said nothing.

Even the Black Killer took only second place in his thoughts that morning. For this was to be an important day for him.

That afternoon James Moore and Andrew would, he knew, be over at Grammoch-town, and, his work finished for the day, he was determined to confront Maggie and decide his fate. If she would have him—well, he would go next morning and thank God for it, kneeling beside her in the tiny village church; if not, he would leave the Grange and all its unhappiness behind, and immediately plunge out into the world.

All through a week of steady work he had looked forward to this hard-earned half-holiday. But, as he was stopping work at noon, his father turned to him and said without warning:

"David, ye will take the Cheviot flock over to Grammoch-town at once."

David answered rudely:

"You must take 'em yourself, if you wish 'em to go today."

"Na," the little man answered; "Wullie and me, we're busy. Ye're to take 'em, I tell ye."

"I won't," David replied. "If they wait for me, they wait till Monday," and with that he left the room.

"I see what it is," his father called after him; "she's meeting ye secretly at Kenmuir. Oh, ye lusty boy, David!"

"You mind your business; I'll mind mine," the boy answered angrily.

Now it happened that on the day before, Maggie had given him a photograph of herself, or, rather, David had taken it and Maggie had objected. As he left the room now, it dropped from his pocket. He failed to notice his loss, but as soon as he was gone, McAdam pounced on it.

"He, he, Wullie! What's this?" he chuckled, holding the photograph to his face. "He, he! It's the wicked woman herself, I warrant; it's the Jezebel!"

He peered into the picture.

"She knows what's what, I'll swear, Wullie. See her eyes— so soft and sad; and her lips—such lips, Wullie!" He held the picture down for the great dog to see: then walked out of the room, still snickering and snapping the face insanely under its cardboard chin.

Outside the house he collided against David. The boy had missed his treasure and was hurrying back for it.

"What've you got there?" he asked suspiciously.

"Only the picture of some lusty queen," his father answered, snapping away at the lifeless chin.

"Give it to me!" David ordered fiercely. "It's mine."

"Na, na," the little man replied. "It's not for such quiet, sober lads as dear David to have any dealings with ladies such as this."

"Give it to me, I tell ye, or I'll take it!" the boy shouted.

"Na, na; it's my duty as yer dad to keep ye from such wicked loose women." He turned, still smiling, to Red Wull.

"There ye are, Wullie!" He threw the photograph to the dog. "Tear her, Wullie, the evil Jezebel!"

The Tailless Tyke sprang on the picture, placed one big paw in the very center of the face, forcing it into the mud, and tore a corner off; then he chewed the scrap with oily, slobbering greed, dropped it, and tore a fresh piece.

David dashed forward.

"Touch it, if you dare, you brute!" he yelled; but his father seized him and held him back.

"'And the dogs of the street,'" he quoted, from the story in the Bible that tells of the wicked Jezebel's violent death.

David turned furiously on him.

"I've half a mind to break every bone in your body!" he shouted, "robbing me of what's mine and throwing it to that black brute!"

"Hush, David, hush!" soothed the little man. "It was only for your own good that your old dad did it. It was your own good that he had in his heart, as he always has. Run off with you now to Kenmuir. She'll make it up to ye, I'm sure. She's quite free with her favors, I hear. You have only to whistle and she'll come."

David seized his father by the shoulder.

"If you give me much more of your sauce…" he roared.

"Sauce, Wullie," the little man echoed in a gentle voice.

"…I'll twist your neck for you!"

"He'll twist my neck for me."

"I'll go away for good, I warn yo', and leave you and yer Wullie on yer own."

The little man began to whimper.

"It'll break yer old dad's heart, lad," he said.

"Nay; yo've got none. But 'twill ruin you, please God. For yo' and yer Wullie will never get a soul to work for you—ye cheese-paring, foul-mouthed miser."

The little man burst into an agony of sham tears, rocking to and fro, his face in his hands.

"Oh, woe is me, Wullie! D'ye hear him? He's goin' to leave us—the son of my heart! My Benjamin! My little Davie! He's goin' away!"

David turned away down the hill; and McAdam lifted his grieving face and waved a hand at him.

"'Adieu, dear amiable youth!'" he cried in a broken voice, quoting again; and immediately went back to sobbing.

Halfway down to the Stony Bottom, David turned.

"I'll give yo' a word o' warning," he shouted back. "I'd advise you to keep a closer eye on what yer Wullie's doing, especially at night, or you might wake to a surprise one morning."

In an instant the little man stopped his fooling.

"And why is that?" he asked, following David down the hill.

"I'll tell you. When I woke this morning I walked to the window, and what d'ye think I see? Why, yer Wullie galloping like a good one up from the Bottom, all foaming at the mouth, too, and splashed with red, as if he'd come from the Screes. What had he been up to, I'd like to know?"

"What should he be doing," the little man answered, "but keepin' an eye on the stock? And that when the Killer might be out."

David laughed harshly.

"Ay, the Killer was out, I'll guarantee, and you may hear about it before this evening, my man," and with that he turned away again.

◆ ◆ ◆

As he had predicted, David found Maggie alone. But in the heat of his indignation against his father, he seemed to have forgotten his original plan, and instead poured his latest troubles into the girl's sympathetic ear.

"There's only one man in the world he wishes more harm to than me," he was saying. It was late in the afternoon, and he was still complaining bitterly about his father and his fate. Maggie sat in her father's chair by the fire, knitting; while he lounged on the kitchen table, swinging his long legs.

"And who may that be?" the girl asked.

"Why, Mr. Moore, to be sure, and the Owd One, too. He'd do either of them harm if he could."

"But why, David?" she asked anxiously. "I'm sure dad never hurt him, or any other man for that matter."

David nodded toward the Dale Cup resting on the mantelpiece in silvery majesty.

"It's that that has done it," he said. "And if the Owd One

wins again, as win he will, bless him! why, look out for 'me and my Wullie'; that's all."

Maggie shuddered, and thought of the face at the window.

"'Me and my Wullie,'" David went on; "I've had about as much of them as I can swallow. It's always the same—'Me and my Wullie,' and 'Wullie and me,' as if I never put my hand to a bit of work! Ugh!"—he made a motion of passionate disgust—"the two of 'em are like to drive me mad. I could strike the one and strangle the other," and he rattled his heels angrily together.

"Hush, David," interrupted the girl; "you mustn't speak that way about yer dad; it's against the commandments."

"It's not against human nature," he snapped in answer. "Why, it was only yesterday morning he says in his nasty way, 'David, my grand fellow, how ye work! ye astonish me!' And on my word, Maggie"—there were tears in the great boy's eyes—"my back was nearly broke with laboring. And the Terror, he stands by and shows his teeth, and looks at me as much as to say, 'Some day, by the grace of goodness, I'll have my teeth in your throat, young man.'"

Maggie's knitting dropped into her lap and she looked up, her soft eyes for once flashing.

"It's cruel, David; so it is!" she cried. "I wonder you stay with him. If he treated me that way, I wouldn't stay another minute. If it meant going to the Poor Folks' Home, I'd go," and she looked as if she meant it.

David jumped off the table.

"Have you never guessed why I stay, lass, and me so happy at home?" he asked eagerly.

Maggie looked down again.

"How should I know?" she asked innocently.

"Nor care, neither, I suppose," he said reproachfully. "Yo' want me to go and leave yo', and go right away; I see how it is. You wouldn't mind, not you, if you was never to see poor David again. I never thought you really liked me, Maggie; and now I know it."

"You silly lad," the girl murmured, knitting steadily on.

"Then you do," he cried, triumphant. "I knew you did." He came close to her chair, his face clouded with eager anxiety.

"But do you like me more than just *liking*, Maggie? Do you?" he bent and whispered in the little ear.

The girl cuddled over her work so that he could not see her face.

"If you won't tell me, you can show me," he coaxed her. "There's other things besides words."

He stood before her, one hand on the chair back on either side. She sat thus, caged between his arms, with drooping eyes and rosy color.

"Not so close, David, please," she begged, fidgeting uneasily; but he paid no attention.

"Do move away a bit," she implored.

"Not till you've showed me," he said stubbornly.

"I cannot, Davie," she cried with laughing impatience.

"Yes, you can, lass."

"Take your hands away, then."

"Nay; not till you've showed me."

A pause.

"Do please, Davie," she begged.

And—

"Do please," he pleaded.

She tilted her face in invitation, but her eyes were still down.

"It's no use, Davie."

"Yes 'tis," he coaxed.

"Never."

"Please."

A long pause.

"Well, then—" She looked up, at last, shy, trustful, happy; and the sweet lips were tilted farther to meet his.

And that is how they were, in the pose of a pair of lovers, when a low, dreamy voice broke in on them—

"'A dear-lov'd lad, convenience snug,
A treacherous inclination.'

"Oh, Wullie, I wish you were here!"

It was little McAdam. He was leaning in at the open window, grinning offensively at the young couple, his eyes squinting, an evil expression on his face.

"The crucial moment! And I interfere! David, you'll never forgive me."

The boy jumped around with a curse; and Maggie, her face flaming, leapt to her feet. The tone, the words, the look of the little man at the window were all unbearable.

"By thunder! I'll teach you to come spying on me!" roared David. Above him on the mantelpiece blazed the Shepherds' Trophy. Searching for any weapon, in his fury, he reached up a hand for it.

"Ay, give it back to me. Ye robbed me of it," the little man cried, holding out his arms as if to receive it.

"Don't, David," pleaded Maggie, putting a hand on her lover's arm to hold him back.

"By the Lord! I'll give him something!" yelled the boy. Nearby, there stood a pail of soapy water. He seized it, swung it, and hurled its contents at the leering face in the window.

The little man stepped back hastily, but the dirty stream of water caught him and soaked him through. The bucket followed, struck him full on the chest, and rolled him over in the mud. After it, with a rush, came David.

"I'll let you know, spying on me!" he yelled. "I'll—" Maggie, whose face was now as white as it had been crimson, clung to him, getting in his way.

"Don't, David, don't!" she begged. "He's your own dad."

"I'll dad him! I'll teach him!" roared David, halfway through the window.

At that moment, Sammel Todd came stumbling furiously around the corner, closely followed by Henry and Our Job.

"Is he dead?" shouted Sammel, seeing the form on the ground.

"Ho, ho!" chimed the other two.

They picked up the wet and muddy little man and hurried him out of the yard like a thief, one man on either side of him and one man behind.

As they forced him through the gate, he struggled to turn around.

"By Him that made ye! ye shall pay for this, David McAdam, you and yer—"

But Sammel's big hand came down on his mouth, and he was carried away before that last evil word could come into being.

CHAPTER 21

Horror of Darkness

IT WAS long past dark, that night, when McAdam staggered home.

All that evening at the Sylvester Arms, his curses against David had made even the hardest of the men shudder. James Moore, Owd Bob, and the Dale Cup were for once forgotten as, in his passion, he swore at his son.

The Dalesmen gathered fearfully away from the dripping little madman. Although usually the sorts of outbursts they were hearing were not enough to silence them, on this evening they were speechless before him; only now and then did they send a quick, secret glance in his direction, as though they were about to carry out some bold action aimed at him. But McAdam noticed nothing, suspected nothing.

When at last he lurched into the kitchen of the Grange, there was no light, and the fire burned low. So dark was the room that he did not see the white ribbon of paper pinned to the table.

The little man sat down heavily, his clothes still sodden, and went back to his endless damnation.

"I've endured more from him, Wullie, than Adam Mc-Adam ever thought to endure from any man. And now it's past bearing. He struck me, Wullie! Struck his own father. Ye saw it yerself, Wullie. Na, ye weren't there. Oh, if only ye had been, Wullie! Him and his missie! But I'll force him to know Adam McAdam. I'll stand no more of it!"

He sprang to his feet and, reaching up with trembling hands, pulled down the old bell-mouthed blunderbuss that hung above the mantelpiece.

"We'll make an end to it, Wullie, so we will, once and for all!" And he banged the weapon down upon the table. It lay right across that slip of quiet, accusing paper, yet the little man did not see it.

Sitting down again, he prepared to wait. His hand groped for the pocket of his coat, and he tenderly fingered a small stone bottle, his beloved companion during all these years alone. He pulled it out, uncorked it, and took a long drink; then placed it on the table next to him.

Gradually the gray head lolled to one side; the wrinkled hand dropped and hung limply down, the fingertips brushing the floor; and he dozed off into a heavy sleep, while Red Wull watched at his feet.

It was not till an hour later that David returned home.

As he drew near the lightless house, which stood in the darkness like a body from which the spirit has flown away, he could not help contrasting this dreary home of his with the bright kitchen and cheerful faces he had left.

Entering the house, he felt his way to the kitchen door and opened it; then struck a match and stood in the doorway looking in.

"Not home, is he?" he muttered, the tiny light above his head. "Wet inside as well as out, by now, I'll bet. By gum! it was a lucky thing for him I didn't get my hands on him this evening. I could have killed him." He held the match above his head.

Two yellow eyes, glowing in the dark like two smoky quartz stones from the Cairngorm mountains, and a small dim figure bunched up in a chair, told him his guess was wrong. Many a time he had seen his father like this before, and now he muttered scornfully:

"Drunk; the little lout! Sleepin' it off, I imagine."

Then he saw his mistake. The hand that hung above the floor twitched and was still again.

There was a clammy silence. A mouse, hearing nothing and thinking it was safe to come out, scuttled across the hearth. One mighty paw lightly moved; a lightning tap, and the tiny beast lay dead.

Again that hollow stillness: no sound, no movement; only those two unwinking eyes fixed steadily on him.

At last, a small voice from the fireside broke the quiet.

"Drunk—the—little—lout!"

Again a clammy silence, and a pause as long as a lifetime.

"I thought you were sleepin'," said David at last, lamely.

"Ay, so ye said. 'Sleepin' it off'; I heard ye." Then, still in the same small voice, now quivering a little. "Would ye be so kind, sir, as to light the lamp? Or, d'ye think, Wullie, that would be soiling his dainty fingers? They're more used, I'm told, to danderin' with the bonnie brown hair of his—"

"I'll not have ye talk of my Maggie so," the boy interrupted passionately.

"*His* Maggie, did ye hear that, Wullie? *His!* I thought it would soon get that far."

"Take care, dad! I'll stand but little more," the boy warned him in a choking voice; and he began to trim the wick of the lamp with trembling fingers.

McAdam then spoke to Red Wull.

"I suppose no man ever had such a son as him, Wullie. Ye know what I've done for him, and ye know how he's repaid it. He's set himself against me; he's said bad things about me; he's robbed me of my Cup; last of all, he struck me—struck me in front of them all. We've worked hard for him, you and I, Wullie; we've slaved to keep him in house and home, and he's spent his time, all the while, in riotous living, carousing at Kenmuir, amusing himself with his—" He broke off short. The lamp was lit, and the strip of paper, pinned to the table, naked and glaring, caught his eye.

"What's this?" he muttered; and loosened the nail that clamped it down.

This is what he read:

"Adam Mackadam yer warned to make an end to yer Red Wull will be best for him and the Sheep. This is the first yoll have two more the third will be the last? —+"

It was written in pencil, and the only signature was a dagger, crudely drawn in red.

McAdam read the paper once, twice, three times. As he slowly understood its meaning, the blood faded from his face. He stared at it and went on staring, with whitening face and pursed lips. Then he shot a glance at David's broad back.

"What d'ye know about this, David?" he asked, finally, in a dry, thin voice, reaching forward in his chair.

"About what?"

"About this"—holding up the slip. "And I'd be pleased to have the truth, for once."

David turned, picked up the paper, read it, and laughed harshly.

"It's come to this, has it?" he said, still laughing, and yet his face, too, was turning pale.

"Ye know what it means. I imagine ye put it there; maybe ye wrote it. Ye'll explain it." The little man spoke in the same small, even voice, and his eyes never moved from his son's face.

"It's plain as day. Have ye not heard?"

"I've heard nothing.... I'd like the truth, David, if ye can tell it."

The boy smiled a forced, unnatural smile, looking from his father to the paper in his hand.

"Yo' shall have it, but yo'll not like it. It's this: Tupper lost a sheep to the Killer last night."

"And what if he did?" The little man rose smoothly to his feet. Each noticed the other's face—it was dead white.

"Why, he—lost—it—on— Where d'yo' think?" He drawled the words out, pausing almost lovingly on each.

"Where?"

"On—the—Red—Screes."

The crash was coming—it was unavoidable now. David knew it, knew that nothing could stop it, and braced himself to meet it. The smile had vanished from his face, and his breath fluttered in his throat like the wind before a thunderstorm.

"What of it?" The little man's voice was calm as a summer sea.

"Why, yer Wullie—as I told you—was on the Screes last night."

"Go on, David."

"And this"—holding up the paper—"tells you that they know, as I know now, as most of them have known for many a day now, that your Wullie, Red Wull—the Terror—"

"Go on."

"Is—"

"Yes."

"The Black Killer."

It was spoken.

The worn string had snapped at last. The little man's hand flashed to the bottle that stood before him.

"Ye—liar!" he shrieked, and threw it with all his strength at the boy's head. David dodged and ducked, and the bottle hurtled over his shoulder.

Crash! it whizzed into the lamp behind, and broke on the wall beyond, the liquor inside trickling down the wall to the floor.

For a moment, darkness. Then the alcohol met the lamp's smoldering wick and blazed into flame.

By the sudden light, David saw his father on the far side of the table, pointing with a crooked forefinger. By his side, Red Wull was standing alert, his hackles up, his yellow fangs bared, his eyes glowing; and, at his feet, the little brown mouse lay still and lifeless.

"Out o' my house! Back to Kenmuir! Back to yer—" The unforgivable word, unmistakable, hovered for a second on his lips like some foul bubble, and never burst.

"No mother this time!" panted David, racing around the table.

"Wullie!"

The Terror leapt to the attack; but David overturned the table as he ran, the blunderbuss crashing to the floor; it fell, and for a moment it was an obstacle in the dog's path.

"Stand off, ye—!" screeched the little man, seizing a chair in both hands; "stand off, or I'll knock yer brains out!"

But David was on him.

"Wullie, Wullie, to me!"

Again the Terror came with a roar like the sea. But David, with a mighty kick catching him full on the jaw, repelled the attack.

Then he gripped his father around the waist and lifted him

from the ground. The little man, struggling in those iron arms, screamed, cursed, and battered at the face above him, kicking and biting in his fury.

"The Killer! Would ye like to know who's the Killer? Go and ask 'em at Kenmuir! Ask yer—"

David swayed slightly, crushing the body in his arms until it seemed that every rib must break; then hurled it from him with all the strength of his passion. The little man fell with a crash and a groan.

The blaze in the corner flared up, flickered, and died. There was a hellish black darkness, and a silence of the dead.

David stood against the wall, panting, every nerve strung as tight as the ropes of a sailing ship.

In the corner lay the body of his father, limp and still; and in the room one other living thing was moving.

He clung close to the wall, pressing it with wet hands. The horror of it all, the darkness, the man in the corner, that moving thing, petrified him.

"Father!" he whispered.

There was no reply. A chair creaked at an invisible touch. Something was creeping, stealing, crawling closer.

David was afraid.

"Father!" he whispered in hoarse agony, "are you hurt?"

The words were stifled in his throat. A chair overturned with a crash; a great body struck him on the chest; a hot, poisonous breath blasted in his face, and wolfish teeth were reaching for his throat.

"Come on, Killer!" he screamed.

The horror of the suspense was past. It had come, and with it he was himself again.

Back, back, back, along the wall he was carried. His hands wrapped themselves around a hairy throat; he forced the great head with its dreadful shining eyes from him; he braced himself for the effort, lifted the huge body from his chest, and heaved it from him.

It struck the wall and fell with a soft thud.

As he recoiled, a hand clutched his ankle and tried to trip him. David kicked back and down with all his strength. There was one awful groan, and he staggered against the door and out.

There he paused, leaning against the wall to breathe.

He struck a match and lifted his foot to see where the hand had clutched him.

God! There was blood on his heel.

Then a great fear took hold of him. A cry was suffocated in his chest by the pounding of his heart.

He crept back to the kitchen door and listened.

Not a sound.

Fearfully he opened it a crack.

Silence of the tomb.

He banged it shut. It opened behind him, and that fact gave wings to his feet.

He turned and plunged out into the night, and ran for his life through the blackness. And a great owl swooped softly by and hooted mockingly:

"For your life! for your life! for your life!"

PART FIVE

Owd Bob of Kenmuir

22

A Man and a Girl

IN THE village, even the Black Killer and the murder on the Screes were forgotten in this new excitement. The mystery surrounding the thing, and the fact that no one knew all of its details, caused everyone to be still more curious. There had been a fight; McAdam and the Terror had been badly hurt; and David had disappeared—those were the facts. But what had started the fight no one could say.

One or two of the Dalesmen had, in fact, a shrewd suspicion. Tupper looked guilty; Jem Burton muttered, "I know how it must have been"; while, as for Long Kirby, he vanished entirely, and did not reappear till three months had passed.

Injured as he had been, McAdam was still recovered enough to appear in the Sylvester Arms on the Saturday following the battle. He entered the taproom silently, without a word to anyone; one arm was in a sling and his head was bandaged. He took a careful look at every man present; and all of them except Tammas, who was shamelessly bold, and Jim Mason, who was innocent, fidgeted beneath the stare.

Maybe it was just as well for Long Kirby that he was not there.

"Anything the matter?" asked Jem, at last, rather lamely, given the obvious marks left by the fight.

"Na, na; nothing out of the ordinary," the little man replied, chuckling. "Only David attacked me, and when I was asleep, too. And"—with a shrug—"here I am now." He sat down, wagging his bandaged head and grinning. "Ye see he's so playful, ma Davie. He slaps ye over the head with a chair, kicks ye in the jaw, stamps on yer belly, and all as merry as the month of May." And they could get nothing more from him, except that if David reappeared, it was McAdam's firm intention to hand him over to the police for attempted parricide.

"'Brutal assault on an old man by his son!' That will look good in the *Argus*; he, he! They couldn't let him off with less than two years, is what I'm thinking."

No one believed the story of the incident as McAdam told it, though they kept quiet. They felt that he had brought his punishment entirely on himself. Tammas, indeed, who always rude when he was not being funny—and, in fact, the difference between the two was not very great—told him directly: "It served you right. And I only wish he'd made an end o' you."

"He did his best, poor lad," McAdam reminded him gently.

"We've had enough o' you," continued the old man, who was not about to soften his opinions. "I'm quite sorry he didn't slice yer throat while he was at it."

At that, McAdam raised his eyebrows, stared, and then broke into a low whistle.

"That's it, is it?" he muttered, as though a new light was dawning on him. "Ah, now I see."

❖ ❖ ❖

The days passed. There was still no news of the missing boy, and Maggie's face became pitifully white and careworn.

Of course she did not believe that David had attempted to murder his father, though she knew he had been desperately tormented. Still, it was a terrible thought that he might at any moment be arrested; and in her imagination she was constantly summoning up dreadful pictures of a trial, a conviction, and all that would follow.

Then Sammel started a wild theory that the little man had murdered his son and thrown the mutilated body down the dry well at the Grange. The story was, of course, ridiculous, and, coming from a man like Sammel, might well have been tossed aside with the mockery it deserved. Yet it was the worst thing the girl had imagined; and she decided, whatever the cost, to visit the Grange, face McAdam, and discover whether he could or would relieve her constant anxiety.

She hid her intention from her father, knowing well that if she revealed it to him, he would gently but firmly forbid her to try it; and on an afternoon some two weeks after David's disappearance, choosing her opportunity, she picked up a shawl, threw it over her head, and hurried with pounding heart out of the farm and down the slope to the Wastrel.

The little plank-bridge rattled as she trotted across it; and she ran faster for fear that someone might have heard and come to look. And, indeed, at that moment it rattled again behind her, and she turned guiltily around. It proved, however, to be only Owd Bob, sweeping after her, and she was glad.

"Comin' with me, lad?" she asked, as the old dog cantered up, thankful to have that gray protector with her.

Around Langholm Hollow the two now ran; over the lower

slopes of the Pike, still clothed in summer, until, at last, they reached the Stony Bottom. Down the bramble-covered bank of the ravine the girl slid; picked her way from stone to stone across the streamlet tinkling in that rocky bed; and scrambled up the opposite bank.

At the top, she halted and looked back. The smoke from Kenmuir was winding slowly up against the sky; to her right, the low gray cottages of the village huddled in the shelter of the Dale; far away over the Marches towered the bleak and rocky Scaur; before her rolled the swelling slopes of the Muir Pike; while behind—she glanced timidly over her shoulder—was the hill, at the top of which squatted the Grange, lifeless, cold, scowling.

Her courage failed her. In her whole life she had never spoken to McAdam. Yet she knew him well enough from all David's stories—ay, and hated him for David's sake. She hated him and feared him, too; feared him intensely—this terrible little man. And, with a shudder, she remembered the dim face at the window, and thought of his famous hatred of her father. But even McAdam could hardly do harm to a girl coming, broken-hearted, to look for her lover. Besides, wasn't Owd Bob with her?

And, turning, she saw the old dog standing a little way up the hill, looking back at her as though he wondered why she was waiting. "Aren't I enough?" the faithful gray eyes seemed to say.

"Lad, I'm afraid," was her answer to the unspoken question.

Yet that look determined her. She clenched her teeth, drew the shawl around her, and set off running up the hill.

Soon her run slowed to a walk, the walk to a few faltering steps, and the steps to a halt. Her breath was coming painfully, and her heart pounded against her side like the wing beats of a caged bird. Again her gray guardian looked up, urging her to come forward.

"Keep close, lad," she whispered, starting on again. And the old dog loped up beside her, pushing against her skirt, as though to let her feel his presence.

So they reached the top of the hill; and the house stood before them, grim, unfriendly.

The girl's face was now quite white, yet determined; she looked very much like her father. With her lips pressed together, breathing fast, she crossed the threshold of the entryway, stepping softly as though entering a house of the dead. There she paused and lifted a warning finger at Owd Bob, asking him to stay outside; then she turned to the door on the left of the entrance and tapped.

She listened, her head wrapped in the shawl, close to the wood paneling. There was no answer; she could hear only the drumming of her heart.

She knocked again. From inside came the scraping of a chair cautiously shoved back, followed by a deep-mouthed, echoing growl.

Her heart stood still, but she turned the handle and entered, leaving a crack open behind.

On the far side of the room, a little man was sitting. His head was bound in dirty bandages, and a bottle was on the table beside him. He was leaning forward; his face was gray, and he stared with naked horror in his eyes. One hand grasped the great dog, who stood at his side with yellow teeth glinting and muzzle hideously wrinkled; with the other he pointed a trembling finger at her.

"My God! Who are ye?" he cried hoarsely.

The girl stood close against the door, her fingers still on the handle; trembling like an aspen tree at the sight of that eerie pair.

The look in the little man's eyes terrified her: his swollen pupils; his eyelids, bare of eyelashes and yawning wide; the broken row of teeth in his gaping mouth, froze her very soul. Rumors of the man's insanity flooded back into her memory.

"I'm—I—" the words came in quivering gasps.

At the first word, however, the little man's hand dropped; he leaned back in his chair and gave a sigh of relief from the bottom of his soul.

No woman had crossed that threshold since his wife died; and, for a moment, when the girl had first entered on silent feet, and awoke him from dreaming of days long past, he had thought this figure wrapped in her shawl, with her pale face and locks of hair peeping out, was no earthly visitor, but the spirit of the one he had loved so long ago and lost, come to blame him for breaking his word.

"Speak up, I can't hear," he said, in tones that were mild compared with those last wild words.

"I—I'm Maggie Moore," the girl quavered.

"Moore! Maggie Moore, d'ye say?" he cried, half rising from his chair, a flush of color sweeping across his face, "the daughter of James Moore?" He paused for an answer, staring angrily at her; and she shrank, trembling, against the door.

The little man leaned back in his chair. Gradually a grim smile crept across his face.

"Well, Maggie Moore," he said, half amused, "you've got pluck, anyway." And his withered face looked at her almost kindly from beneath its dirty crown of bandages.

At that, the girl's courage returned with a rush. After all, this little man was not so very terrible. Perhaps he would be kind. And in the relief of the moment, the blood swept back into her face.

There was not to be peace yet, however. The blush was still hot upon her cheeks, when she caught the patter of soft steps in the passageway outside. A dark muzzle flecked with gray pushed in at the crack of the door; two anxious gray eyes followed.

Before she could wave him back, Red Wull had seen the intruder. With a roar, he tore himself from his master's hand, and dashed across the room.

"Back, Bob!" screamed Maggie, and the dark head retreated. The door slammed with a crash as the great dog flung himself against it, and Maggie was hurled, breathless and white-faced, into a corner.

McAdam was on his feet, pointing with a shriveled finger, a fiendish expression on his face.

"Did you bring him? Did you bring *that* to my door?"

Maggie huddled in the corner, shaking with fear. Her eyes gleamed big and black in the white face peering from the shawl.

Red Wull was now beside her, snarling horribly. With his nose to the bottom of the door and his paws busy, he was trying to get out; while, on the other side, Owd Bob, also snuffling at the crack, scratched and pleaded to get in. Only two miserable inches of wood separated the pair.

"I brought him to protect me. I—I was afraid."

McAdam sat down and laughed abruptly.

"Afraid! I'm surprised you weren't afraid to bring him here. It's the first time he's ever set foot on my land, and it had best be the last time." He turned to the great dog. "Wullie, Wullie, do ye hear me?" he called. "Come here. Lay ye down—so— under my chair—good lad. Now's not the time to settle with him"—nodding toward the door. "We can wait for that, Wullie; we can wait." Then, turning to Maggie, "If ye want him to make a show at the Trials two months from now, he'd best not come here again. If he does, he'll not leave my land alive; Wullie will see to that. Now, what is it ye want of me?"

The girl in the corner, scared almost out of her senses by this last occurrence, remained silent.

McAdam saw her hesitation and grinned scornfully.

"I see how it is," he said; "yer dad sent ye. Once before he wanted something from me, and did he come to get it himself like a man? Not he. He sent the son to rob the father." Then, leaning forward in his chair and glaring at the girl, "Ay, and more than that! The night the lad attacked me he came"—speaking each word with hissing distinctness—"straight from Kenmuir!" He paused and stared at her intently, and she was still silent before him. "If I'd been killed, Wullie'd not have been allowed to compete for the Cup. With Adam McAdam's Red Wull out of the way—now do ye see? Now do ye understand?"

She did not, and he saw it and was satisfied. She did not know what he had been saying, and she did not care. She only remembered the reason she had come here; she only saw before her the father of the man she loved; and a wave of emotion rose up in her chest.

She moved timidly toward him, holding out her hands.

"Eh, Mr. McAdam," she begged, "I come to ask ye about David." The shawl had slipped from her head and lay loose upon her shoulders; and she stood before him with her sad face, her pretty hair all tousled, and her eyes big with tears—a touching figure.

"Won't ye tell me where he is? I wouldn't ask it, I wouldn't trouble you, but I've been waiting an awful long time, it seems, and I'm craving for news of him."

The little man looked at her curiously. "Ah, now I remember," he said to himself; and then to her, "You're the lass who's thinking of marrying him?"

"We're engaged," the girl answered simply.

"Well," the other remarked, "as I said before, ye're a brave one." Then he went on, in a tone of voice which sounded both cynical and vaguely sad, "If he's as good a husband to you as he has been a son to me, ye'll have made a most remarkable match, my dear."

Maggie's anger flared up instantly.

"A good father makes a good son," she answered almost boldly; and then, with infinite tenderness, "And I'm praying that a good wife will make a good husband."

He smiled mockingly.

"I'm afraid that won't help ye much," he said.

But the girl paid no attention to this last sneering remark, she was so set on her purpose. She had heard of the one tender place in the heart of this little man with the tired face and mocking tongue, and she resolved to accomplish her purpose by appealing to it.

"You loved a lass yourself once, Mr. McAdam," she said. "How would you have felt if she had gone away and left you? You'd have been driven mad by it; you know you would. And, Mr. McAdam, I love the lad yer wife loved." She was kneeling at his feet now with both hands on his knees, looking up at him. Her sad face and trembling lips pleaded for her more powerfully than any words.

The little man was clearly touched by her.

"Ay, ay, lass, that's enough," he said, trying to avoid looking at those big imploring eyes, which were impossible to avoid.

"Won't ye tell me?" she begged.

"I can't tell ye, lass, because I don't know," he answered crossly. But in truth, he was moved to the heart by her misery.

The girl's last hopes were dashed. She had played her last card and failed. She had clung despairing to this last possibility, and now it was taken from her. She had hoped, and now there was no hope. In the anguish of her disappointment she remembered that this was the man who, with his constant cruelty, had driven her love away.

She rose to her feet and stood back.

"You don't know, and you don't care!" she cried bitterly.

At these words, all the softness vanished from the little man's face.

"You are unfair to me, lass; you are indeed," he said, looking up at her with a false innocence which, if she had known him better, would have warned her to be on her guard. "If I knew where the lad was, I'd be the very first to tell you—and the police, too; eh, Wullie! He, he!" He chuckled at his wit and rubbed his knees, ignoring the scorn that blazed in the girl's face.

"I cannot tell ye where he is now, but maybe ye'd like to hear about the last time I saw him." He turned his chair in order to speak directly to her. "It was like this: I was sitting in this very chair, asleep, when he crept up behind me and leapt on my back. I knew nothing about it till I found myself on the floor and him kneeling on me. I saw by the look of him that he was determined to finish me off, so I said—"

The girl waved her hand at him, superbly scornful.

"You know you're lying, every word of it," she cried.

The little man hitched up his trousers, crossed his legs, and yawned.

"An honest lie for an honest purpose is something any man

may be proud of, as you'll know by the time you're as old as I am, my lass."

The girl slowly crossed the room. At the door she turned.

"Then you won't tell me where he is?" she asked with a heartbreaking tremble in her voice.

"On my word, lass, I don't know," he cried, now agitated.

"On your word, Mr. McAdam!" she said with a quiet scorn in her voice that might have stung even the worst of scoundrels.

The little man spun around in his chair, an angry red coloring his cheeks. In another moment he was calm and smiling again.

"I can't tell you where he is now," he said, smoothly; "but maybe I could let ye know where he's going to."

"Can you? Will you?" cried the simple girl, quite unsuspecting. In a moment she was across the room and at his knees.

"Come closer, and I'll whisper." The little ear, peeking from its nest of brown, moved tremblingly closer to his lips. The little man leaned forward and whispered one short, sharp word, then sat back, grinning, to watch the reaction to his revelation.

He had his revenge, though it was an unworthy revenge on such a victim. And, as he watched the girl's face, in which cruel disappointment combined with the heat of her anger, he still had enough nobility of character to regret his triumph.

She sprang away from him as though he were unclean.

"And you are his father!" she cried in burning tones.

She crossed the room, and at the door she paused. Her face was white again, and she was quite self-possessed.

"If David did strike you, you drove him to it," she said, speaking calmly and gently. "You know—no one knows better—whether you've been a good father to him, him with no mother, poor laddie! Whether you've been to him what she would have wanted you to be. Ask your conscience, Mr. McAdam. And if he was a bit troublesome at times, wasn't there a reason? He had a heavy cross to bear, David had, and you know best if you helped to ease it for him."

The little man pointed to the door; but the girl paid no attention.

"Do you think that when you were cruel to him, mocking and sneering, he never felt it, because he was too proud to show you? He had a big, soft heart, David, beneath the surface. Many's the time when mother was alive, I've seen him throw himself into her arms, sobbing, and cry, 'Eh, if only I had my mother! It was different when mother was alive; he was kinder to me then. And now I have no one; I'm alone.' And he'd sob and sob in mother's arms, and she, weeping herself, would comfort him, while he, little laddie, would not be comforted, crying, 'There's no one to care for me now; I'm alone. Mother's left me and eh! I'm praying to be with her!'"

The clear, girlish voice shook. McAdam, sitting with his face turned away, waved at her, silently ordering her to be gone. But she held on, gentle, sorrowful, unstoppable.

"And what'll you say to his mother when you meet her, as you must soon, now, and she asks you, 'And what about David? What about the lad I left with you, Adam, to guard and keep for me, faithful and true, till this Day?' And then you'll have to speak the truth, God's truth; and you'll have to answer, 'Since the day you left me I never said a kind word to the lad. I never was patient with him, and never tried to be. And in the end, by my hard treatment of him, I drove him to try and murder me.' Then maybe she'll look at you—you best know how—and she'll say, 'Adam, Adam! is this what I deserved from you?'"

The gentle, unyielding voice fell silent. The girl turned and slipped softly out of the room; and McAdam was left alone with his thoughts and the memory of his dead wife.

"Mother and father, both! Mother and father, both!" rang pitilessly in his ears.

CHAPTER 23

The Owd One

THE BLACK Killer still cursed the land. Sometimes the crimes would stop for a while; then a shepherd, making his rounds, would notice his sheep herding together, pressing close in squares, as they never usually did; a raven, stuffed full up to his gullet, would rise into the air before him and flap wearily away, and he would come upon the murderer's latest victim.

The Dalesmen were in despair, so completely useless had their efforts been. There was no proof; no hope, nothing to say that these crimes might soon be coming to an end. As for the Tailless Tyke, the only piece of evidence against him had vanished along with David, who, as it happened, had told no one what he had seen.

The £100 reward that had been offered had brought no result. The police had done nothing. The Special Commissioner had done no better. After the incident in the Scoop, the Killer never ran a risk, yet never missed a chance.

Then, as a last resort, Jim Mason made his attempt. He took

time off from his duties and disappeared into the wilderness. For three days and three nights, no one saw him.

On the morning of the fourth day he reappeared, looking worn and exhausted, his hair wild and clothes creased, a sly and shifty expression in his eyes, gloomy for once, and irritable—he who had never been irritable before—and confessed his failure. Questioned further, he answered with a fierceness that was not like him: "I saw nothing, I tell ye. Which of you liars said I did?"

But that night, his wife heard him in his sleep puzzling over something to himself in a slow, fearful whisper, "Two of 'em; one behind the other. The first big, like a bull; the other—" At which point Mrs. Mason struck him a smashing blow in the ribs, and he woke in a sweat, crying terribly, "Who said I saw—"

◆ ◆ ◆

The days were slipping away; the summer was hot upon the land, and with it the Black Killer was forgotten; David was forgotten; everything else sank into oblivion before the consuming interest of the coming Dale Trials.

The battle for the Shepherds' Trophy, which everyone had been looking forward to for so long, was looming close; soon everything that depended on the outcome of that struggle would finally be decided. Whether the Owd One had a right to claim his proud title would be settled forever. If he won, he would win for good—a thing that had never happened before in the history of the Cup; if he won, the place of Owd Bob of Kenmuir as first and foremost in his profession would be guaranteed for all time. Above all, it would be the last event in the six years of struggle between Red and Gray. It was the last time those two great rivals would meet in battle. The superiority of one would be decided once and for all. For, whether he won or lost, it was to be the last public appearance of the Gray Dog of Kenmuir.

And as every hour brought the great day closer, nothing else was talked about in the countryside. The Dalesmen's enthusiasm was all the stronger because of their feverish anxiety. Many of them would lose more than they wanted to admit if the Owd One was beaten. But he wouldn't be! Nay; old, indeed, he was—two years older than his great rival; there were a hundred risks, a hundred chances; but still: "What's the odds against Owd Bob o' Kenmuir? I'm taking 'em. Who'll bet against the Owd Un?"

And now that the air was filled with this endless talk about the old dog, these announcements, made over and over, that he was certainly going to win; now that McAdam's ears throbbed with the repeated boast that the gray dog was the best in the North, he became once again the silent man he had been six months before—gloomy, brooding, suspicious, muttering about conspiracy, plotting revenge, planning evil.

The scenes at the Sylvester Arms were the same as in earlier years. Usually the little man sat by himself in a far corner, silent and scowling, with Red Wull at his feet. Now and then he burst into a fit of insane giggling, slapping his thigh and muttering, "Ay, it's likely they'll beat us, Wullie. Yet maybe there's a little something—a little something we know and they don't, Wullie—eh! Wullie, he, he!" And sometimes he would leap to his feet and address his tavern audience, speaking to them passionately, or sarcastically, or tearfully, depending on his mood; and his subject was always the same: James Moore, Owd Bob, the Cup, and the plots against him and his Wullie; and always he ended with that hint of the surprise to come.

Meanwhile, there was no news of David; he had vanished as utterly as a ship sinking in the middle of the Atlantic. Some said he had joined the army; some, that he had gone to sea. And "So he has," Sammel agreed, "floating with his heels uppermost."

Having no gleam of comfort, Maggie's misery was so deep that all hearts were sorry for her. She no longer went about her work singing cheerfully; and all the bounce had gone from her step. The people of Kenmuir competed with one another trying to comfort their young mistress.

❖   ❖   ❖

Maggie was not the only one whose life now had a great empty place in it because David was gone. Though he would have been the last to admit it, McAdam felt the boy's loss painfully. It may have been that he missed having someone who was always there to be mocked and scolded; but it may have been a nobler feeling. Alone with Red Wull, now, too late, he felt how lonely he was. Sometimes, sitting by himself in the kitchen, thinking of the past, he experienced the sharp pangs of remorse; and this was especially so after Maggie's visit. After that day, the little man, to be fair to him, was never known to hint by word or glance any mean thing about his enemy's daughter. Once, indeed, when Melia Ross was speaking about Maggie with all the resources of her dirty imagination, McAdam shut her up with: "You're a most amazing big liar, Melia Ross."

Yet, though he now had no evil thoughts about the daughter, his hatred for the father had never been so stubborn.

He grew reckless in what he said. His life was one long threat against James Moore's life. Now he openly declared his belief that, on the eventful night of the fight, James Moore, for a reason that was easy to guess, had urged David on to murder him.

"Then why don't you go and tell him so, you great liar?" roared Tammas at last, driven wild with rage.

"I will!" said McAdam. And he did.

◆ ◆ ◆

It was on the day before the great summer sheep fair at Grammoch-town that he carried out his promise.

That day is always a big field-day at Kenmuir; and James Moore and Owd Bob had been up and working on the Pike from sunrise on. Throughout the widespread lands of Kenmuir the Master went with his untiring helper, rounding up the sheep, separating out some, moving part of the flock to better grasslands. It was already noon when the flock started from the yard.

As they came up, McAdam was sitting on the gate, next to the wooden steps over the wall.

"I have something to say to you, James Moore," he announced, as the Master approached.

"Say it then, and quick. I have no time to stand gossiping here, if you have," said the Master.

McAdam leaned forward till he nearly fell off the gate.

"It's a queer thing, James Moore, that you should be the only one to escape this Killer."

"You're forgetting yourself, McAdam."

"Ay, there's me," the little man agreed. "But you—how do you explain your luck?"

James Moore swung around and pointed proudly at the gray dog, now pacing watchfully around the flock.

"There's my luck!" he said.

McAdam laughed unpleasantly.

"So I thought," he said, "so I thought! And I suppose ye're thinking that yer luck"—nodding at the gray dog—"will win you the Cup for certain a month from now."

"I hope so!" said the Master.

"Strange if he doesn't, after all," said the little man thoughtfully.

James Moore looked at him suspiciously.

"What do you mean?" he asked sternly.

McAdam shrugged his shoulders.

"There's many a slip twixt the Cup and the lip, that's all. I was thinking some bit of bad luck might come to him."

The Master's eyes flashed dangerously. He recalled the many rumors he had heard, and the attempt to poison the old dog early in the year.

"I can't think anyone would be coward enough to murder him," he said, standing tall.

McAdam leaned forward. There was a nasty glitter in his eye, and his face was quivering.

"You wouldn't think anyone would be coward enough to get the son to murder his father. Yet someone did—someone set the lad to do me in. He failed, and next, I suppose, he'll have a go at Wullie!" There was a flush on the pale face, and a vengeful ring to the thin voice. "One way or the other, fair or foul, Wullie or me, one or both, has got to go before Cup Day, eh, James Moore! Eh?"

The Master put his hand on the latch of the gate. "That'll do, McAdam," he said. "I won't stay to hear any more from you, or I might get angry. Now get off this gate; you're trespassing as it is."

He shook the gate. McAdam tumbled off and went sprawling among the sheep that were clustered below. Picking himself up, he dashed on through the flock, waving his arms, kicking wildly, and scattering confusion everywhere.

"Just wait till I get them through, will you?" shouted the Master, seeing the danger.

When one man asked this of another, the rules of courtesy and consideration among shepherds demanded that he oblige. But McAdam rushed on anyway, dancing and spinning like a windmill. If it hadn't been for the lightning-quick watchfulness of Owd Bob, the flock would have broken apart.

"I think yo' might ha' waited!" the Master scolded, as the little man burst his way through.

"Now I've forgot something!" the other cried, and he turned back toward the gate.

This was more than human nature could stand.

"Bob, keep him off!"

A flash of teeth; a blaze of gray eyes; and the old dog had leapt forward to stand in the way of the little man.

"Move out o' my light!" he cried, trying to dash past.

"Hold him, lad!"

And hold him the old dog did, while his master opened the gate and put the flock through, the dog and the little man dodging back and forth in front of each other like players in a game of rugby.

"Out o' my path, or I'll strike!" shouted the little man in a fury, as the last sheep passed through the gate.

"I wouldn't do that if I were you," warned the Master.

"But I will!" yelled McAdam; and, darting forward as the gate swung shut, struck furiously at the dog.

He missed, and the gray dog charged at him like a mail-train.

"Hi! James Moore—" but over he went like a toppled wheelbarrow, while the old dog turned again, raced at the gate, flew over it magnificently, and galloped up the lane after his master.

At McAdam's yell, James Moore had turned.

"Served yo' right!" he called back. "He'll teach ye yet that it's not wise to get in the way of a gray dog or his sheep. It's not the first time he's knocked ye over, I'm thinkin'!"

The little man raised himself painfully onto his elbow and crawled toward the gate. The Master, up the lane, could hear him cursing as he dragged himself along. Another moment, and a head was poked through the bars of the gate, and a devilish little face looked after him.

"Knocked me down, by God he did!" the little man cried passionately. "I owed ye both something before this, and now, by God, I owe ye something more. And mind ye, Adam McAdam pays what he owes!"

"I've heard the opposite," the Master replied calmly, and turned away up the lane toward the Marches.

CHAPTER 24

A Shot in the Night

IT WAS only three short weeks before Cup Day when, one afternoon, Jim Mason brought a letter to Kenmuir. James Moore opened it as the postman lingered in the doorway.

It was from Long Kirby—still in hiding—begging him for mercy's sake to keep Owd Bob safe inside at night; at least until after the great event was over. For Kirby knew, as did every Dalesman, that the old dog slept in the entryway, between the two doors of the house, and that the outer door was only loosely closed by a chain, so that the ever-watchful guardian could slip in and out and go his rounds at any moment of the night.

This was how the blacksmith ended his poorly spelled note: "Look out for McAdam i tell you i know hell tri to git the old wun before cup day—ef he cant git you. if the ole dog is beat i'm a ruined man i say so for the luv o God keep yer eyes peeld."

The Master read the letter and handed it to the postman, who studied it carefully.

"I tell you what," said Jim at last, speaking with a seriousness that made the other man stare, "I wish you'd do what he asks you: keep the Owd One in at night, I mean, just for now."

The Master shook his head and laughed, tearing the letter to pieces.

"Nay," he said; "McAdam or no McAdam, Cup or no Cup, the Owd One has the run of my land same as he's had since he was a puppy. Why, Jim, the first night I shut him up, that'll be the night the Killer comes, I'll bet."

The postman turned away, discouraged, and the Master stood looking after him, wondering what had happened lately to his friend, who used to be so cheerful.

Those two were not the only warnings James Moore received. During the weeks just before the Trials, the danger signal was sounded over and over beneath his nose.

Twice did Watch, the black mongrel chained in the straw-yard, sound a bold challenge on the night air. Twice did the Master, with lantern, Sammel, and Owd Bob, go out and search every hole and corner on the place—and find nothing. One of the dairy-maids quit her job, swearing that the farm was haunted; that several times in the early morning, she had seen an evil spirit flitting down the slope to the Wastrel—a sure sign, Sammel declared, that someone in the house was about to die. And one time a sheep-shearer, coming up from the village, told how he had seen, in the half-light of dawn, a ghostly little figure, thin and nervous, stealing silently from tree to tree in the grove of larches by the lane. The Master, however, irritated by these constant alarms, chose not to believe the story.

"One thing I'm certain of," he said. "Not a creature moves on Kenmuir at night without the Owd One knowing about it."

Yet, even as he said it, a little man with tired eyes, wet and dirty, smeared with dew and dust, was limping in at the door of a house barely a mile away. "No luck, Wullie, curse it!" he cried, throwing himself into a chair and speaking to someone who was not there—"no luck. And yet I'm as sure of it as I am that there's a God in heaven."

◆ ◆ ◆

McAdam had turned into an old man, in the last few months. Though he was hardly over fifty, he looked as though he had come to the end of his life. His thin hair was completely white, his body was shrunken and stooped, and his thin hand shook like the leaves on an aspen as it groped its way to the familiar bottle.

In another way, too, he was different. In the old days, whatever his faults, he had been the hardest-working man in the countryside. At all hours, in all weathers, you might have seen him with his gigantic companion tending to his business. Now all that had changed: he never put his hand to the plow to turn the soil, and with no one to help him, the fields were completely uncared-for; so that men said that, for sure, there would be a farm for rent on the March Mere Estate by the time autumn came.

Instead of working, the little man sat all day in the kitchen at home, brooding about the injuries people had done to him, and planning vengeance. He even stopped going to the Sylvester Arms, but instead stayed where he was with his dog and his bottle. Only when the curtain of night had come down to cover him, would he slip out and away on a mysterious errand, leaving even Red Wull behind.

◆ ◆ ◆

So the time glided on, till the Sunday before the Trials came around.

All that day, McAdam sat in his kitchen, drinking, muttering, scheming revenge.

"Curse it, Wullie! curse it! The time's slippin'—slippin'—slippin' away! Next Thursday—only three days more! and I don't have the proof—I don't have the proof!"—and he rocked back and forth, biting his nails in the agony of his helplessness.

All day long, he never moved. Long after sunset he still sat there; long after dark had blotted out the features of the room.

"They're all against us, Wullie. It's you and I alone, lad. McAdam's to be beaten somehow, anyhow; and Moore's to win. So they've settled it, and so it will be—unless, Wullie, unless—but curse it! I don't have the proof!"—and he hammered the table before him and stamped on the floor.

At midnight he stood up, a mad, desperate plan looming in his muddled brain.

"I swore I'd pay him back, Wullie, and I will. Though I may hang for it I'll get even with him. I don't have the proof, but I *know*—I *know*!" He groped his way to the mantelpiece with blind eyes and a reeling brain. Reaching up with fumbling hands, he took down the old gun from above the fireplace.

"Wullie," he whispered, chuckling hideously, "Wullie, come on! You and I—he, he!" But the Tailless Tyke was not there. At nightfall he had silently padded out of the house on business only he knew about. So his master crept out of the room alone—on tiptoe, still chuckling.

The cool night air refreshed him, and he walked silently along, his quaint old weapon over his shoulder: down the hill; across the Bottom; around the Pike; till he reached the plank-bridge over the Wastrel.

He crossed it safely, for the kindly spirit that looks after drunkards was placing his footsteps for him. Then he went quietly up the slope like a hunter stalking his prey.

Having arrived at the gate, he raised himself cautiously and peered over into the moonlit yard. There was no sign or sound of a living creature. The little gray house slept peacefully in the shadow of the Pike, all unaware of the man with murder in his heart who was slowly and with great effort climbing to the top of the yard-gate.

The door to the entryway was wide open, the chain hanging limply down, unused; and the little man could see, inside, the moon shining on the iron nail heads of the inner door, and the blanket of the one who should have been sleeping there, *and was not*.

"He's not there, Wullie! He's not there!" He jumped down from the gate. He abandoned all caution and staggered recklessly across the yard. He was drunk, and dizzy, and ready for battle. His veins were flushed with the fever of the victory that he was sure would be his. At last, he would be paid back for the injuries he had suffered for so many years.

Another moment, and he was in front of the good oak door, battering it madly with the butt of his gun, yelling, dancing, screaming vengeance.

"Where is he? What's he up to? Come and tell me that, James Moore! Come down, I say, ye coward! Come and meet me like a man!"

"'Scots wha hae wi' Wallace bled,
Scots wham Bruce has aften led—
Welcome to your gory bed
        Or to victorie!'"

(Scots who have with Wallace bled!
Scots whom Bruce has often led!
Welcome to your gory bed
    Or to victory!)

The soft moonlight streamed down on the white-haired madman thundering at the door, screaming his war-song.

The quiet farmyard, startled from its sleep, awoke in an uproar. Cattle shifted in their stalls; horses whinnied; fowl chattered, stirred up by the din and the dull thudding of the blows: and above the rest, loud and piercing, the shrill cry of a terrified child.

Maggie, wakened from a vivid dream of David chasing the police, hurried to put a shawl around her, and in a minute had the baby in her arms and was comforting her—vaguely fearing all the while that the police were after David.

James Moore flung open a window, and, leaning out, looked down on the wild-haired, rumpled figure below him.

McAdam heard the noise, looked up, and saw his enemy. He immediately stopped his attack on the door, and, running beneath the window, shook his weapon up at the man.

"There ye are, are ye? Curse ye for a coward! Curse ye for a liar! Come down, I say, James Moore! Come down—I dare ye to do it! Once and for all, let's settle our account."

The Master, looking down from above, thought that at last the little man had lost his mind.

"What is it yo' want?" he asked, as calmly as he could, hoping to gain time.

"What is it I want?" screamed the madman. "Listen to him! He crosses me in everything; he plots against me; he robs me of my Cup; he sets my son against me and goads him on to murder me! And in the end he—"

"Come, then, come! I'll—"

"Give me back the Cup ye stole, James Moore! Give me back my son that ye've took from me! And there's another thing. What's yer gray dog up to? Where's yer—"

The Master interrupted again:

"I'll come down and talk things over with you," he said soothingly. But before he could withdraw, McAdam had jerked his weapon to his shoulder and aimed it full at his enemy's head.

The threatened man looked down the gun's great quivering mouth, completely unmoved.

"You must hold it steadier, little man, if you want to hit your target!" he said grimly. "There, I'll come help you!" He drew back slowly; and all the time was wondering where the gray dog was.

In another moment he was downstairs, undoing the bolts and bars of the door. On the other side stood McAdam, his blunderbuss at his shoulder, his finger trembling on the trigger, waiting.

"Master! Stop, or he'll kill you!" roared a voice from the loft on the other side of the yard.

"Father, Father! Get back!" screamed Maggie, who saw it all from the window above the door.

Their cries were too late. The blunderbuss went off with a roar, belching out a storm of sparks and smoke. The shot peppered the door like hail, and the whole yard seemed for a moment to be wrapped in flame.

"Aw! Oh! My God! I'm wounded! I'm a goner! I'm shot! Help! Murder! Eh! Oh!" bellowed a lusty voice—and it was not James Moore's.

The little man, the cause of the uproar, lay quite still on the ground, with another figure looming over him. As he had stood, his finger on the trigger, waiting for that last bolt to be drawn, a gray form, leaping from out of the blue, had suddenly and silently attacked him from behind, and jerked him backward to the ground. With the shock of the fall, the blunderbuss had gone off.

The last bolt was thrown back with a clatter, and the Master came out. With a glance he took in the whole scene: the fallen man; the gray dog; the still-smoking weapon.

"So it was you, was it, Bob lad?" he said. "I was wondering where you were. You came just at the right moment, as you always do!" Then, in a loud voice, addressing the darkness: "You're not hurt, Sammel Todd—I can tell that by yer noise; it was only the shot off the door that warmed ye. Come down now and give me a hand."

He walked up to McAdam, who still lay gasping on the ground. The shock of the fall and recoil of the weapon had knocked the breath out of the little man's body; beyond that he was barely hurt.

The Master stood over his fallen enemy and looked sternly down at him.

"I've put up with more from you, McAdam, than I would from any other man," he said. "But this is too much—coming here at night with a loaded gun, scaring the women and children out of their minds, and I can't help thinking you meant even worse. If you were half a man, I'd give you the finest beating you ever had in yer life. But, as you know well, I could no more hit you than I could a woman. Why you've got it in for me, you know best. I never did you or any other man any harm. As for the Cup, I've got it and I'm going to do my best to keep it—it's for you to win it from me if you can on Thursday. As for what you say about David, you know it's a lie. And as for what you're trying to tell me with your hints and your mysteries, I have no more idea than an unborn baby. Now I'm going to lock you up, you're not safe out and about. I'm thinking I'll have to hand ye over to the police."

With the help of Sammel, he half dragged, half carried the stunned little man across the yard, and shoved him into a little room half underground, at the far end of the row of farm buildings, used for storing coal.

"You think it over on that side of the door, my lad," called the Master grimly, as he turned the key in the lock, "and I'll do the same on this side." And with that he went back to bed.

◆ ◆ ◆

Early in the morning, he went to release his prisoner. But he was a minute too late. For scuttling down the slope and away was a figure black with coal dust, unsteady on his feet, his white hair blowing in the wind. The little man had broken off a wood hatch that covered a manhole in the wall of his prison-house, squeezed his small body through, and so escaped.

"It's probably just as well," thought the Master, watching the flying figure. Then, "Bob, lad!" he called; for the gray dog, ears back, tail streaming, was hurtling down the slope after the runaway.

On the bridge, McAdam turned, and, seeing the dog nearly upon him, screamed, missed his footing, and fell with a loud splash into the stream—in almost the same spot in which, years before, he had plunged in order to save Red Wull.

On the bridge, Owd Bob stopped short and looked down at the man struggling in the water below. He made a move as though to leap in and rescue his enemy; then, seeing it was unnecessary, turned and trotted back to his master.

"You only did right, I'm thinking," said the Master. "Like as not he came here planning to make an end of you. Well, after Thursday, I pray God we'll have peace. It's getting beyond a joke." The two turned back into the yard.

But down below them, along the edge of the stream, for the second time in this story, a little dripping figure was tottering toward home. The little man was crying—the hot tears mingling on his cheeks with the undried waters of the Wastrel—crying with rage, shame, and exhaustion.

CHAPTER 25

The Shepherds' Trophy

CUP DAY.

It dawned calm and beautiful, with not a cloud on the horizon, not a threat of storm in the air; just the sort of day on which the Shepherds' Trophy must be won for good.

And a fortunate thing it was. For never since the founding of the Dale Trials had such a crowd gathered on the north bank of the Silver Lea. From the Highlands they came; from the far Campbell country; from the Peak; from Yorkshire, "the county of many acres." From all along the silvery water of the Solway to the north they came, gathering in that quiet corner of the earth to see the famous Gray Dog of Kenmuir fight his last great battle for the Shepherds' Trophy.

By noon, the bleak and rocky Scaur looked down on such a gathering as it had never seen before. The paddock at the back of the Dalesman's Daughter was packed with a tumultuous, chattering crowd: lively groups of farmers; clusters of solid countryfolk; sharp-faced townspeople; loud-voiced bookmakers; giggling girls; amorous boys—thrown together like toys in a bath of sawdust; while here and there, on the edges of the crowd, stood a lonely man and wise-faced dog, who had come from far away to take his proud title from the best sheepdog in the North.

At the back of the enclosure were parked an impressive range of carts and carriages, as different from one another in quality and kind as their owners. There was the Squire's gracefully curving landau rubbing axle-boxes with Jem Burton's modest donkey cart; and there was Viscount Birdsaye's flaring barouche side by side with the red-wheeled wagon of Kenmuir.

In that wagon, Maggie, sad and sweet in her simple summer dress, leaned over to talk to Lady Eleanour; while golden-haired little Anne, delighted with the milling crowd, trotted around the wagon, waving to her friends and shouting from joy.

Thick as flies clustered that colorful mass of people on the north bank of the Silver Lea, while on the other side of the stream was a little group of judges, inspecting the racecourse.

This was the course that every dog would have to run: the three sheep must first be found in the big fenced enclosure to the right of the starting flag; then they must be taken up the slope and away from the spectators; around a flag and slant-wise down the hill again; through a gap in the wall; along the hillside, parallel to the Silver Lea; sharply to the left through a pair of flags—the most difficult turn of them all; then down the slope to the pen, which was set up close to the bridge over the stream.

The day's competitions began with the Local Stakes, won by Rob Saunderson's experienced old dog, Shep. There followed the Open Juveniles, won by Ned Hoppin's young dog. It was late in the afternoon when, at last, the great event of the meeting was reached.

In the enclosure behind the Dalesman's Daughter, the

clamor of the crowd grew to be ten times as great, and the yells of the bookmakers announcing the odds on the bets became still louder.

"Walk up, gen'lemen, walk up! The old firm! Rasper? Yessir—twenty to one, bar two! Twenty to one, bar two! Bob? What price Bob? Even money, sir—no, not a penny longer, couldn't do it! Red Wull? Who says Red Wull?"

On the far side of the stream, clustered around the starting flag, is the finest range of sheepdogs ever seen together.

"I've never seen such a field, and I've seen fifty," is Parson Leggy's conclusion.

There, beside the tall form of his master, stands Owd Bob of Kenmuir, watched by everyone. His silvery tail fans the air, and he holds his dark head high as he gazes at his challengers, proudly aware that today will make his fame or spoil it. Below him, the mean-looking, smooth-coated black dog is the unbeaten Pip, winner of the renowned Cambrian Stakes at Llagollen—many think him the best of all the good dogs that have come from sheep-dotted Wales. Beside him, that handsome sable collie, with the tremendous coat and slash of white on throat and face, is the famous MacCallum More, fresh from his victory at the Highland contest. The hearty brown dog, who seems to be of many breeds, is from Yorkshire, the land of the Tykes—Merry, on whom the Yorkshiremen are betting as though they loved him. And Jess, the wiry black-and-tan, is the favorite of the men of the Derwent and Dove. Tupper's big blue Rasper is there; Londesley's Lassie; and many more—too many to mention: big and small, grand and mean, smooth and rough—and not a bad dog there.

And alone, his back to the others, stands a stooped little figure, very noticeable indeed—Adam McAdam; while the great dog beside him, hideously scowling his defiance, is Red Wull, the Terror of the Border.

The Tailless Tyke had already shown what a fighter he was. For MacCallum More, going up to examine this great rival who stood there so alone, had right away taken a violent dislike to him, and had spun at him with all the fury of the Highland bandit, who attacks first and explains afterward. Red Wull had immediately turned on him with savage, silent greed; bob-tailed Rasper was racing up to join in the attack; and in another second the three would have been locked together and no one could have separated them—but just in time McAdam stepped in and stopped them.

One of the judges came hurrying up.

"Mr. McAdam," he cried angrily, "if that brute of yours starts fighting again, hang me if I don't throw him out of the competition! Only last year at the Trials he killed the young Cossack dog."

A dull flash of passion swept across McAdam's face. "Come here, Wullie!" he called. "If that Highland tyke attacks ye again, ye're to be tossed out of the Trial."

No one paid any attention to him. The battle for the Cup had begun—little Pip starting it off.

On the opposite slope, the uproar had died down now. Trades people left their goods, and the bookmakers their stools, to watch the struggle. Every eye was fixed upon the moving figures of man and dog and three sheep on the far side of the stream.

One after another, the competitors ran their course and penned their sheep—there wasn't a single failure. And all of them received their fair reward of applause, except for Adam McAdam's Red Wull.

Last of all, when Owd Bob trotted out to defend his title, there rose a shout that made Maggie's pale cheeks blush with pleasure and little Anne scream at the top of her lungs.

His was a show beyond compare with any other. Sheep

should be handled gently rather than hurried; persuaded, rather than forced. And when a sheepdog can subdue his own personality, when he can lead his sheep by pretending that they are leading him, then he has reached the high point of his art. The hearts of the Dalesmen swelled with pride as they watched their favorite at his work; Tammas pulled out that well-worn phrase of his—"As clever as any person, and as gentle as the spring sunshine"; the crowd bawled their enthusiasm, and Long Kirby puffed his cheeks and rattled the money in his trousers pockets; and rightly so.

But it is enough to say, about this part of the contest, that Pip, Owd Bob, and Red Wull were chosen to fight out the struggle one more time.

◆ ◆ ◆

The course was changed and made more difficult. On the far side of the stream it was the same as before: up the slope; around a flag; down the hill again; through the gap in the wall; along the hillside; down between the two flags; a turn; and to the stream again. But the pen was taken away from its earlier position, carried over the bridge, and up the near slope, and the hurdles were put together right below the spectators.

The sheep had to be driven over the plank-bridge, and the penning was done beneath the very nose of the crowd. A difficult course, if ever there was one; and the time allowed was ten short minutes.

◆ ◆ ◆

The spectators hustled and elbowed in their attempts to move into a good position. And they were right to do so; what was about to begin was the finest show of sheep-handling that anyone there would ever see.

◆ ◆ ◆

Evan Jones and little Pip were the first to go.

Those two, who had won on many a hard-fought field, worked together as they had never worked before. Smooth and swift, like a racing boat in Southampton Water; around the flag, through the gap, they brought their sheep. Down between the two flags—performing that awkward turn very well; and back to the bridge.

There they stopped: the sheep would not face that narrow plank. Once, twice, and again, they broke and scattered; and each time the gallant little Pip, his tongue out and tail quivering, brought them back to the head of the bridge.

At last one faced it; then another, and—but it was too late. The time was up. The judges signaled; and the Welshman called off his dog and left the course.

Out of sight of everyone, in a hollow of the ground, Evan Jones sat down and took the small dark head between his knees—and you may be sure the dog's heart was as heavy as the man's. "We did our best, Pip," he cried brokenly, "but we're beat—for the first time ever!"

◆ ◆ ◆

There was no time to linger.

James Moore and Owd Bob were off on their last run.

There was no applause this time; not a voice was raised; faces were anxious; fingers twitched; the whole crowd was tense as a stretched wire. One wrong turn, one stubborn sheep, one ill-tempered judge, and the gray dog would be beaten. And everyone there knew it.

Yet on the far side of the stream, master and dog went about their business as quietly as never before, as calmly as never before; it was as though they were rounding up a flock of their own on the Muir Pike.

The old dog found his sheep in a twinkling of the eye, and a wild, scared threesome they turned out to be. Rounding the first flag, one bright-eyed fellow made a dash for the open. He was quick; but the gray dog was quicker: it was a splendid recovery, and a sound like a sob came up from the people watching on the hill.

Down the slope they came toward the gap in the wall. A little below the opening, James Moore took up his position to stop them and turn them; while some distance behind his sheep Owd Bob came slowly along, seeming to follow them rather than drive them, yet watchful of every move-ment and knowing in advance what they were going to do. On he came, one eye on his master, the other on his sheep; never hurrying them, never exciting them, yet bringing them quickly along.

Not a word was spoken; barely a movement of the hand or arm was made; yet master and dog worked like a single being.

Through the gap, along the hill parallel to the spectators, playing into one another's hands like a team at polo.

They made a wide sweep for the turn at the flags, and the sheep wheeled as though obeying a command, dropped through them, and traveled rapidly toward the bridge.

"Steady!" whispered the crowd.

"Steady, man!" muttered Parson Leggy.

"Hold 'em, for God's sake!" croaked Kirby, his voice hoarse. "Damn! I knew it! I saw it coming!"

The pace down the hill had grown quicker—too quick. Close to the bridge, the three sheep made an effort to break and scatter. A dash—and two were stopped; but the third went away like the wind, and after him Owd Bob, a gray streak against the green grass. Tammas was cursing silently; Kirby was white to his lips; and in the stillness, you could plainly hear the Dalesmen's panting breath as it fluttered in their throats.

"Gallop! They say he's old and slow!" muttered the Parson. "Dash! Look at that!" For the gray dog, racing like a storm over the sea, had already brought the runaway back again.

Man and dog were coaxing the three sheep one step at a time toward the bridge.

One dared to step onto it—the others followed.

In the middle, the leader stopped and tried to turn—and time was flying, flying, and there was still to come the penning of the sheep, which alone would take minutes. Many hands were reaching for their watches, but they could not take their eyes off the group below to look.

"We're beaten! I've won my bet, Tammas!" groaned Sammel. (The two had a long-standing bet on the event.) "I always knew how 'twould be. I always told you the owd tyke—" Then breaking into a bellow, his honest face red with enthusiasm: "Come on, Master! Good for you, Owd One! That's the way!"

For gray dog had leapt on the back of the sheep farthest behind; it had plowed forward against the next, and they were over the bridge and going up the slope in the midst of a thunder of applause.

At the pen, it was a sight to see shepherd and dog working together. The Master, his face stern and a little whiter than usual, reaching forward with both hands, herding the sheep in; the gray dog, his eyes big and bright, dropping to the ground; crawling and creeping, closer and closer.

"They're in!—No—Yes—dang me! Stop 'er! Good, Owd Un! Ah-h-h, they're in!" And the last sheep reluctantly passed through—just on the stroke of time.

A roar went up from the crowd; Maggie's white face turned pink; and the Dalesmen mopped their wet foreheads. The crowd surged forward, but the stewards held them back.

"Back, please! Don't pass the barriers! McAdam's still to come!"

From the far bank, the little man watched the scene. His coat and cap were off, and his hair gleamed white in the sun; his sleeves were rolled up; and his face was twitching but calm, as he stood—ready.

The uproar over the stream at last died down. One of the judges nodded to him.

"Now, Wullie—now or never!—'Scots wha hae'!"—and they were off.

"Back, gentlemen! Back! He's off—he's coming! McAdam's coming!"

They might well shout and push; for the great dog was on to his sheep before they knew it; and they went away with a rush, with him right on their backs. Up the slope they swept and around the first flag, already galloping. Down the hill toward the gap, and McAdam was flying ahead to turn them. But they passed him like a hurricane, and Red Wull was in front with a rush and turned them alone.

"McAdam wins! Five to four McAdam! I bet against Owd Bob!" rang out a clear voice in the silence.

Through the gap they rattled, ears back, feet twinkling like the wings of game birds driven by the hunt.

"He's lost 'em! They'll break! They're away!" was the cry.

Sammel was halfway up the wheel of the Kenmuir wagon; every man was on his toes; ladies were standing in their carriages; even Jim Mason's face flushed with momentary excitement.

The sheep were tearing along the hillside, all together, like a white cloud driven by the wind. After them, galloping like a winner of the famous Waterloo dog race, came Red Wull. And last of all, leaping over the ground like a demon, heading not toward the two flags, but toward the plank-bridge, was the white-haired figure of McAdam.

"He's beat! The Killer's beat!" roared a harsh voice.

Red Wull was now racing parallel to the sheep and above them. All four were traveling at a terrific rate; while the two flags were barely twenty yards in front, below the line of flight and almost parallel to it. To manage the turn, a change of direction had to be made almost at a right angle.

"He's beat! He's beat! McAdam's beat! He can't make it no-how!" was the roar.

From across the stream came a yell—

"Turn 'em, Wullie!"

At the word, the great dog swerved down on the flying three. They turned, still at the gallop, like a troop of horsemen, and came down through, clean and neat, between the flags; and on down to the stream they rattled, passing McAdam on the way as though he were standing still.

"Well done, Wullie!" came the scream from the far bank; and from the crowd rose a burst of applause, for they were clapping in spite of themselves.

"My word!"

"Did you see that?"

"By gob!"

It was a turn, indeed, to make the smartest team of

galloping horsemen proud. If he had been just a moment later, the sheep would have been too far past to strike the mark; a moment sooner, and they would have missed it.

"It hasn't been even two minutes so far. We're beaten—don't you think so, Uncle Leggy?" asked Muriel Sylvester, looking up sadly into the parson's face.

"It's not what I think, my dear; it's what the judges think," the parson answered; and anyone could read, plainly written on his face, what he thought their verdict would be.

Right on to the center of the bridge the lead sheep galloped and—stopped short.

Up above in the crowd, there was utter silence; staring eyes; rigid fingers. The sweat was dripping off Long Kirby's face; and, at the back, a green-coated bookmaker slipped his notebook in his pocket, and glanced behind him. James Moore, standing in front of them all, was the calmest one there.

Red Wull had to have his way. Like the gray dog, he leapt on the back of the sheep farthest behind. But the red dog was heavy, whereas the gray dog was light. The sheep staggered, slipped, and fell.

Almost before it had touched the water, McAdam, his face blazing and eyes bright, was in the stream. In a second, he had hold of the struggling creature, and, with an almost superhuman effort, had half thrown, half shoved it onto the bank.

Again there was a round of applause, led by James Moore.

The little man scrambled, panting, onto the bank and raced after sheep and dog. His face was white beneath the sweat; his breath came in trembling gasps; his trousers were wet and clinging to his legs; he was shaking in every part of his body, and yet he would not be beaten.

They were up to the pen, and the last struggle began. The

crowd, silent and motionless, craned forward to watch the strange, white-haired little man and the huge dog, working so close below them. McAdam's face was white; his eyes staring, unnaturally bright; his bent body leaning forward; and he tapped with his stick on the ground like a blind man, coaxing the sheep in. And the Tailless Tyke, his tongue out and sides heaving, crept and crawled and worked his way up to the opening, more patient than he had ever been before.

They were in at last.

There was a lukewarm, half-hearted cheer; then silence.

Exhausted and trembling, the little man leaned against the pen, one hand on it; while Red Wull, his sides still heaving, gently licked the other hand. Quite close stood James Moore and the gray dog; above was the black wall of people, utterly still; below, the judges comparing notes. In the silence you could almost hear the panting of the crowd.

Then one of the judges went up to James Moore and shook him by the hand.

The gray dog had won. Owd Bob of Kenmuir had won the Shepherds' Trophy for good.

There was a second of quivering silence; then a woman's high-pitched laugh—and a deep bellow rang out through the waiting air: followed by shouts, screams, hat-tossings, back-clappings, blending in a noise that made the many-winding waters of the Silver Lea quiver and quiver again.

Owd Bob of Kenmuir had won the Shepherds' Trophy for good and all.

Maggie's face flushed red. Little Anne flung her fat arms toward her triumphant Bob, and screamed with the best of them. Squire and parson, both red-cheeked, were shaking hands wildly. Long Kirby, who had not prayed for thirty years, exclaimed with heartfelt earnestness, "Thank God!" Sammel Todd bellowed in Tammas's ear, and almost killed him with his pounding. Among the Dalesmen some laughed like drunken men; some cried like children; all joined in that roaring song of victory.

To little McAdam, standing with his back to the crowd, that storm of cheering came as the first announcement of defeat.

A wintry smile, like the sun over a March sea, crept across his face.

"We might have known it, Wullie," he muttered, soft and low. The tension eased, the battle lost, the little man almost broke down. There were red spots of color in his face; his eyes were big; his lips pitifully quivering; he was close to sobbing.

An old man—utterly alone—he had put everything he had into this one last chance—and lost.

Lady Eleanour noticed the wretched little figure standing alone on the edge of the wild mob. She noticed the expression on his face; and her tender heart went out to the man in his defeat.

She went up to him and laid a hand upon his arm.

"Mr. McAdam," she said timidly, "won't you come and sit down in the tent? You look *so* tired! I can find you a corner where no one shall disturb you."

The little man wrenched his arm roughly away. The unexpected kindness, coming at that moment, was almost too much for him. A few steps away, he turned again.

"It's very kind of yer ladyship," he said hoarsely; and stumbled away to be alone with Red Wull.

◆ ◆ ◆

Meanwhile, the victors stood like rocks in the tide. About them surged a continually changing crowd, shaking the man's hand, patting the dog.

Maggie had carried little Anne to offer her congratulations; Long Kirby had come; Tammas, Saunderson, Hoppin, Tupper, Londesley—all but Jim Mason; and now, elbowing through the press, came Squire and parson.

"Well done, James! Well done, indeed! Knew you'd win! told you so—eh, eh!" Then, playfully, to Owd Bob: "Knew you would, Robert, old man! Ought to—Robert the Devil—mustn't be a naughty boy—eh, eh!"

"The first time ever the Dale Cup's been won outright!" said the Parson, "and I daresay it never will be again. And I think Kenmuir's the very fittest place for its final home, and a Gray Dog of Kenmuir for its winner."

"Oh, by the way!" the Squire interrupted. "I've arranged for the Manor dinner to be two weeks from today, James. Tell Saunderson and Tupper, will you? I want all the tenants there." He disappeared into the crowd, but in a minute had fought his way back. "I'd forgotten something!" he shouted. "Tell your Maggie perhaps you'll have news for her after it—eh, eh!"—and he was gone again.

Last of all, James Moore was aware of a white, blotchy, grinning face at his elbow.

"I must congratulate ye, Mr. Moore. Ye beat us—you and the gentlemen—you and the judges."

"It was a close thing, McAdam," the other answered. "And you made a grand fight. In all my life I never saw a finer turn than yours by the two flags yonder. No hard feelings, I hope?"

"Hard feelings! Me? Is it likely? No, no. 'Do unto every man as he does unto you—and something more besides,' that's my motto. I owe ye many a good turn, which I'll pay ye yet. No, no; there's no good quarreling with fate—or with judges. Well, I wish you well for your victory. Perhaps it'll be our turn next."

Then a rush of men, headed by Sammel, roughly hustled

little McAdam out of the way and bore the other one off on their shoulders in noisy triumph.

❖ ❖ ❖

In giving the Cup away, Lady Eleanour made a prettier speech than ever. Yet all the while she was haunted by a white, miserable face; and all the while she was conscious of two black moving dots in the Murk Muir Pass opposite her—alone, abandoned, a contrast to the cheering crowd around her.

❖ ❖ ❖

That is how the champion challenge Dale Cup, the world-renowned Shepherds' Trophy, came to rest for good and all; won outright by the last of the Gray Dogs of Kenmuir—Owd Bob.

Why he was the last of the Gray Dogs will now be told.

PART SIX

The Black Killer

CHAPTER 26
Red-Handed

THE SUN was hiding behind the Pike. Over the lowlands, the feathery breath of the night still hovered. And the hillside was shivering in the chill of dawn.

Down on the silvery meadow beside the Stony Bottom there lay the ruffled body of a dead sheep. All around the victim, the dewy ground was dark and patchy like rumpled velvet; coarse ferns trampled down; stones dislodged as though by struggling feet; and the whole spotted with red on all sides.

Twenty or so yards up the hill, in a twisting and turning confusion of red and gray, two dogs had death-holds on each other. While yet higher, a pack of wild-eyed hill-sheep watched the bloody drama, fascinated.

The fight raged on. Red and gray, blood-spattered, murderous-eyed; the crimson foam dripping from their jaws; now rearing up high with arching crests and wrestling paws; now rolling over in tumbling, tossing, twisting disorder— the two fought out their blood-feud.

Above, the close-packed flock huddled and stamped, edging

nearer and nearer to see the outcome. In just this way, the women of Rome must have craned their necks around the arenas to see two men fighting to the death.

The first cold flicker of dawn stole across the green. The red eye of the morning peered, horrified, over the shoulder of the Pike. And from the sleeping valley there arose the yodeling of a man driving his cattle home.

Day was upon them.

◆ ◆ ◆

James Moore was waked by a little whimpering cry beneath his window. He leapt out of bed and rushed to look; for he knew that the old dog would not be calling for no reason.

"Lord o' mercy! Whatever's happened to you, Owd One?" he cried in anguish. And, indeed, his favorite, splotched with blood and earth, almost unrecognizable, was a pitiful sight.

In a moment, the Master was downstairs and out of the house, examining him.

"Poor old lad, you've caught it this time!" he cried. There was a ragged tear on the dog's cheek; a deep gash in his throat from which the blood still came out, staining the white patch on his chest; while his head and neck were clotted with the red.

The Master quickly called for Maggie. After her, Andrew came hurrying down. And a little later a tiny, nightgown-wearing, barefooted figure appeared wide-eyed in the door-way, and then ran off screaming.

They treated the old warrior on the table in the kitchen. Maggie tenderly washed his wounds and bandaged them with gentle, pitying fingers; and he stood all the while grateful yet fidgeting, looking up into his master's face as if begging to be gone.

"He must have had a rare fight with someone—eh, dad?" said the girl as she worked.

"Ay; and with whom? It wasn't for nothing he got into a fight, I'm sure. Nay; he has a tale to tell, has the Owd Un, and— Ah-h-h! I thought as much. Look there!" For in bathing the bloody jaws, he had come upon a cluster of tawny red hair, hiding in the corners of the lips.

The secret was out. Those few hairs told their own accusing tale. There was only one creature in the Daleland they could belong to—"The Tailless Tyke."

"He must have been trespassing!" cried Andrew.

"Ay, and up to some of his bloody work, I'll bet my life," the Master answered. "But the Owd Un shall show us."

The old dog's hurts proved less severe than had at first seemed possible. His good gray coat, thick as a forest around his throat, had never been so useful to him. And at last, the wounds washed and sewn up, he jumped down from the table, all in a hurry, and made for the door.

"Now, old lad, you may show us," said the Master, and, with Andrew, hurried after him down the hill, along the stream, and over Langholm Hollow. And as they came near the Stony Bottom, the sheep, clustering in groups, raised frightened heads to stare.

Suddenly, a cloud of poisonous flies rose, buzzing, before them; and there in a hollow of the ground lay a murdered sheep. Abandoned by its comrades, the glassy eyes staring helplessly upward, the throat horribly torn, it slept its last sleep.

The matter was plain to see. At last the Black Killer had visited Kenmuir.

"I guessed as much," said the Master, standing over the mangled body. "Well, it's the worst night's work the Killer has ever done. I suppose the Owd Un must have come upon him while he was at it; and then they fought. And my word! It must have been quite a fight, too." For all around were traces of that terrible struggle: the earth torn up and tossed, ferns uprooted, and throughout, little tufts of wool and of tawny hair, mingling with dark-stained iron-gray wisps.

James Moore walked slowly over the battlefield, stooping down as though he were searching for clues. And searching he was.

He bent down a long time, and finally stood up.

"The Killer has killed his last," he muttered; "Red Wull has done his worst and will do no more." Then, turning to Andrew: "Run on home, lad, and get the men to carry that away"—pointing to the carcass. "And Bob, lad, you've done your work for today, and right well, too; go on home with him. I'm off to see to this!"

He turned and crossed the Stony Bottom. His face was set like a rock. At last the proof was in his hand. Once and for all, the hill country would be rid of its killer.

As he stalked up the hill, a dark head appeared at his knee. Two big gray eyes, half doubting, half remorseful, wholly wistful, looked up at him, and the silvery brush of his waving tail signaled a silent request.

"Eh, Owd One, yo' should have gone with Andrew," the Master said. "However, since yo're here, come along." And he walked on up the hill, his thin face hard and threatening, with the gray dog at his heels.

As they came near the house, McAdam was standing in the doorway, sucking his twig as always. James Moore looked at him closely as he came, but the sour face framed in the door revealed nothing. Sarcasm, surprise, defiance were all written there, plain to read; but no guilty awareness of why James Moore had come, no storm of passion to hide a frightened heart. If this was an act, it was very well done.

As man and dog passed through the opening in the hedge, the expression on the little man's face changed again. He started forward.

"James Moore, as I live!" he cried, and advanced with both hands out, as though welcoming a long-lost brother. "Indeed, it has been a long while since ye've honored my poor house." And, in fact, it was nearly twenty years. "I take it most kind in ye to look in on a lonely old man. Come along in and let's have a chat. James Moore knows very well how welcome he always is in my little home."

The Master ignored the greeting.

"One of my sheep has been killed in back of the Dyke," he announced shortly, jerking his thumb over his shoulder.

"The Killer?"

"The Killer."

The friendliness beaming in every wrinkle of the little man's face was transformed into wondering interest; and that in turn gave way to sorrowful sympathy.

"Dear, dear! It's come to that, has it—at last?" he said gently, and his eyes wandered to the gray dog and rested sadly upon him. "Man, I'm sorry—I can't tell ye I'm surprised. Myself, I knew it all along. But if Adam McAdam had told ye, ye wouldn't have believed him. Well, well, he's lived his life, if any dog ever did; and now he must go where he has sent many before him. Poor man! Poor dog!" He heaved a sigh, deeply melancholy, tender, and sympathetic. Then, brightening up a little: "Ye've come to get the gun?"

James Moore listened to this speech, at first puzzled. Then he understood McAdam's meaning, and his eyes flashed.

"Ye fool, McAdam! Did ye ever hear of a sheepdog attacking his own master's sheep?"

The little man was smiling and calm again now, rubbing his hands softly together.

"Ye're right, I never did. But your dog is not like other dogs—'There's none like him—none,' I've heard ye say so yerself, many a time. And I say you're right. There's none like him—for devilment." His voice began to quiver and his face to blaze. "It's his cursed cleverness that has fooled everyone but me—child of Satan that he is!" He stood up to his tall adversary. "If it wasn't him, who else would have done it?" he asked, looking up into the other's face as if daring him to speak.

The Master's shaggy eyebrows lowered. He towered above the other like the Muir Pike above its surrounding hills.

"Who, ye ask?" he answered coldly, "and I'll tell you. Your Red Wull, McAdam, your Red Wull. It's your Wull that's the Black Killer! It's your Wull that has been the plague of the land all these months! It's your Wull that has killed my sheep back there!"

At that, all the little man's false good humor vanished.

"Ye lie, man! Ye lie!" he cried in a dreadful scream, dancing up to his antagonist. "I knew how 'twould be. I said so. I see what ye're up to. Ye've found out at last—blind as ye've been!—that it's your own hell's tyke that's the Killer; and now ye think by yer lyin' accusations to throw the blame on my Wullie. Ye rob me of my Cup, ye rob me of my son, ye treat me unfairly in everything; I have only one thing left to me—Wullie. And now ye want to take him away, too. But ye shall not—I'll kill ye first!"

He was shaking, bobbing up and down like a cork in water, and almost sobbing.

"Have ye not wronged me enough without that? You long-legged liar, with yer skulking, murdering tyke!" he cried. "You say it's Wullie. Where's yer proof?"—and he snapped his fingers in the other man's face.

The Master was now as calm as his foe was passionate.

"Where?" he answered sternly; "why, there!"—holding out his right hand. "There's proof enough to hang a hundred." And lying in his broad palm was a little bundle of that damning red hair.

"Where?"

"There!"

"Let's see it!" The little man bent to look closer.

"There's what I think of yer proof!" he cried, and he spat straight down into the other man's bare palm. Then he stood back, facing his enemy in a way that would have earned him respect, if his act had been a nobler one.

James Moore stepped forward. It looked as if he were about to make an end of his miserable adversary, so angry was he. His chest heaved and his blue eyes blazed. But just when it seemed that he would take his foe in the hollow of his hand and crush him, who should come stalking around the corner of the house but the Tailless Tyke?

He was a pathetic sight, laughable even at that moment. He limped badly, his head and neck were wrapped in bandages, and beneath their ragged edges the little eyes gleamed out fiery and bloodshot.

Around the corner he came, unaware of strangers; then, immediately recognizing his visitors, he stopped short. His hackles went up, each hair stood on end till his whole body looked like a newly mown wheat field; and a snarl, like a rusty brake shoved down hard, escaped from between his teeth. Then he trotted heavily forward, his head sinking lower and lower as he came.

And Owd Bob, eager to accept the challenge of a fight, stepped forward, glad and brave, to meet him. Delicately he picked his way across the yard, head and tail up, perfectly calm. Only the long gray hair around his neck stood up like the great collar of a noble lady in the court of Queen Elizabeth.

But the battle-weary warriors were not going to be allowed to have their way.

"Wullie, Wullie, stop!" cried the little man.

"Bob, lad, come in!" called the other. Then he turned and looked down at the man beside him, scorn showing in every feature of his face.

"Well?" he said shortly.

McAdam's hands were opening and shutting; his face was quite pale beneath his sun-browned skin; but he spoke calmly.

"I'll tell ye the whole story, and it's the truth," he said slowly. "I was up there this morning"—pointing to the window above—"and I saw Wullie crouching down alongside the Stony Bottom. (Ye know he can run free on my land at night, same as your dog.) In a minute, I saw another dog coming along on your side of the Bottom. He creeps up to the sheep on the hillside, chases 'em, and knocks one down to the ground. The sun was risen by then, and I see the dog clear as I see you now. It was that dog there—I swear it!" His voice rose as he spoke, and he pointed an accusing finger at Owd Bob.

"Now, Wullie! I thought. And before you could clap yer hands, Wullie was over the Bottom and onto him as he gorged himself—the bloody-minded murderer! They fought and fought—I could hear the roaring where I stood. I watched till I could watch no longer, and, all in a sweat, I ran down the stairs and out. When I got there, there was yer tyke racing for Kenmuir, and Wullie coming up the hill to me. It's God's truth, I'm telling ye. Take him home, James Moore, and let his dinner be an ounce o' lead. It will be the best day's work ye ever done."

The little man had to be lying—clearly lying. Yet he spoke with an earnestness, a seeming belief in his own story, that might have convinced anyone who did not know him so well. But the Master only looked down on him with greater scorn.

"It's Monday today," he said coldly. "I'll give ye till Saturday. If you've not done your duty by then—and you know very well what it is—I shall come and do it for ye. In any case, I shall come and see. I'll remind ye again on Thursday—you'll be at the Manor dinner, I suppose. Now I've warned yo', and you know best whether I mean it or not. Bob, lad!"

He turned away, but turned back again.

"I'm sorry for ye, but I have to do my duty—and so have you. Till Saturday I shall breathe no word to any soul about this business, so that if you see good to put him out of the way without bother, no one need ever know as how Adam McAdam's Red Wull was the Black Killer."

He turned away for the second time. But the little man sprang after him, and clutched him by the arm.

"Look ye here, James Moore!" he cried in a thick, shaky, horrible voice. "You're big, I'm small; you're strong, I'm weak; you have everyone behind you, I have no one; you tell your story, and they'll believe ye—for you go to church; I tell mine, and they'll think I'm lying—for I don't. But one word in your ear! If ever again I catch ye on my land, by God!"—he swore a great oath—"I won't spare you. You know best if I mean it or not." And his face was dreadful to see in its hideous determination.

CHAPTER 27

For the Defense

THAT NIGHT, a vague story was whispered in the Sylvester Arms. But Tammas, when he was questioned, pursed his lips and said: "Nay, I've sworn to say nothing." Which was the old man's way of declaring that he knew nothing.

♦ ♦ ♦

On Thursday morning, James Moore and Andrew came down dressed in their best clothes. It was the day of the Squire's annual dinner for his tenants.

The two, however, were not allowed to start upon their way until they had been thoroughly inspected by Maggie; for the girl liked her menfolk to represent Kenmuir honorably on these occasions. So she brushed Andrew's jacket, tied his scarf, saw that his boots and hands were clean, and generally neatened him up till she had changed the awkward adolescent into a thoroughly "proper young man."

And all the while, she was thinking of that other boy—on such gala days, she had done the same for him. And her father, seeing the tears in her eyes, and remembering the Squire's mysterious hint, said gently:

"Cheer up, lass. I might have news for you tonight!"

The girl nodded, and smiled sadly.

"Maybe so, dad," she said. But in her heart she was doubtful.

Still, it was with a cheerful face that, a little later, she stood in the door with little Anne and Owd Bob and waved good-bye to the travelers; while the golden-haired girl, fiercely gripping the old dog's tail with one hand and her sister with the other, cried out to them a wordless farewell.

◆ ◆ ◆

The sun had reached its highest point in the sky when the two who had walked from Kenmuir passed through the massive gray front doors of the Manor.

In the grand entrance hall, so impressive with all its painted portraits and other evidences of the many generations of the Squire's honored family, were now gathered the numerous tenants of the wide March Mere Estate. They were weather-beaten, rent-paying sons of the soil; most of them native-born, many of them like James Moore, whose fathers had for generations owned and farmed the land they now leased from the Sylvesters—there in the old hall they were gathered, in great numbers. And standing apart from the others, placing himself, as though deliberately, beneath the frown of one of those armored warriors, guardian of the entrance, was little McAdam, always small and weak, wretched now, mocking his own manhood.

The door at the far end of the hall opened, and the Squire entered, smiling broadly at everyone.

"Here you are—eh, eh! How are you all? Glad to see ye! Good-day, James! Good-day, Saunderson! Good-day to you all! Bringing a friend with me—eh, eh!" and he stood aside to allow his agent, Parson Leggy, to pass, and then, last of all, shy and blushing, a fair-haired young giant.

"If it ain't David!" people cried out. "Eh, lad, we's happy to see you! And yer lookin' well, surely!" And they crowded around the boy, shaking him by the hand and asking him for his story.

It was a simple tale. After he had run away on that eventful night, he had gone south, working as a drover of cattle, taking them to market. He had written to Maggie and had been surprised and hurt to receive no answer. In vain he had waited, and, too proud to write again, he had not known about his father's recovery, and had neither wanted to return, nor dared to. Then, by mere chance, he had met the Squire at the York cattle-show; and that kind man, who knew his story, had quieted his fears and made him promise to return as soon as his employment was finished. And there he was.

The Dalesmen gathered around the boy, listening to his story, and in return telling him the home news, and teasing him about Maggie.

Of all the people present, only one seemed unmoved, and that was McAdam. When David had first entered the hall, the little man had started forward, a flush of color warming his thin cheeks; but no one had noticed his emotion; and now, back again beneath his armor, he watched the scene, a sour smile playing about his lips.

"I think the lad might have the grace to come and say he's sorry for trying to murder me. However"—with his usual shrug—"I suppose I'm being unreasonable."

Then the gong rang out the summons for dinner, and the Squire led the way into the great dining-hall. At one end of the long table, heavy with all the solid delicacies of such a feast, he took his seat with the Master of Kenmuir on his right. At the other end was Parson Leggy. While down either side settled the strong, dependable Dalesmen, with McAdam a little lost figure in the center.

At first they hardly talked, as shy as children; knives cut, glasses tinkled, the men carving the roasts worked away, only the tongues were quiet. But the Squire's ringing laugh and the parson's cheery tones soon made them feel comfortable; and a confusion of voices rose and grew loud.

Of them all, only McAdam sat silent. He talked to no one, and you may be sure that no one talked to him. His hand crept more often to his glass than to his plate, until his pale face grew rosy and the dim eyes became unnaturally bright.

Toward the end of the meal, there was a loud tapping on the table, calls for silence, and men pushed back their chairs. The Squire had risen to his feet, to make his yearly speech.

He started by telling them how glad he was to see them there. He mentioned Owd Bob and the Shepherds' Trophy, at which the men clapped loudly. He mentioned the Black Killer, and said he had a solution to propose: that the Owd One should be set upon the criminal's track—a suggestion that was received with enthusiasm, while McAdam's cackling laugh could be heard high above the rest.

From there, he went on to speak about the present state of agriculture, and its economic depression, which he felt was the fault of the recent Radical Government. He said that now, with the Conservatives in office, and a government made up of "honorable men and gentlemen," he was convinced that things would get better. The Radicals' only ambition, he said, was to set class against class, landlord against tenant. Well, during the last five hundred years, his own family, the Sylvesters, had almost never been—he was sorry to say—good men (at this, there was laughter and disagreement); but he had never yet heard of a Sylvester—though he shouldn't say it—who was a bad landlord (at this, there was loud applause).

This was a free country, and any tenant of his who was not happy (a voice called out, "Who says we ain't?")—"thank you, thank you!"—well, there was plenty of room for him elsewhere in the world. (Cheers.) He thanked God from the bottom of his heart that, during the forty years he had been responsible for the March Mere Estate, there had never been any bad feeling or difficulty between him and his people (cheers), and he didn't think there ever would be. (Loud cheers.)

"Thank you, thank you!" And his motto was, "Avoid a Radical as you would avoid the devil!"—and he was very glad to see them all there—very glad; and he wished to propose a toast to "The Queen! God bless her!" and—wait a minute!— along with her Majesty's name, to join to it another—he was sure that gracious lady would wish it—"Owd Bob of Kenmuir!" Then he sat down suddenly in the midst of thundering applause.

The men drank in honor of the Squire's toasts, and then James Moore, as was his right, as Master of Kenmuir, rose to answer.

He began by saying that he spoke "as representing all the tenants"—but he was interrupted.

"Na," came a shrill voice from halfway down the table. "All except me, James Moore. I'd as soon be represented by Judas the traitor!"

There were cries of "Hold yer gab, little man!" and the Squire's voice spoke, "That'll do, Mr. McAdam!"

The little man held his tongue, but his eyes gleamed like a ferret's; and the Master went on with his speech.

He spoke briefly and clearly, in short phrases. And all the while McAdam kept muttering a steady stream of comments.

At last he could not control himself any longer. Half rising from his chair, he leaned forward with hot face and burning eyes, and cried: "Sit down, James Moore! How dare ye stand there like an honest man, ye whitewashed sepulcher?"—quoting the Bible and meaning that Moore was a hypocrite, fair on the outside, corrupt on the inside. "Sit down, I say, or"—threateningly—"would ye have me come to ye?"

At that, the Dalesmen laughed loudly, and even the Master's grim face relaxed. But the Squire's voice rang out sharp and stern.

"Keep silence and sit down, Mr. McAdam! D'you hear me, sir? If I have to speak to you again, it will be to order you to leave the room."

The little man obeyed, ill-humored and vengeful, like a beaten cat.

The Master ended his speech by asking everyone present to give three cheers for the Squire, her ladyship, and the young ladies, their daughters.

The men responded enthusiastically, everyone standing. Just as the noise was at its height, Lady Eleanour herself, with her two pretty girls, walked gracefully out onto the balcony at the end of the hall; at which the cheering became deafening.

Slowly the noise quieted. One by one the tenants sat down again. At last there was left standing only one lonely figure—McAdam.

His face was rigid, and he gripped the chair in front of him with thin, nervous hands.

"Mr. Sylvester," he began in a low yet clear voice, "ye said this is a free country and we're all free men. And that being so, I'll take the liberty, with yer permission, to say a word. It's maybe the last time I'll be with ye, so I hope ye'll listen to me."

The Dalesmen looked surprised, and the Squire looked uncomfortable. But he nodded his agreement.

The little man straightened up. His face was tense, as though determined to do something difficult. All the passion had vanished from it, all the bitterness was gone; and what was left was a strange, noble seriousness. Standing there in the silence of that great hall, with every eye upon him, he looked like some prisoner in a court of law about to plead for his life.

"Gentlemen," he began, "I've been among ye now twenty years or so, and I can truly say there's not a man in this room I can call 'Friend.'" He looked along the rows of upturned faces. "Ay, David, I see you, and you, Mr. Hornbut, and you, Mr. Sylvester—every one of you, and not one who would defend me like a comrade if a trouble came upon me." There was no reproach in the grave little voice—it merely stated a hard fact.

"There's not a single one of ye, I doubt, who does not have someone—friend or family—he can turn to when things are going bad with him. I have no one.

"'I bear alane my lade o' care—' alone with Wullie, who stands by me, wind or snow, rain or shine. And now I'm afraid he'll be taken from me." He spoke this last half to himself, a sorrowful, puzzled expression on his face, as though lately he had dreamed some evil dream.

"Except for Wullie, I've no friend on God's earth. And, mind ye, a bad man often makes a good friend—but ye've never given me the chance. It's a miserable thing, that, gentlemen, to have to fight the battle of life alone: no one to pat ye on the back, no one to say 'Well done.' It hardly gives a man a chance. For if he does try and yet fails, men pay no attention to the trying, they see only the failing.

"I don't blame ye. There's something bred in me, it seems, that sets everyone against me. It's the same with Wullie and the other dogs—they're down on him same as men are on me. I suppose we was made that way. Since I was a lad, it's always been the same. From school days on, I've had every-one against me.

"In my life I've had three friends. My mother—and she died; then my wife"—he gave a great swallow—"and she's gone; and I may say they're the only two human beings as have lived on God's earth in my time that ever tried to put up with me—and Wullie. A man's mother—a man's wife—a man's dog! It's often all he has in this world; and the more he cares for them, the more likely they are to be took from him." The serious little voice shook, and the dim eyes filled with tears.

"Since I've been among ye—twenty-odd years—can any man here remember speaking any word that wasn't ill to me?" He paused; there was no answer.

"I'll tell ye. All the time I've lived here, I've had one kindly word spoke to me, and that two weeks ago, and not by a man then—but by her ladyship, God bless her!" He glanced up into the balcony. No one could be seen there; but a curtain at one end shook as though someone behind it were sobbing.

"Well, I'm thinking we'll be going in a little while now, Wullie and me, alone and together, as we've always done. And it's time we went. Ye've had enough of us, and it's not for me to blame ye. And when I'm gone, what'll ye say about me? 'He was a drunkard.' I am. 'He was a sinner.' I am. 'He was everything he shouldn't be.' I am. 'We're glad he's gone.' That's what ye'll say about me. And it's what I deserve."

The gentle, condemning voice stopped, and began again.

"That's what I am. If things had been different, maybe I'd have been different. Do ye know Robbie Burns? That's a man I've read, and read, and read. Do ye know why I love him as some of you do your Bibles? Because there's something hu-man and generous about him. A weak man himself, always slipping, slipping, slipping, and trying to hold himself up; sorrowing one minute, sinning the next; doing bad things

and wishing he could undo them—just a plain human man,
a sinner. And that's why I'm thinking he's tender towards us
who are like him. *He understood*. It's what he wrote—after one
of his tumbles, I'm thinking—that I was going to tell ye:

> 'Then gently scan yer brother man,
>   Still gentler sister woman,
>   Though they may gang a kennin' wrang,
> To step aside is human—'

> (Then gently study your fellow man,
>   Still gentler your fellow woman,
>   Though they may knowingly go wrong,
> To stray from the path is human—)

the teaching of forgiveness. Give him his chance, says Robbie,
though he be a sinner. Many a man would be different, many
a bad man would be good, if only they had their chance. Give
them their chance, says he; and I'm with him. As it is, ye see
me here—a bad man with still a streak of good in him. If I'd
had my chance, maybe it would be—a good man with just a
spice of the devil in him. All the difference between what is
and what might have been."

CHAPTER 28

The Devil's Bowl

HE SAT down. In the great hall there was silence, except for a tiny sound from the balcony like a sob stifled.

The Squire stood up quickly and left the room.

After him, one by one, the tenants drifted out.

At last, only two were left—McAdam, sitting alone with a long row of empty chairs on either side; and, at the far end of the table, Parson Leggy, stern, upright, motionless.

When the last man had left the room, the parson rose, and with lips tight-set strode across the silent hall.

"McAdam," he said quickly and almost roughly, "I've listened to what you've said, as I think we all have, with a sore heart. You hit hard—but I think you were right. And if I haven't done my duty by you as I should have—and I fear I have not—it's now my duty as God's minister to be the first to say I'm sorry." And it was clear from his face what an effort the words cost him.

The little man tilted back his chair, and raised his head.

It was the old McAdam who looked up. The thin lips were

curled; a grin was crawling across the mocking face; and he wagged his head gently, as he looked at the speaker through the slits of his half-closed eyes.

"Mr. Hornbut, I believe ye thought I was serious, indeed I do!" He leaned back in his chair and laughed softly. "Ye swallowed it all down like good butter. Dear, dear! To think of that!" Then, stretching forward: "Mr. Hornbut, I was only playing with ye."

The parson's face, as he listened, was ugly to watch. He shot out a hand and grabbed the mocking man by his coat; then dropped it again and turned abruptly away.

As he passed through the door, a little sneering voice called after him:

"Mr. Hornbut, I ask ye how you, a minister of the Church of England, can with a good conscience think—even for a minute—that there can be any good in a man who doesn't go to church? Sir, ye're a disbeliever—not to say a heathen!" He snickered to himself, and his hand crept to a half-empty wine decanter.

◆ ◆ ◆

An hour later, James Moore, his business with the Squire completed, passed through the hall on his way out. The only person there was now McAdam, and the Master walked straight up to his enemy.

"McAdam," he said gruffly, holding out a muscular hand, "I'd like to say—"

The little man knocked aside the token of friendship.

"Na, na. No sweet talk, if ye please, James Moore. Maybe that'll go down with the parsons, but not with me. I know you and you know me, and all the whitewash in the world will not fool us."

The Master turned away, and his face was as hard as a millstone. But the little man went after him.

"I nearly forgot," he said. "I've a surprise for ye, James Moore. But I hear it's yer birthday on Sunday, and I'll keep it till then—he, he!"

"Ye'll see me before Sunday, McAdam," the other answered. "On Saturday, as I told you, I'm comin' to see if you've done yer duty."

"Whether ye come, James Moore, is your business. Whether ye'll ever leave again, once you're there, will be my business. I've warned ye twice now"—and the little man laughed that harsh, cackling laugh of his.

At the door of the hall, the Master met David.

"Now, lad, you're coming along with Andrew and me," he said; "Maggie'll never forgive us if we don't bring you home with us."

"Thank you kindly, Mr. Moore," the boy answered. "I have to see Squire first; and then you may be sure I'll be along after you."

The Master hesitated for a moment.

"David, have you spoke to yer father yet?" he asked in a low voice. "You should, lad."

The boy made a gesture of disagreement.

"I can't," he said impatiently.

"I would, lad," the other advised. "If you don't, you may be sorry later."

As he turned away, he heard the boy's steps, dull and muffled, as he crossed the hall; and then a thin, falsely pleasant voice in the emptiness:

"I declare if it isn't David! The return of the Prodigal Son—he, he! So ye've seen yer old dad at last, and the last; the proper place, ye say, for yer father—he, he! Eh, lad, I'm happy to see ye. Do ye remember when we was last together? Ye was kneeling on my chest: 'Your time's come, dad,' says you, and strikes me on the face—he, he! I remember it as if it was yesterday. Well, well, we'll say no more about it. Boys will be boys. Sons will be sons. Accidents will happen. And if at first ye don't succeed, why, try, try again—he, he"

◆　◆　◆

Dusk was changing to dark when the Master and Andrew reached the Dalesman's Daughter. It had been dark for a long time when they came out again from the cozy parlor of the inn and plunged into the night.

As they crossed the Silver Lea and trudged over that familiar ground, where, just two weeks before, the battle of the Cup had been fought, the wind fluttered past them in fitful gusts.

"There's trouble in the wind," said the Master.

"Ay," answered his son, who was quiet by nature.

All day there had been not a breath of air, and the sky was dangerously blue. But now a world of black was surging up from the horizon, smothering the starlit night; and small dark clouds, like puffs of smoke, separating themselves from the main body, were driving wildly forward—the front of the oncoming storm.

In the distance, there was a low tumbling like heavy carts rolling over the floor of heaven. All around, the wind sounded hollow like a mighty blade sweeping across the wheat. The air was heavy with a leaden blackness—no glimmer of light anywhere; and as they began climbing the Pass, they reached out blind hands to feel along the rock face.

A cool wet mist, coming inland from the sea, descended around them. A few big raindrops splashed heavily down. The wind rose with a leap and roared past them up the rocky track. And the water-gates of heaven were flung wide open.

Wet and tired, they battled on; thinking sometimes of the cozy parlor behind them; sometimes of the home in front; wondering whether Maggie, in complete disobedience of her father's orders, would be waiting up to welcome them home; or whether only Owd Bob would come out to meet them.

The wind shot rapidly past them like rounds of gunfire. The rain stormed at them from above; spat at them from the rock face; and leapt up at them from their feet.

Once, they stopped for a moment, finding a miserable bit of shelter in a crevice in the rock.

"It's a Black Killer's night," panted the Master. "I'll bet he's out."

"Ay," the boy gasped, "I bet he is."

Up and up they climbed through the blackness, blind and knocked about by the wind. The eternal thunder of the rain was all around them; the uproar of the gale above; and far beneath, the roar of angry waters.

Once, in a quiet moment in the storm, the Master turned and looked back into the blackness along the path they had come.

"Did ye hear anything?" he roared above the muffled moaning of the wind.

"Nay!" Andrew shouted back.

"I thought I heard a step!" the Master cried, peering down. But he could see nothing.

Then the wind leaped to life again like a giant from his sleep, drowning all sound with its hurricane voice; and they turned and set off again.

Coming near the summit, the Master turned once more.

"There it was again!" he called; but his words were swept away on the storm; and they started walking again.

Every now and then the moon gleamed down through the storm-tossed sky. Then they could see the wet wall above them, with the water tumbling down its steep face; and far below, in the roaring channel of the Pass, a brown-stained torrent. Hardly, however, had they time to glance around when a mass of cloud would hurry jealously up, and all would again be blackness and noise.

At length, nearly exhausted, they came over the top of the last and steepest part of the Pass, and emerged into the Devil's Bowl. There, overcome by that last effort, they flung themselves down on the soaking ground to catch their breath.

Behind them, the wind rushed with a gloomy roar up the funnel of the Pass. It screamed above them like ten million devils on horseback; and exploded out onto the wild Marches beyond.

As they lay there, still panting, the moon gleamed down in a moment of kindness. In front, through the lashing rain, they could make out the little hills that squat like witches around the Devil's Bowl; and lying in the heart of it was the Lone Tarn, its white waters, usually so still, now plowed into a thousand furrows.

The Master raised his head and craned forward at the ghostly scene. Suddenly he raised himself up onto his arms and stayed motionless awhile. Then he dropped as though dead, forcing Andrew down with an iron hand.

"Lad, did you see?" he whispered.

"Nay; what was it?" the boy answered, startled by his father's tone.

"There!"

But as the Master pointed forward, a blur of cloud came across and all was dark. Quickly it passed; and again the lantern of the night shone down. And Andrew, looking with all his eyes, saw indeed.

There, in front, by the rumpled waters of the Tarn, packed in a solid mass, with every head turned in the same direction, was a flock of sheep. They were motionless, transfixed, staring with horror-bulging eyes. A column of steam rose from their warm bodies into the rain-pierced air. Panting and trembling, yet they stood with their backs to the water, as though determined to defend themselves to the death. Beyond them, less than fifty yards away, crouched a humpbacked boulder, casting a long, misshapen shadow in the moonlight. And beneath it were two black objects, one still struggling weakly.

"The Killer!" gasped the boy, and, all ablaze with excitement, began plunging forward.

"Steady, lad, steady!" urged his father, dropping a hand on the boy's shoulder to hold him back.

Above them, a huddle of clouds flung furiously across the night, and the moon was hidden.

"Follow me, lad!" ordered the Master, and began to crawl silently forward. As quietly, Andrew came after him. And over the soaked ground they crept, one behind the other, like two night-hawks on some foul errand.

On they crawled, lying on their bellies during the blinks of moonlight, and stealing forward in the dark; until, at last, the swish of the rain on the waters of the Tarn, and the panting of the flock in front, warned them they were near.

They crept around the trembling pack, passing so close as to brush against the flanks of the sheep; and yet unnoticed, for the sheep were engrossed in the tragedy occurring before them. Only, when the moon was covered, Andrew could hear them huddling and stamping in the darkness. And again, as it shone out, fearfully they edged closer to watch the bloody drama.

Along the edge of the Tarn the two crept. And still the gracious moon hid their approach, and the drunken, riotous wind drowned out the noise of their coming.

So they stole on, on hands and knees, with hearts dismayed and fluttering breath; until, suddenly, in a pause of the wind, they could hear, right before them, the smack and slobber of bloody lips, mouthing their bloody meal.

"Say thy prayers, Red Wull. Thy last minute has come!" muttered the Master, rising to his knees. Then, in Andrew's ear: "When I rush, lad, follow!" for he thought, when the moon shone out again, to jump in on the great dog, and, surprising him as he lay gorged and unsuspicious, to deal him one terrible sweeping blow, and put an end, forever, to the lawless doings of the Tailless Tyke.

The moon flung off its veil of cloud. White and cold, it stared down into the Devil's Bowl; on murderer and murdered.

Within a hand's reach of the two men as they crept forward bent on revenge, rose the black boulder. On the edge of its shadow lay a dead sheep; and standing beside the body, his coat all ruffled by the hand of the storm was—Owd Bob—Owd Bob of Kenmuir.

Then the light vanished, and darkness covered the land.

CHAPTER 29

The Devil's Bowl

IT WAS Owd Bob. There could be no mistake. In the whole, wide word there was only one Owd Bob of Kenmuir. The silver moon gleamed down on the dark head and rough gray coat, and lit the patch of white on his chest.

And in the darkness James Moore was lying with his face pressed downward so that he would not see.

Once he raised himself on his arms; his eyes were shut and his face uplifted, like a blind man praying. He passed a tired hand across his forehead; his head dropped again; and he moaned and moaned like a man in everlasting pain.

Then the darkness lifted a moment, and he took a quick, secret glance, like a murderer's glance at the gallows where he will be hanged, at the scene in front of him.

It was no dream; clear and cruel in the moonlight was the humpbacked boulder; the dead sheep; and that gray figure, beautiful, motionless, damned for all eternity.

The Master turned his face and looked at Andrew, a dumb, pitiful prayer in his eyes; but in the boy's white, horror-stricken face there was no comfort to be found. Then his head drooped down again, and the strong man was whimpering.

"He, he, he! Excuse me for laughing, Mr. Moore—he, he, he!"

A little man, all wet and shrunk, sat hunching on a mound above them, rocking his shriveled form to and fro in his fits of merriment.

"Ye rascal—he, he! Ye rogue—he, he!" and he shook his fist in fun at the gray dog, who paid no attention. "I owe ye another grudge for this—you've beaten me to it"—and he leaned back and shook this way and that in his laughter.

The man below him rose heavily to his feet, and stumbled toward the little mocking man, his great figure swaying from side to side as though in a blind fever, still moaning as he went. And there was something on his face that no man can mistake. Though he was only a boy, Andrew recognized it.

"Father! Father! Don't!" he begged, running after his father and laying helpless hands on him.

But the strong man shook him off like a fly, and rolled on, swaying and groaning, with that awful expression plain to see in the moonlight.

In front, the little man squatted in the rain, still bowed over; and had no idea of running away.

"Come on, James Moore! Come on!" he laughed, evil joy in his voice; and something gleamed bright in his right hand, and was hidden again. "I've been waiting for this a long time now. Come on!"

Then, in the dreadful lonesomeness of the Devil's Bowl on that night, something worse than sheep-murder would have been committed; but all of a sudden, there sounded the splash of a man's foot falling heavily behind; a hand like a falling tree struck the Master on the shoulder; and a voice roared above the noise of the storm:

"Mr. Moore! Look, man! Look!"

The Master tried to shake off that grasp; but it pinned him where he stood, immovable.

"Look, I tell you!" cried that great voice again.

A hand pushed past him and pointed; and grimly he turned, ignoring the figure at his side, and looked.

The wind had dropped as suddenly as it had risen; the little man on the mound had stopped laughing; Andrew's sobs were hushed; and in the background, the huddled flock edged closer. The world hung balanced on the pinpoint of the moment. Every eye was turned in one direction.

With dull, uncomprehending gaze James Moore stared as he was told. There was the gray dog alone in the moonlight, still paying no attention to the witnesses; there was the murdered sheep, lying half in and half out of that twisted shadow; and there was the humpbacked boulder.

He stared into the shadow, and still stared. Then he started as though struck. The shadow of the boulder had moved!

Motionless, with head forward and bulging eyes, he gazed.

Ay, ay, ay; he was sure of it—a huge dim outline, as though of a lion crouched on the ground, in the very thickest of the blackness.

At that he was seized with such a fit of trembling that he would surely have fallen if it hadn't been for the strong arm around his waist.

That crouching figure grew clearer every moment; till at last they could plainly see the line of arching underbelly, the crest as thick as a stallion's, the massive, wagging head. There was no mistake this time. There he lay in the deepest black, gigantic, lolling in his horrid pleasure—the Black Killer!

And they watched him at his feast. Now he burrowed into the spongy flesh; now he turned to lap the dark pool of blood that glittered in the moonlight beside him like red wine in a silver cup. Now lifting his head, he snapped irritably at the raindrops, and the moon caught his wicked, rolling eye and the red shreds of flesh dripping from his jaw. And again, raising his great mouth as if about to howl, he let the delicious nectar trickle down his throat and delight his palate.

So he went on, all unsuspicious, wisely nodding in slow-mouthed gluttony. And in the stillness, between the gusts of wind, they could hear the smacking of his lips.

While all the time the gray dog stood before him, motion-less, as though carved in stone.

At last, as the murderer rolled his great head from side to side, he saw that still figure. At the sight, he leaped back, alarmed. Then with a deep-mouthed roar that shook the waters of the Tarn, he was up and across his victim with teeth bared, his coat standing straight up in wet, rigid furrows from his head to his tail.

So the two stood, face to face, with maybe a yard of rain-pierced air between them.

The wind hushed its sighing to listen. The moon stared down, white and speechless. Away at the back, the sheep edged closer. While, except for the everlasting thunder of the rain, there was complete silence.

It seemed an age that they waited like that. Then a voice, clear yet low and far away, like a bugle in a distant city, broke the stillness.

"Eh, Wullie!" it said.

There was no anger in the tone, only a terrible blame; it was the sound of the man's heart breaking.

At the call, the great dog leapt around, snarling in hideous passion. He saw the small, familiar figure, clear against the tumbling sky; and for the only time in his life, Red Wull was afraid.

His blood-enemy was forgotten; the dead sheep was forgotten; everything was sunk in the agony of that moment. He crouched in fear upon the ground, and a cry like that of a lost soul was forced from him; it rose on the still night air and floated, wailing, away; and the white waters of the Tarn trembled in cold pity; out of the lonely hollow; over the dismal Marches; into the night.

On the mound above stood his master. The little man's white hair was bared to the night wind; the rain trickled down his face; and his hands were folded behind his back. He stood there, looking down into the hollow below him, as a man may stand at the grave of his lately buried wife. And there was an expression on his face that I cannot describe.

"Wullie, Wullie, to me!" he cried at last; and his voice sounded weak and far away, like a distant memory.

At that, the huge brute came crawling toward him on his belly, whimpering as he came, very pitiful in his suffering. He knew what was going to happen to him, as every sheep-dog knows it. That was not what troubled him. His pain, his unbearable pain, was that this man, his friend and father, who had trusted him, should have discovered him in his sin.

He crept up to his master's feet; and the little man never moved.

"Wullie—my Wullie!" he said very gently. "They've always been against me—and now you! A man's mother—a man's wife—a man's dog! They're all I ever had; and now one of the three has turned against me! Indeed I am alone!"

At that, the great dog raised himself, and placing his fore-paws on his master's chest tenderly, for fear that he should hurt the man who was already hurt beyond healing, stood towering above him; while the little man laid his two cold hands on the dog's shoulders.

So they stood, looking at each other, like a man and his love.

◆ ◆ ◆

At McAdam's word, Owd Bob looked up, and for the first time saw his master.

He did not seem at all startled, but trotted over to him. There was nothing fearful in the way he held himself, no haunting blood-guilt in the true gray eyes which never told a lie, which never, dog-like, failed to look you in the face. Yet his tail was down, and, as he stopped at his master's feet, he was quivering. For he, too, knew, and was moved.

For weeks he had tracked the Killer; for weeks he had followed him as he crossed Kenmuir, on his way to perform his bloody acts; yet always he had lost him on the Marches. Now, at last, he had hunted him down. Yet his heart went out to his enemy in his suffering.

"I thought it was you, lad," the Master whispered, his hand on the dark head at his knee—"I thought it was you!"

◆ ◆ ◆

Rooted to the ground, the three watched the scene between McAdam and his Wull.

In the end, the Master had tears in his eyes; Andrew was crying; and David had turned his back.

At last, silent, they moved away.

"Had I—should I go to him?" asked David hoarsely, nodding toward his father.

"Nay, nay, lad," the Master answered. "That's not a matter for a man's friends."

So they walked out of the Devil's Bowl, and left those two alone together.

◆ ◆ ◆

A little later, as they walked along, James Moore heard the sound of lightly pattering, uneven footsteps behind.

He stopped, and the other two went on.

"Man," a voice whispered, and a face, white and pitiful, like a mother's begging for her child, looked into his—"Man, you won't tell them? I wouldn't want 'em to know it was my Wullie. Think if it had been yer own dog."

"You may trust me!" the other answered, his voice choking.

The little man stretched out a trembling hand.

"Give us yer hand on it. And G-God bless ye, James Moore!"

So these two shook hands in the moonlight, with no one to witness it but the God who made them.

And that is why the mystery of the Black Killer is still unsolved in the Daleland. Many have guessed; but besides those three, only one other knows—knows now which of those two that he saw upon a summer night was the guilty one, and which the innocent. And Postie Jim tells no man.

CHAPTER 30

The Tailless Tyke at Bay

ON THE following morning, there was a sheep auction at the Dalesman's Daughter.

Though many of the farmers arrived early, there was one man even earlier. Tupper, the first to enter the sand-floored parlor, found McAdam there before him.

He was sitting a little forward in his chair; his thin hands rested on his knees; and on his face was a gentle, dreamy expression such as no man had ever seen there before. All the harsh wrinkles seemed to have disappeared in the night; and the sour face, stamped deep with the bitterness of life, was softened now, as if finally at peace.

"When I came down this morning," said Teddy Bolstock in a whisper, "I found him sitting just so. And he hasn't moved or spoke since."

"Where's the Terror, then?" asked Tupper, awed somehow into speaking quietly too.

"In the paddock out back," Teddy answered, "marching up and down, up and down, for all the world like a sentry soldier. And so he was when I looked out the window when I woke up."

Then Londesley entered, and after him, Ned Hoppin, Rob Saunderson, Jim Mason, and others, each with his dog. And each man, as he came in and saw the little lone figure for once without his huge companion, put the same question; while the dogs sniffed about the little man, as though suspecting some trick. And all the time, McAdam sat as though he neither heard nor saw, lost in some sweet, sad dream; so quiet, so silent, that more than one of them thought he was asleep.

After the first glance, however, the farmers paid him little attention, gathering around the tavern-keeper at the far end of the room to hear the latest story about Owd Bob.

It seemed that one week before, James Moore with a pack of sheep had met the new Grammoch-town butcher at the Dalesmen's Daughter. They had made a bargain, and the butcher had started home with the flock. Since he had no dog, the Master offered him the Owd One. "And he'll find me in the town tomorrow," he said.

Now the butcher was a stranger in the land. Of course he had heard of Owd Bob of Kenmuir, yet it had never struck him that this handsome gentlemanly dog with the quiet, confident manner, who handled sheep as he had never before seen them handled, was that hero—"the best sheepdog in the North."

It is certain that by the time the flock was penned in the enclosure behind the shop, he longed to own that dog—ay, would even offer ten pounds for him!

Immediately the butcher locked him up in a shed—most undignified; determined to make his offer the next day.

When the next day came, he found no dog in the shed, and, worse, no sheep in the enclosure. A missing board showed him how the dog had escaped, and a missing bar of the fence showed him how the sheep had got out. And as he was making the discovery, a gray dog and a flock of sheep, traveling along the road toward the Dalesman's Daughter, met the Master.

From the first, Owd Bob had mistrusted the man. The attempt to lock him up had confirmed his suspicions. His master's sheep were not meant for such a rascal; and he worked his own way out and took the sheep along with him.

The men responded to the story as it went along with constant exclamations—"Ma word! Good, Owd Un!—Ho, ho! Did he do that?"

Of them all, only McAdam sat strangely silent.

Rob Saunderson, always glad to tease the little man, noticed it.

"And what do you think of that, Mr. McAdam, for a wonderful story of a wonderful tyke?" he asked.

"It's a good tale, a very good tale," the little man answered dreamily. "And James Moore didn't invent it; he read it in the Christmas issue of the *Flock-keeper*, yonder in Saxty." (On the following Sunday, old Rob, out of pure curiosity, took down from his shelf that issue of the paper. To his amazement he found the little man was right. There was the story almost exactly the same. Still, it was also true of Owd Bob of Kenmuir.)

"Ay, ay," the little man went on, "and in a day or two James Moore will have another tale to tell ye—a better tale, ye'll think—more laughable. And yet—ay—no—I won't believe it! I never loved James Moore, but I think, as Mr. Hornbut once said, that he'd rather die than tell a lie. Owd Bob of Kenmuir!" he went on in a whisper. "Up to the end, I can't shake him off. I half think that where I'm going, there'll be gray dogs sneaking around me in the twilight. And they're always behind and behind, and I can't, can't—"

Teddy Bolstock interrupted, lifting his hand for silence.

"Do you hear that?—Thunder!"

They listened; and from outside came a gurgling, jarring roar, horrible to hear.

"It's coming nearer!"

"Nay, it's going away!"

"That's not thunder!"

"More like the Lea in flood. And yet— Eh, Mr. McAdam, what is it?"

The little man had moved at last. He was on his feet, staring around him, wild-eyed.

"Where's yer dogs?" he almost screamed.

"Here's my—Nay, by God! he's not here!" was the astonished cry.

So interested had they been in the story of Owd Bob and the butcher, no man had noticed that his dog has risen from his side; no one had noticed a line of shaggy figures creeping out of the room.

"I tell ye it's the tykes! I tell ye it's the dogs! They're on my Wullie—fifty to one they're on him! My God! My God! And me not there! Wullie, Wullie!"—in a scream—"I'm coming, I'm with ye!"

At the same moment, Bessie Bolstock rushed in, white-faced.

"Oh, Father! Mr. Saunderson! All of you! The tykes are fighting mad! Listen!"

There was no time for listening. Each man seized his stick and rushed for the door; and McAdam led them all.

❖　❖　❖

It was a rare thing for McAdam and Red Wull to be apart. So rare, that others besides the men in the little tap-room had noticed it.

Saunderson's old Shep walked quietly to the back door of the house and looked out.

There on the slope below him, he saw what he was looking for, pacing up and down, bony and grim, like a lion at feeling-time. And as the old dog watched, his tail was gently swaying, as though he were well pleased.

He walked back into the bar just as Teddy began his tale. Twice he walked around the room on silent feet. From dog to dog he went, stopping at each one as though urging him on to some great endeavor. Then he headed for the door again, looking back to see if any of them were following.

One by one, the others stood up and trailed out after him: big blue Rasper, Londesley's Lassie, Ned Hoppin's young dog; Grip and Grapple, the tavern-keeper's bull-terriers; Jim Mason's Gyp, foolish and flirting even now; there were others; and last of all, waddling heavily in the rear, that scarred warrior, the Venus.

Out of the house they pattered, silent and unseen, with murder in their hearts. At last they had found their enemy alone. And slowly, in a black cloud, like the shadow of death, they dropped down the slope upon him.

And he saw them coming, knew what they were after— and who would know better than the Terror of the Border?— and was glad. It might be death, and the kind of death he would wish to die—at the very least, it took his mind away from that endless, haunting pain. And he smiled grimly as he looked at the approaching crowd and saw that he had defeated every single one of them in his time.

He stopped his restless pacing, and waited for them. His great head was high as he gazed at them scornfully, daring them to come on.

And on they came, marching slow and silent like soldiers at a funeral: young and old; bob-tailed and bull; terrier and collie; flocking like vultures to the dead. And the Venus, heavy with her years, rolled after them on her bowed legs, panting in her hurry for fear that she should be late. For didn't she have to avenge the blood of her own kin?

So they came around him, slow, certain, murderous, spreading out to cut off his escape on every side. There was no need for that. He never thought of escape. The odds were heavily against him—crushingly heavy; yet he loved them for it, and was trembling already with the glory of the coming fight.

They were up to him now; the sheepdogs walking around him on their toes, stiff and short like cats on hot coals; their backs a little humped; heads turned aside; yet watching him to see what he would do.

And he remained stock-still and did not look at them. His great chin was cocked, and his muzzle wrinkled in a dreadful grin. As he stood there, shivering a little, his eyes rolling back, his breath grating in his throat to set every bristle on end, he certainly looked like a devil.

The Venus came up alongside him. There was no hesitating, for her; she never walked if she could stand, or stood if she could lie down. But now she had to stand, breathing hard through her nose, never taking her eyes off that pad of flesh she had marked for her own. Close beside her were crop-eared Grip and Grapple, looking up at the line above them where hairy neck and shoulder came together. Behind was big Rasper, and close to him Lassie. Each of the others had marked his place, each had taken up his position.

Last of all, old Shep took his stand full in front of his enemy, their shoulders almost rubbing, head by head.

So the two stood for a moment, as though they were whispering together; each devilish, each rolling back his eyes to watch the other. While from the little mob there rose a snarling, bubbling snore, like some giant breathing noisily in his sleep.

Then, like lightning, each one struck. Rearing high, they wrestled with reaching paws and the expression of fiends. Down they went, Shep underneath and the great dog with a dozen of these wolves of hell upon him. Rasper, devilish, was riding on his back; the Venus—luck for him!—had struck and missed; but Grip and Grapple had hold of him; and the others, like leaping demons, were plunging into the spinning whirlpool of the fight.

And there, where just two weeks before he had fought and lost the battle of the Cup, Red Wull was now battling for his life.

He didn't have much chance of winning. But what did he care? The endless agony of the night was forgotten in that glorious, feverish excitement. Years of hatred came bubbling forth. In that supreme moment, he would pay them back for the wrongs they had done him. And he went in to fight, rejoicing like a giant in the red lust for killing.

Not much of a chance! Never before had he faced such a crowd of enemies. His one chance lay in quickness: to stop the swarming mob from getting hold of him till he had at least got rid of a few of them.

Then it was a sight to see the great brute, huge as a bull calf, strong as a bull, rolling over and over and up again, quick as a kitten; leaping here, striking there; shaking himself free; swinging his back end; fighting with feet and body and teeth—every inch of him at war. More than once, he broke right through the mob; only to turn again and face it. He wasn't about to run away; he didn't even think of it.

Up and down the slope the dark mass surged, like some huge, heavy ship tossed by the waves. Black and white, sable and gray, they snapped and gnashed at the great hulk in the center. Up and down, roaming wide, leaving everywhere a trail of red.

He had pinned Gyp and hurled him over his shoulder. Grip followed; he shook her till she rattled, then flung her far away; and she fell with an awful thud, not to rise again; while Grapple, to avenge that death, hung on all the tighter. In a scarlet, soaking patch of the ground lay Big Bell's mongrel, curled in a dreadful ball. And Hoppin's young dog, who just three hours before had been the children's affectionate playmate, now evil to look at, dragged after the huddle up the hill. Back the mob rolled, right over her. When it had passed, she lay quite still, grinning; a handful of tawny hair and flesh in her dead mouth.

So they fought on. And every now and again, a great figure rose up from the heaving, hellish storm all around him; rearing to his full height, his head ragged and bleeding, the red foam dripping from his jaws. This was how he would appear for a moment, like some dark rock in the midst of a raging sea; and then down he would go again.

Silent, now, they fought, mute and determined. Only you might have heard the rip of tearing flesh; a hoarse gurgle as some dog went down; the panting of dry throats; and now and then a sob from that figure in the center. For he was fighting for his life. The Terror of the Border was at bay.

All those who really meant it were on him now. The Venus, blinded with blood, had got hold of him at last; and only once in her long life of battles had she ever let go; Rasper, his breath coming in rattles, had seized him horribly by the thigh; while a dozen other devils with red eyes and wrinkled nostrils still clung to him.

Not much of a chance! And down he went, smothered beneath the weight of numbers, yet struggled up again. His great head was torn and dripping; his eyes a gleam of rolling red and white; the little tail straight and stiff like the gallant stump of a flagpole that has been shot away. He was desperate, but wouldn't be beat; and he sobbed as he fought stubbornly on.

Not much of a chance! It could not last. And down he went finally, still silent—they would never force a cry from him in his agony, the Venus holding tight to that mangled pad of flesh; Rasper beneath him now; three at his throat; two at his ears; a crowd on his legs and body.

The Terror of the Border was down at last!

◆   ◆   ◆

"Wullie, my Wullie!" screamed McAdam, leaping down the slope a couple of yards in front of the rest of them. "Wullie! Wullie! To me!"

At the shrill cry, the huddle below shook violently. It heaved and swelled and dragged back and forth, like the sea lashed into life by some dying monster of the deep.

A gigantic figure, tawny and red, fought its way to the surface. A great tossing head, so bloody it was unrecognizable, flung itself out from the mob. One quick glance he shot from his ragged eyes at the little flying figure in front; then with a roar like a waterfall plunged toward it, shaking off the bloody leeches as he went.

"Wullie! Wullie! I'm with ye!" cried that little voice, now so near.

Through—through—through!—a huge effort, and his last. They hung onto his throat, they clung to his muzzle, they were all around him. And down he went again with a sob and a little suffocating cry, looking up at his master with one quick, begging glance as the sea of blood closed over him—grasping, shaking, smothering, tearing, like fox-hounds at the kill.

The men left the dead dogs where they lay and pulled away

the living. And it was no easy job, for the pack of dogs were mad for blood.

At the bottom of the wet mess of hair and red and flesh was old Shep, stone-dead. And as Saunderson pulled the body out, his face was twisting with emotion; for no man can lose in a moment the friend he has had for a dozen years, and not be moved.

The Venus lay there, her teeth still clenched in death; smiling that she had paid him back at last. Big Rasper, no longer blue, was gasping out his life. Two more came crawling out to find a quiet spot where they could lie down and die. Before the night had fallen, another had gone. And there was not a single dog who had fought on that day that did not bear the scars of it with him to his grave.

The Terror of the Border, terrible in his life, like Samson in the Bible, was even more terrible in his dying.

❖ ❖ ❖

Down at the bottom lay what had once been Adam McAdam's Red Wull.

At the sight of him, the little man did not scream or swear: it was past that, for him. He sat down on the soaking ground, and took the torn and bloodied head in his lap very tenderly.

"They've done you in at last, Wullie—they've done you in at last," he said quietly; he was convinced, and nothing could change his mind, that the attack had been organized while he was kept shut away in the tap-room.

On hearing the sound of the loved little voice, the dog gave one weary wag of his stump-tail. And with that, the Tailless Tyke, Adam McAdam's Red Wull, the Black Killer, was gone for good.

One by one, the Dalesmen took away their dead, and the little man was left alone with the body of his last friend.

Dry-eyed he sat there, nursing the dead dog's head; hour after hour—alone—singing to himself:

> "'Monie a sair daurk we twa hae wrought,
> An' wi' the weary warl' fought!
> An' mony an anxious day I thought
> We wad be beat.'

> (Many a hard day's work we two have done,
> And with the vexed world fought!
> And many an anxious day I thought
> We would be beat.)

"And now we are beat, Wullie—now we are!"

So he went on, saying the lines over and over again, always with the same sad ending.

"A man's mother—a man's wife—a man's dog! They three are all little McAdam ever had to stand by his side! Do ye remember the old mother, Wullie? And what she said? 'Never be down-hearted, Adam; ye've always got yer mother.' And one day I had not. And Flora, Wullie (ye remember Flora, Wullie? Na, na; ye wouldn't) with her laughing, playful manner, crying to me: 'Adam, ye say ye're alone. But ye've got me—isn't that enough for any man?' And God knows it was enough—while it lasted!" He broke down and sobbed a while. "And you, Wullie—and you!—the only man friend I ever had!" He felt for the dog's bloody paw with his right hand.

"'An' here's a hand, my trusty fier,
And gie's a hand o' thine;
An' we'll tak' a right guid willie-waught,
For auld lang syne.'"

(And here's a hand, my trusty friend
And give us a hand of thine;
And we'll take a right good draft of ale,
For the days long past.)

◆　◆　◆

He sat there, muttering and stroking the poor head upon his lap, bending over it, like a mother over a sick child.

"They've done ye in at last, lad—done ye sore. And now I'm thinkin' they won't be content till I'm gone too. And oh, Wullie!"—he bent down and whispered—"I dreamed such an awful thing—that my Wullie—but there! 'Twas only a dream."

So he went on sitting, murmuring to the dead dog; and no man came near him. Only Bessie of the inn watched the little lone figure from afar.

It was long past noon when at last he stood up, laying the dog's head carefully down, and stumbled away toward that bridge which once the dead thing on the slope had defended against a crowd of a thousand people.

He crossed it and turned; there was a look upon his face, half hopeful, half fearful, very piteous to see.

"Wullie, Wullie, to me!" he cried; only the tones, formerly so fiery, were now weak as a dying man's.

For a while he waited, uselessly.

"Aren't ye comin', Wullie?" he asked at last in trembling tones. "It's not like ye to leave me."

He walked away a step, then turned again and whistled that shrill, sharp call, only now it sounded like a broken echo of itself.

"Come to me, Wullie!" he begged, very pitifully. "It's the first time ever I've known ye not to come when I whistle. What's wrong with ye, lad?"

He crossed back over the bridge, walking blindly like a sobbing child; and yet dry-eyed.

Over the dead body he stooped.

"What's the matter with ye, Wullie?" he asked again. "Will you, too, leave me?"

Then Bessie, watching fearfully, saw him bend, heave the great body on his back, and stagger away.

Limp and hideous, the carcass hung down from the little man's shoulders. The huge head, with its grim, wide eyes and lolling tongue, jolted and swayed with the motion, seeming to grin a ghastly defiance at the world it had left. And the last Bessie saw of them was that bloody, rolling head, with the puny legs staggering beneath their load, as the two passed out of sight and out of the knowledge of that world.

◆ ◆ ◆

In the Devil's Bowl, next day, they found the pair: Adam Mc-Adam and his Red Wull, face to face; dead, not divided; each, save for the other, alone. The dog, his bitter expression glazed and ghastly in the fixedness of death, propped against that humpbacked boulder beneath which, a while before, the Black Killer had met his fate; and, close by, his master lying on his back, his dim dead eyes staring up at the heaven, one hand still clasping a crumpled photograph; the weary body at rest at last, the mocking face—mocking no longer—lit up by a whole-souled, transfiguring happiness.

Postscript

A<small>DAM</small> M<small>C</small>A<small>DAM</small> and his Red Wull lie buried together: one just inside the sacred ground of the church cemetery, the other just outside.

The only mourners at the funeral were David, James Moore, Maggie, and a gray dog peering through the gate.

During the service, a carriage stopped at the churchyard, and a lady with a graceful figure and a gentle face stepped out and came across the grass to pay her last respects to the dead. And Lady Eleanour, as she joined the little group around the grave, seemed to notice that the parson's voice was more solemn than usual as he spoke the words: "Earth to earth—ashes to ashes—dust to dust; in sure and certain hope of the Resurrection to eternal life."

◆ ◆ ◆

When you wander in the gray hill-country of the North, in the loneliest corner of that lonely land you may happen to come upon a low farmhouse, lying in the shadow of the Muir Pike.

When you enter, a tall old man comes out to greet you—the Master of Kenmuir. His shoulders are bent, now; the hair that was so dark is frosted; but the blue-gray eyes look you in the face as proudly as they ever did.

And while the girl with the crown of yellow hair is preparing food for you—they are welcoming in the extreme, these Northerners—you will notice on the mantelpiece, standing alone, a massive silver cup, with a dent in it.

That is the world-famous Shepherds' Trophy, won outright, as the old man will tell you, by Owd Bob, the last and best of the Gray Dogs of Kenmuir. The last because he is the best; because once, for an eternally long moment, James Moore had thought he was the worst.

When at length you leave the house, the old man will go with you to the top of the slope to show you the way.

"You cross the stream; over Langholm Hollow, yonder; past the Bottom; and up the hill on the far side. You'll come upon the house on top. And you might meet the Owd One on the road. Good-day to you, good-day."

So you go as he has told you; across the stream, around the edge of the Hollow, over the Bottom and up the hill again.

On the way, as the Master has predicted, you come upon an old gray dog, trotting soberly along. The Owd One, indeed, seems to spend the evening of his life going thus between Kenmuir and the Grange. The black muzzle is almost white now; the dog who used to trot so smooth and strong, is now stiff and slow; ancient and honored, indeed, he is, and people still talk about him as the best sheepdog in the North.

As he passes, he stops to look at you. The noble head is high, and one foot is raised; and you look into two big gray eyes like none you have ever seen before—soft, a little dim, and infinitely sad.

That is Owd Bob of Kenmuir; as many stories are told

about him as there are flowers in May. And with him dies the last of the immortal line of the Gray Dogs of Kenmuir.

❖ ❖ ❖

You travel on up the hill, somewhat thoughtful, and knock at the door of the house at the top.

A woman, blooming with the loveliness of motherhood, opens the door to you. And nestling in her arms is a little boy with golden hair and a happy face, like one of the cherubs painted by Correggio.

You ask the child his name. He kicks and squeals, and looks up at his mother; and in the end he whispers shyly, as if it was the funniest joke in all this merry world, "Adum Mataddum."

THE END

Bob, as he appeared in the 1901 edition of *Bob, Son of Battle.*
Photograph by A. Radclyffe Dugmore

Afterword

I FIRST read *Bob, Son of Battle* when I was eleven or twelve years old, or maybe older—I can't be sure. But I never forgot the story or the experience of reading it, in all the years after that. I was so moved by the story, I felt as though I had lived through it myself.

The strange thing is, though, that the characters which moved me the most were not the "good" master and the "good" dog, and the "good" daughter of the master, and the other good people in the story, but the "bad" shepherd, Adam McAdam, and his "bad" dog, Red Wull. I suppose this was because there were so many moments in the story when I could see that with just a little love and patience and help from others, the bad man would have been able to change. There were good qualities in him: He was capable of love and affection and loyalty, he was strong and brave, he was a hard worker, he was expert at handling his sheep. But fate was against him—things had not gone his way. And the same was true of his dog, Red Wull, who was an excellent sheepdog, loved his master, was loyal to him, defended him, and craved his affection and attention: There were good qualities in Red Wull, too, and it was not really the fault of that fierce and courageous tiny puppy that he grew up to be what he was. No one—no person and no dog—is all good, and no one is all bad, and this book reflects the truth of that.

Some writers are sure, from a very early age, that they want to be writers. This was not the case for the author of *Owd Bob*. The Englishman Alfred Ollivant was headed for quite a different career, and this book would never have been written if he had not suffered a very serious accident that caused him to change the direction of his life. Ollivant had just graduated from military school. He had finished his training to be an officer in the British army. He was an expert horseback rider and had won a special prize for his skill while still in school. He was only nineteen years old and preparing to begin his career. It is most likely that he would have gone off to faraway India, where other men in his family had also gone as military officers. We can guess that he was now spending the months before his move gathering the things he would need to take with him: trunks and boxes of clothing and other supplies. But one day, during this time, he was out riding in the English countryside when he had a bad fall from his horse. No one is sure how it happened, but in this fall he hurt his spine very seriously.

For many months, he was under the care of doctors and nurses. Still, he thought he might get better and return to his career in the army. At last, he saw that if he recovered at all, it would take many years, and he might never be strong enough for life in the army. He gave up any idea of becoming an officer.

Because of his injury, Ollivant had to spend his days lying flat on his back. There was very little he could do but read.

One book he read was by the Scottish writer Robert Louis Stevenson, the author of the adventure stories *Treasure Island* and *Kidnapped*. But what Ollivant was reading was not an adventure story; it was a book Stevenson had written when he was much older, and looking back on his life, recalling things that had happened to him and that he liked to remember. It was called *Memories and Portraits*. One of the stories was about a shepherd he had become friends with long ago.

When he was a young man, Stevenson used to take long walks over a hill called Allermuir, in the rolling Pentland Hills to the southwest of the city of Edinburgh, and there he often came upon this shepherd, whose name was John Todd. Although the old shepherd was often cross with city people who came walking in the country, and angry at the world in general, he and young Stevenson grew to be friends. Stevenson would walk with the shepherd and watch him as he worked. On one of their walks, John Todd told him the story of a fine sheepdog he had known. It was not his sheepdog but one belonging to another shepherd. This sheepdog was young but talented, and learning quickly to be very good at his job—and the job of a sheepdog is complicated and important: He must not only understand his master's orders, and even sometimes read his master's mind, but also use his own wits and judgment. Without a dog, a shepherd would not be able to control his flock.

But this dog had turned into something that shepherds dread, and that is a sheep-killer. Sometimes even the best dog may turn into a sheep-killer. This dog, as John Todd told Stevenson, would go roaming far away from his master's land and flocks, and find a sheep from another flock to kill. The way he discovered it was this: As he was resting one day under a bush, near a small pool that was used for bathing sheep, he saw a young collie come skulking down the hillside, as though secretly. He knew the dog. What was it doing so far from home, and why did it look so guilty? John Todd watched as it came to the water's edge and then plunged in, washing away from its mouth and head the evidence of its crime. Now John Todd had to tell the owner of the dog what he had seen. And that was the end of that young and talented sheepdog— because the shepherds know that once a dog turns into a sheep-killer, that dog will never change.

Ollivant, lying on his back, slowly healing, often in pain, was moved and impressed by this story. The idea came to him that he could write a story himself, an invented story, about a brave and skillful sheepdog that turned into a sheep-killer. He did not mean to write a novel, only a short story. But the story grew and grew, until he saw that only a novel would be large enough to hold all the parts of it that he had imagined. He wrote the novel lying on his back, often out in his backyard because the doctors wanted him to get a lot of fresh air. He wrote on a board that had been made into a sort of writing desk and set up across his chest. Sometimes the wind blew his pages away.

When he was finished writing the novel, he sent it to publishers in both the United States and England. It was accepted for publication in both countries. In the States, it was called *Bob, Son of Battle*, while in England, it had a different title: *Owd Bob, the Gray Dog of Kenmuir*. Also, the English publisher asked him to rewrite the book and change many parts of it. In the English version, the book starts with McAdam in the kitchen with his old dog Cutty Sark. In the American version, it starts with the farmworkers of Kenmuir working in the farmyard. Even the tiny puppy Red Wull comes into McAdam's life differently in the English version: McAdam finds him out in the hills, crouching in the grass by the side of his dead mother. In the American version, a man passing through town is offering him for sale in the local tavern. We do not yet know why the English publisher wanted Ollivant to tell the story in a slightly different way. The most important scenes, and the end of the story, are the same.

In America, the book was a big success right away, and it soon was in England, too. It went on being bought and read by hundreds and even thousands of people for many, many years. It was made into a movie, and then later into another movie, and then another, and then another—four movies altogether. It also came out as a Dell comic book and in other versions that were shorter and sometimes simpler than the original. Even though it was a sad story, in many ways, it was very popular with grown-ups and children both. Some people said—and some people still say—that it is the greatest dog story of all time. It is hard to believe, now, that the story was written more than a hundred years ago, because it is still so exciting and moving.

As for Ollivant, fourteen years went by before he recovered enough from his injuries to return to a more or less normal life, and even then he was often not in good health. But he was no longer interested in joining the army. He was now a writer. He had written several more books in those fourteen years. And he went on writing, book after book. I've read one more, so far, called *Boy Woodburn*. It is about a girl, an expert horseback rider, who disguises herself as a boy so that she can compete in one of the most important races in England, called the Grand National. It is another gripping story.

Even though I had never forgotten *Bob, Son of Battle*, I began to think that not many people knew it anymore. I would ask friends who loved to read if they had read it, but most of them had never even heard of it. I was sure that not many children had read it. I wondered if that was because the book was too hard to read nowadays.

I remembered how difficult parts of the book were, most of all the speech of the characters. The story takes place in the north of England, out in the country, and in those days, country people, especially the working people, like the shepherds, spoke their own kind of English, with their own words for many things. If you were visiting from London, or from America, you might understand some of what they said, but there would be many more things you would not understand at all. Instead of "know" they would say "ken." Instead of "nothing" they would say "nowt," instead of "must" they would say "mun," and instead of "old" they would say "owd."

If you have read *The Secret Garden*, by Frances Hodgson Burnett, you may remember the Yorkshire speech of Dickon and his family, and how one of the other main characters, Mary, likes to learn it and practice it because she likes the way it sounds. Yorkshire, where that book takes place, is not very far from Cumberland, where *Owd Bob* takes place, and in some ways the speech sounds the same.

But one of the most important characters, the angry and unhappy shepherd McAdam, is not from the north of England but from even farther north, over the border in Scotland, and his way of speaking is even more different. He uses words that even the English do not understand, such as "aiblins" for "maybe" and "gey" for "very." To him, "naethin' ava" means "nothing at all." Here is something McAdam says about his son, David (McAdam is speaking to his dog, Red Wull, as he often does in the book): "I've tholed mair fra him, Wullie, than Adam M'Adam ever thocht to thole from ony man." This means: "I have endured more from him, Wullie, than Adam

McAdam ever thought he would have to endure from any man." You can begin to understand it if you try, as Mary in *The Secret Garden* began to understand the speech of Yorkshire, but you might not have the patience.

I did not want Ollivant's powerful story to be forgotten simply because it was difficult to read, so I had an idea. I would go through the whole book, and change the speech of the characters from their Cumbrian or Scottish way of speaking to regular, standard English, so that it would not be so hard to read. And that is what I began to do. But once I started, I saw that there were other things about the way the story was written that made it hard to read. The book was written a long time ago, and habits of writing and speaking were different then. Sentences were often more complicated. The author, Ollivant, also uses expressions that we do not use anymore and might not understand nowadays. He uses words we know, but in a different way from the way we use them. For instance, he sometimes uses "without" to mean "outside": where he writes "She bid him halt without" we would write, "She told him to stay outside." There are other words he uses that we won't understand at all because they are words used only by people whose business is raising sheep—words like "wether," "gimmer," "tup," and "hogg." Others are words for things in the landscape of Cumberland, like "fell," "ghyll," "beck," and "scaur" (meaning "stretch of open country," "ravine," "small brook," and "steep, rocky place"). And then there are quite standard words that we simply may not know, like debouch, wraith, smithy, anent, worsted, inanition, erstwhile, asseverated, hearken, and so on.

The odd thing is that because the story is so powerful, you can read right over these hard words and puzzling expressions and not mind, because you are so eager to know what happens next. That is what I did when I first read it. But not everyone will keep going when they come to a hard sentence. They may give up, and put the book away, and never go back to it. So I decided that I would not only change the speech of the characters but also change the way the story was told, just enough so that almost everything could be understood without any problem, and there would be nothing to get in the way of the story. And that is what I did. I tried not to change it more than I had to, because the way Ollivant had written it was very good, and I did not want to lose that. I even left in some of the hard words and sentences. Lastly, I gave the book a new title that combined the American title and the English title.

I hope that if people like reading *Bob, Son of Battle* in this version, they will try reading it in the original, exactly the way Ollivant wrote it, so as to enjoy the speech of Cumberland and Scotland and every word of the story the way it was first written. But more than anything else, I hope the story will have a new life and find many more readers.

—LYDIA DAVIS

ALFRED OLLIVANT (1874–1927) was born in Old Charlton, Kent, the son of a colonel in the Royal Horse Artillery. Shortly after he graduated from the Royal Military Academy at Woolwich, intending to pursue a career in the army, he was thrown from his horse and seriously injured. While beginning his recuperation from the accident (he was to remain under his doctors' care for the next fourteen years), he wrote *Owd Bob: The Grey Dog of Kenmuir* (known in the United States as *Bob, Son of Battle*), which was a best seller both in the United Kingdom and the United States when it came out in 1898. Ollivant would go on to publish fourteen more novels, as well as various occasional essays, poems, and other works, including, during the First World War, a series of articles describing wartime life in England for an American audience.

MARGUERITE KIRMSE (1885–1954) was born in Bournesmouth, England. She emigrated to the United States as an accomplished harpist in order to continue her musical education, but instead embarked on a highly successful career as an illustrator. She is best known for her drawings of dogs, including those in *Lassie, Come-Home* by Eric Knight.

LYDIA DAVIS is the author of seven collections of stories, including *Break It Down*, *Samuel Johnson Is Indignant*, and, most recently, *Can't and Won't*, as well as one novel, *The End of the Story*. Her *Collected Stories* were published as a single volume in 2009, and in 2013 she was awarded an American Academy of Arts and Letters Award of Merit Medal for the Short Story, as well as the Man Booker International Prize. She is also the translator of many books from the French, most notably Proust's *Swann's Way* and Flaubert's *Madame Bovary*.